T0390744

THAT KIND of GIRL

Also by Natalie C. Anderson

City of Saints & Thieves

Let's Go Swimming on Doomsday

THAT KIND of GIRL

NATALIE C. ANDERSON

Nancy Paulsen Books

NANCY PAULSEN BOOKS
An imprint of Penguin Random House LLC
1745 Broadway, New York, New York 10019

First published in the United States of America by Nancy Paulsen Books,
an imprint of Penguin Random House LLC, 2025

Visit us online at PenguinRandomHouse.com.

Library of Congress Cataloging-in-Publication Data
Names: Anderson, Natalie C., author. | Title: That kind of girl / Natalie C. Anderson.
Description: New York: Nancy Paulsen Books, 2025. | Audience term: Teenagers
Summary: "Two teenage girls from opposite worlds both end up as prime suspects when a rich classmate is murdered"—Provided by publisher.
Identifiers: LCCN 2024044276 (print) | LCCN 2024044277 (ebook)
ISBN 9780593406298 (hardcover) | ISBN 9780593406304 (ebook)
Subjects: CYAC: Murder—Fiction. | Mystery and detective stories.
LCGFT: Detective and mystery fiction. | Thrillers (Fiction) | Novels.
Classification: LCC PZ7.A528 Th 2025 (print) | LCC PZ7.A528 (ebook) | DDC [Fic]—dc23
LC record available at https://lccn.loc.gov/2024044276
LC ebook record available at https://lccn.loc.gov/2024044277

Manufactured in the United States of America

ISBN 9780593406298

1 3 5 7 9 10 8 6 4 2

BVG

Edited by Stacey Barney
Design by Nicole Rheingans
Text set in FS Brabo

for Siara

Inez

The amount of blood Inez has managed to get all over herself is really quite amazing.

She keeps finding it. Crusted in her earring. Threaded into her shoelace. You would think that with all the practice she's had cleaning, she'd be better at this.

Her stained clothes are long gone, but when it came to dumping her shoes, she'd hesitated. Shoes are expensive, and these were practically brand-new. She'd kept them, scrubbed the pleather with an old toothbrush dipped in bleach, but the spots were stubborn. The shoes have to go. After all, what if she becomes a suspect and the cops put that luminol stuff on them? She's seen it on TV.

She hates to ditch the shoes. They represent . . . what? A blow job? Two hand jobs and some change?

Inez has developed the annoying habit of measuring all her earthly treasure in the slapping transactions of flesh. The clothes she's wearing tonight: a puck and a half. Rent on her trailer: five pucks, or around eight blow jobs. (She cannot bring herself to call them fucks. It's absurd, she knows. A twenty-one-year-old sex worker who can't say *fuck,* even in her head. Oh, the irony.)

Inez has two jobs: cleaning and pucking, and she wishes she could think in terms of hallways mopped, toilets brushed, trash cans emptied, but no.

Her mother had been a cleaner until she got too sick to work. Inez tries not to imagine what Mama—God rest her tired soul—must think about her now. She's sure that her mama looks down on her from heaven and sees everything. *Everything.* Inez believes in heaven in a vague sort of way, if only because she needs to think about her mother as being some*place*. Instead of some*thing*: bones and flesh and masses of decaying abnormal cells.

She checks the time on her phone. (It had been free; a client had left it in her car. Which begs the question, was it really free? But she hadn't asked for it. QED: zero pucks. Yes, she's a redneck cleaning lady whore, but she knows how to use the phrase *QED*.)

It's 3:48 in the morning. A good time for dumping evidence. The garbage trucks come at five. Inez pulls the shoes off and drops them regretfully into the industrial trash bag, which is already half full from cleaning the first- and second-floor bathrooms. The cheap flip-flops she'd bought that afternoon (0.5 hand jobs) go on her feet. She has good feet. Good legs. Good everything, really. (Just being honest, not bragging.) She wiggles her bare toes, and for a moment she's a kid, back when flip-flops were all she wore, if she wore shoes at all. Running around the trailer park, her soles permanently tinged pink from the iron-red clay.

She leaves her trolley full of spray bleach and paper towels in the hallway and lets herself out of the building. She walks around the side alley to the dumpsters. It's dark back here, and when she tosses the bag in, it bangs and something scurries away. She catches the flash of a hairless pink tail. Possum. They grow them big here at the university, feed them on rich cafeteria garbage. Everything thrown out on a use-by schedule, no exceptions.

The cleaning agency she works for put her on the cafeteria shift for a while. She and her coworkers would take stuff home that was supposed to go to the dumpsters even though their boss told them it was against the rules. It was a perk of the job, bringing home stale cake, dented industrial-sized cans of tomatoes. It helped stretch her paycheck. But not enough to make her want to give up pucking. After all, you can't buy shoes with stale bagels.

There. Done, she thinks as she hurries back into the tangerine lights illuminating the building entrance. She'll shower again when she gets home.

Then there will be nothing else left to tie her to the body.

Maybe she should feel guilty, but when she scans her emotions, all she finds is relief.

By the time she finishes her shift at six a.m., the garbage trucks have come and gone in a great clanging harassment of the dawn. By then the flip-flops have rubbed a blister raw between her toes. But this time the blood she spills on her shoes is entirely her own.

Roxie

I scan the sidewalk for a target. A man approaches at speed, eyes glued to his phone.

I dig deep, find a smile and a chirpy voice. Both are rusty but serviceable. “Hello, sir! Can you spare a minute for the environment?”

Shiny, happy me, saving the world.

The business-bro shoulders past, close enough for me to see his shaving mistakes. He never even looks up.

Whew.

I let a few more prospects slide by.

Then, “Good morning!” I wave vigorously at a woman pushing a stroller. “It only takes a second to make a world of difference!”

She zombie-stares at me over a screaming infant. Chugs coffee from a thermos the size of a paint bucket and walks on.

Another well-chosen mark.

I adjust my XXL leprechaun-green T-shirt and check my phone. The foot traffic at this end of Biltmore Avenue is light, not the best place to gather signatures for—I glance at my clipboard—Save the Porpoises. In fact, my clipboard holds exactly one signature: Mr. Claude Huber. My partner, an earnest college kid with a man-bun, told me Claude owns a nearby guitar shop and always dutifully signs every petition that comes under his nose. I didn't even have to ask. Or explain what he was signing. He just strode up, ballpoint clicking.

"Go for the younger people. Students. Nobody on their phone." Man-bun is really into this mentorship thing. "You have to sort of bring them in, like an embrace." He demonstrates, angling himself across the sidewalk with his arms open wide like he's about to break into some tai chi. "If you just sort of slow people down a little . . ."

He drones. I mm-hmm at appropriate intervals.

The bell I've been waiting for tinkles. Up the street a guy wearing a maroon hoodie emerges from a pet store. His face is hidden. Under his arm he carries what looks like a fluffy football.

I follow my mentor's advice and move into the man's trajectory. "Excuse me, sir, but can I tell you some disturbing news about our cetaceous friends?"

I catch a brief glimpse under the hood. Pale face. Mud-brown eyes and a lurid face tattoo.

Zero eye contact. He's past me and gone.

Finally. Bingo.

My partner gives a sympathetic shake of the head. "You start to get a feel for this the longer you do it. Now, that guy, you know he's never going to sign, because—"

"Hold this?" I say, pushing my clipboard into Man-bun's hands. "I need to find a bathroom. Too much coffee. Back in a sec." I'm gone before he can protest.

I follow Hoodie, keeping a block between us. I yank my long dark hair out of a ponytail. My ugly green shirt gets dunked into a trash can. Hoodie glances back, but only sees one more girl staring at her phone as she walks.

There is no better invisibility cloak than carrying a clipboard and asking people if they have a minute for the environment.

I lift my phone to my ear. "I've got him," I say.

"Oh, praise the Lord. Is Teddy with him? Where are they?"

"I'm following. I'll let you know when I have an address."

"Don't you dare lose him, Roxie," Chloe Hamilton tells me. "I paid two thousand dollars for that dog; there's no way I'm letting some hood rat sell him for drug money."

It's the third time she's told me how much the dog cost. Still floors me. I refrain from pointing out that, actually, it was her father who paid. *Two hundred bucks,* I tell myself. *Keep your mouth shut and your feet moving. Two hundred bucks when you get Teddy-Boo back.*

"Roxie? Are you there?"

"I'll text."

Hoodie walks fast, the pup's tiny manicured feet bouncing. The dog-napper is leading me out of Asheville's central district, where all the breweries and restaurants and shops selling healing crystals are clustered.

The historic buildings give way to a nouveau strip mall. Soon the sidewalks end and I'm following Hoodie along the road shoulder. Garages, a pipe-fitting store, cracked asphalt sprouting head-high weeds. It's a section I've always found weirdly empty for all its proximity to downtown. When Hoodie cuts through a municipal parking lot, I have to slow further. If he turns around now, it'll be obvious I'm following.

He ducks through a break in a chain-link fence. When he's out of sight, I sprint after him.

The street I emerge onto is a surprise. Here, life switches back on. It's Saturday, and kids are out riding bicycles in the middle of the road. They're making the most of an anemic playground. Teenagers perch on the park's picnic tables, chattering loud as blue jays, singing along to music playing on their phones. I hear lawn mowers, catch sight of two grannies on front porches. It's clearly a low-income neighborhood, but it has a homey feel to it, a place where you know you can't get up to too much trouble because everybody's somebody's auntie.

Hoodie strides up the walk to a deflated-looking house.

As he knocks on the door, I slouch against a parked car. *This* is where he's selling the dog? Nobody who lives in that house has the money to buy a purebred Pomeranian. Unless, as Chloe put it, the dog's being sold at a rock-bottom price to service a rock-bottom habit. But I didn't get "addict" in the brief look I had under Hoodie's hood. No twitchy red eyes and acne-pocked skin.

He shifts the dog gently, cradling it against his chest. He's bought it a new collar at the pet store. Hot pink with rhinestones. He pulls his hood back, revealing the black swirls of his ill-considered faux-tribal tat. It goes from his temple down into his shirt. Zero chance of mistaken identity. He really should have considered another career besides petty larceny, one where he wouldn't be instantly recognizable on security cameras.

He knocks on the front door again, harder this time.

I lift my phone camera, framing him, the dog, and the door. A before-shot of him going in with a pooch, a bookend of him emerging empty-handed. Or if I'm lucky, still counting his profits. Chloe is driving around with her boyfriend. Matt is steroid-marinated flesh in a backward baseball hat. Chloe has hinted that photos might not be necessary if they can catch him on the street. Matt has a lacrosse stick. Why involve the police?

I agree that police involvement is rarely a good idea, but I am nothing if not thorough.

Once I send the photos, my part is over. My business is to find. That's it. I traced Hoodie from the carpentry job on Chloe's pool house to the handoff as promised, and what happens to him now is not my problem.

I appraise the house for hints about who the buyer is. Its paint is peeling but there are flowerpots on the porch. A Ford Escort sags to the pavement out front. There are toys in the yard—a broken doll stroller and a rusted bike with training wheels.

Those toys.

I am suddenly not liking the direction this is going.

The front door opens, and a bright pink blur shoots out, grabs Hoodie in a hug around the waist. The little girl is eight-ish. Growth-spurt skinny with soft corkscrews of black hair. Head-to-toe pink sparkles. I'm close enough to hear her squeal when Hoodie crouches down, revealing the squirming dog, whose collar, I note, has been chosen to match the girl's color palette.

Seriously? I curse under my breath.

I creep closer, staying inconspicuous behind parked cars, but I'm not sure Hoodie would notice if I came up and tap-danced across the porch.

I see the little girl point to herself. Her lips say, *"For me?"* Hoodie nods and she flings her arms around his neck again, nearly knocking him over. He could not look any happier if it started raining hundred-dollar bills. Their heads side by side, I notice that they have exactly the same jawlines.

My phone buzzes with a text.

Chloe H: WELL? WHERE IS HE?
Matt's ready to kick his sorry ass.

I look from the words to the family. The dog is frantically licking the girl's chin. The door opens wider, and a woman comes out to stand over the scene, arms crossed over her chest. She's wearing purple scrubs. A CNA. Or she works at a nursing home. Something demanding that doesn't pay well. Her face says, *You have got to be kidding me.*

My sentiments exactly.

The vibrations from my phone are insistent.

Chloe H: Rox where are you.
Send location

I raise my gaze in an appeal to the sky. I don't expect help, but old habits die hard. The heavens are blue, and the September day is beautiful. Crisp and breezy. Leaves are already starting to turn the hillsides red and gold. Tourists all over town will be raising craft beers and Instagramming their faces off right now.

Why couldn't it have been a drug dealer behind that door? Is that really so much to ask?

I reach in my pocket, find Mama's lighter, and roll the wheel under my thumb. The grating scrape resonates through my finger bones, up my arm.

Two hundred bucks.

The little girl's mom is in the process of succumbing to Teddy-Boo's cuteness, though she's clearly trying to keep from showing it. I can't hear what she's saying from this far, but I can imagine: "*. . . And you're responsible for feeding him and walking him and picking up his poop EVERY DAY, you hear me?*"

Chloe H: ROXIE!! Where r u?!

I take a last long look at the family, then turn and start the trek back toward Biltmore Avenue. I can get a bus from there. I won't return to my post on the street. I've got another job to get to and I'm late as it is.

Before turning my phone to silent, I send one final text.

Me: Sry. Lost him.

Roxie

I burst through the front door of the restaurant. "Look, I know I'm late, but you wouldn't believe the interest people have in saving porpoises. They're like the polar bears of the estuary. So cute, so cuddly. None of the psychotic tendencies of dolphins . . ." I stop talking because no one is yelling at me. "Uncle Len?"

I find my uncle sitting in one of the back booths, paperwork fanned on the table. I finish knotting my apron and drop in across from him. Why is he just sitting here? At this hour on a Saturday he should be working up to an aneurysm, slinging things and shouting at us to hurry it the hell up. The Rusty Nail opens in fifteen minutes.

I check my watch, just to be sure I haven't stepped through a time warp. Nope. Still late.

"Uncle Lenny? You okay?" I sniff for disaster. We got evicted. We're bankrupt. I have to go back to foster care. A million ugly thoughts flip through my mind as I try to read him. Usually I'm pretty good at this. I spent much of my childhood divining the weather in people's body language: twitchy noses, the little muscles around the eyes. My only clue is that Len has his ex-FBI-agent face on: grumpy with a side of impatience.

He rouses himself. "I just got off the phone with Aunt Regina's lawyer. He found an addendum to her will. She left us something after all."

I relax. That doesn't sound so bad. "What is it?" I grab a napkin and silverware from the stack that's being ignored at the other end of the table and start to roll them together. I like rolling silverware. I like the orderly origami of it. "A tea set? Ooh—her freaky animal head collection? Please let it be that."

Great-Aunt Regina died last Wednesday with only Uncle Lenny and Aunt Lori as potential heirs, but when Regina's lawyer read her will, they found she'd decided to leave her entire estate to the North Carolina Arts Foundation. Lori had started crying. Uncle Len had just rolled his eyes. ("Typical.")

"A diamond necklace worth two million dollars," my uncle says.

I laugh.

He doesn't.

I stop rolling napkins. "Wait, are you serious?" After a glance at the kitchen, where Marcus is prepping for lunch, I lean in. He probably can't hear us, but I figure it's bad practice to discuss anything of value—in, say, the millions—within earshot of ex-cons. Even the perfectly nice, reformed ex-cons that the restaurant is staffed with. "Her diamond necklace? The one she always wore at Christmas? It's worth two *million*? Why aren't you busting a happy hernia?" I demand. "Pop some champagne, man!"

"Because it's not that easy," my uncle growls. "It never is with Aunt Regina. She's hidden it."

I go still. A strange coldness washes over me. "Hidden it? What do you mean?"

"I mean before she died, she literally tucked it away somewhere on the estate. And now she wants us to play treasure hunt to find it. Apparently she thinks she's the posthumous star of an Agatha Christie novel." He shakes his head. "So typical."

"Treasure hunt." My stomach begins to knot.

"She's left a trail of *bread crumbs*," my uncle goes on. "Her will included a *clue* to get us started." He makes *clue* sound like it's a hair he's found in the potato salad. He swivels a piece of paper so I can see his choppy handwriting:

And I will give thee the treasures of darkness,
and hidden riches of secret places

The words swim in front of my eyes.

There's more, but I don't see it. I push back from the table, fumbling to get out, fighting limbs that have gone limp.

"Rox?"

I manage to walk to the kitchen. Marcus looks up, but I keep going, past storage, past Uncle Lenny's office. I'm running by the time I throw myself out the back door. I emerge into a too-bright parking lot, sucking in air, trying like hell to get oxygen into my lungs. I put my hands on my knees, puffing, riding waves of nausea.

"Roxie! Are you okay?" I feel Lenny hovering behind me. I put a hand up to keep him back.

Images like flashbulbs assault me. My mother smiling at me in the car's rearview mirror. Me digging into the chickens' roosting boxes. The crinkle of a Jolly Rancher wrapper. Red flames. Blue lights. Bits of burning paper floating down through the trees like snow.

"Here, sit." Uncle Lenny guides me to an overturned milk crate, careful not to touch me. I hang my head between my knees and try to take deep, normal breaths. One Jerusalem, two Jerusalem. I'm sweaty all over.

"I'm going to get you some water."

He comes back a minute later with a cup and I manage a small sip. "Sorry."

"There's nothing to be sorry for." He brings another crate and sits beside me. He gives me a little more time, then asks, "Want to talk about it?"

I lean my head back against the brick wall. "We used to play a game."

He sucks in a breath. "Shit. Your mom."

I nod.

He lets out the breath in a deep sigh. "She played treasure hunt with you." He shakes his head, looks out at the half-empty parking lot. "I'm sorry. I had no idea."

For a little while we don't speak. We watch heat shimmer off of the asphalt. Marcus comes out, slings a bag of trash into the dumpster. He gives us a look but doesn't ask, goes back inside. Beyond the lot is a wild green scrubland, and farther, glints of the French Broad River.

"She learned the game from Great-Aunt Regina?" I ask.

Uncle Lenny nods. "We used to play it at Montgomery House when we were little. Your mom was always the best."

I wipe my brow with the back of my sleeve. "What does it say?" I ask. "What's the clue?"

"Rox, I don't think—"

"Show me."

He hesitates, then hands over the wrinkled piece of paper, watches me closely.

I don't let myself see the first, familiar line. It's always the same anyway; I know the words from Isaiah by heart. But the rest I read slowly, carefully.

> *Around four heads the angels flew*
> *Silent in their keeping*
> *Vanity thy name is mine*
> *And paint masked all the weeping*

I clear my throat. "Does it mean anything to you?"

He's still watching me. "No." He takes the paper back. "Let's forget about it, okay?"

I check my watch. "You should go, you've got to open."

"It's fine, don't worry about opening."

"Uncle Len, you've never opened late once in five years. Don't start now, just because some poetry is making me vomity."

He looks toward the kitchen, stands reluctantly. "Do you want to come sit in my office?"

"No, I'm good here." I wave at the stinky dumpster. "I'm going to enjoy the fresh air."

"Do you want to go home? You can take the car."

"No, really. Go. You heard Dr. Adams, he said this sort of thing would happen. It was a trigger. It's normal. It just . . . surprised me."

"I'll get things up and running and come back to check on you in a few. Okay?" He gives me a last long look, then hurries away.

I blow out a long breath, lean against the wall. I'm sixteen now and the scars on my back are more than five years old, but they feel fresh. Puffy and hot like they're infected. Like my childhood is a virus I'll never get rid of.

Cars are starting to pull into the parking lot. Groups of people stroll toward the front entrance. In the kitchen I hear the clang and hustle of meals being created. Orders going back and forth. The restaurant will soon be humming with life.

I put my hand in my pocket, roll the wheel on Mama's lighter.

I try to scratch the words from my brain, but they keep coming back.

I whisper to no one:

"And I will give thee the treasures of darkness . . ."

Inez

Inez has been checking the news on her phone every five minutes for days now, but there's no mention of a body found. If they'd found a body, it would be news, right?

She's still waiting for the guilt to hit her.

She flicks through TV channels, seeing nothing but light and color. A glass of iced green tea, sweetened to the point a spoon would stand up in it, sits beside her. It's rich in antioxidants, apparently.

If only her mother had drunk more tea.

She wishes she had a shift scheduled tonight. Anything to give the day structure, some sort of destination.

The housekeeping agency she works for contracts with universities, nursing homes, occasionally private clients. She never knows how many hours they'll give her or where she'll be working that week until they post the schedule Sunday night. The hours are never enough. She keeps asking for more, and they always say, *Sure, honey, no problem.* But then the next week rolls around and it's the same old shit. She knows it has something to do with not paying benefits, the cheap bastards.

Mostly they give her nights at the university—she's one of the few on staff who doesn't complain about third shift. If she's lucky, they send her to clean rich people's homes. She's going to a new one tomorrow. But mostly it's mucking university dorm bathrooms for minimum wage. She can make five times that in half as long servicing one of her clients. It's hard to argue with the math. She often thinks, while scrubbing puke off the inside rim of a toilet, that she should just quit. Go full-time with the sex stuff. But then she couldn't pretend to her dead mother that she's paying the bills with "honest" work.

She lives in the same rented trailer on the outskirts of town she's always lived in. And because the trailer is where her mother spent her final weeks wheezing and dying, it's pretty much the last place she wants to be today. Or any day. And yet, here she is. Because she can't figure out how to be anywhere else. Anywhere else costs money.

While the TV babbles, she checks the messages on the XXX site she uses to see if she has any potential customers. It's the usual slush of grammatically appalling trash: *CUM ride thiz faty blondie!!!!!!!*

Yes, but where? What time? Can you please be more specific? They're not real clients, just jerks getting their jocks off looking at profiles. She deletes them all.

She scans the forums, too. Users warn each other about customers or scams, ask advice, and swap gossip. She never posts, but the threads are fascinating. Everything from dating advice to how to get semen stains out of suede. The chatter today is all about how to construct your own glory hole with Home Depot materials. Very instructive.

Some girls do internet only, which is appealing, but they say it's hard to make money that way. You can't simply make a video and walk away. You have to put in hours of social media time and "cultivate a fan base." Just thinking about it exhausts her. She doesn't want a fan base. And even if she did do all her sessions online, people could always record it, and then she'd show up on one of those free porn websites. She's not doing this shit for nothing.

After the incident over the summer, she stopped for a while. But the credit card bills from paying for her mom's medical stuff kept coming, and Pammy Jones let her know that she couldn't wait for rent any longer. ("Everybody here's got issues, sweetheart, or they wouldn't be living in a trailer park.") So she went back to work.

She's been sticking to her regulars. She has a few. College boys mostly, word of mouth from that first quasi-disastrous encounter.

She wishes she could be more choosy. Once, she set up a session with a woman her mom's age. It was strange but sort of nice. Simpler, somehow. The woman had really looked like a mom, too. Capri pants and a bedazzled T-shirt. She'd been nervous, and Inez had found herself in the strange role of comforter, encourager, leading the woman to the very mom-like bedroom by the hand.

After, the woman had offered Inez lasagna in a Tupperware container to take home. She overpaid her by twenty bucks. ("Use it for gas." Such a mom thing to say that Inez almost choked up.) She had sort of hoped the lady would become a regular, but she hadn't called again. If only she could just service the sweet, sad moms of Asheville. There really weren't enough to go around. At least not enough willing to buy sex.

Eventually Inez drives to the mall for a new pair of shoes, just to give herself something to do. She can't show up for work tomorrow in flip-flops. The house she'll be cleaning is fancy, and her flip-flops are the sort of thing made for wearing in the shower. The only other shoes she has are sneakers and four-inch heels.

When she's done, she walks back across the hot asphalt to her car. The new loafers she wears are cheap but comfy black pleather and look like something a grandmother would approve of. She will not be wearing them on dates. She likes them, even though they're sort of ugly. Maybe for that reason.

She doesn't want to get in her car. She stands there with her keys in her hand. She can't stop herself from looking at the back seat, seeing herself there.

She turns abruptly and walks to the end of the lot, where an overgrown bank pitches steeply down to a murky creek. She keeps walking, following the flow of the water. Above, a blue sky is being threatened by encroaching thunderheads and the wind has picked up, a relief.

She walks for five minutes and then she walks some more, thinking she'll turn around soon. She follows the creek. She walks through parking lots, on the shoulder of the road, in the grass with beer cans and McDonald's cartons. It's not easy going. She has to push through tall grasses, navigate fenced-in lots. Eventually the nameless creek joins the French Broad, swollen and brown. She comes to an old bridge, perched only a few feet above the water. Not many cars use it, preferring the newer overpass. She can hear them in an endless low scream above.

The bridge has no sidewalks, only inches of shoulder. You would think that a town built around luring tourists with outdoor activities would be more pedestrian friendly. But here under the overpass there's no reason to walk. This creek is wild and choked with trash. There are no hip new breweries in this part of town, no art galleries. Nothing but warehouses on the flood level.

She stands on the bridge and watches plastic bags caught on low-hanging witch hazel struggle in the stream. The water looks like chocolate milk.

For a long time, she doesn't move. She knows this river. Knows she lives up to her name: both broad and deep. That catfish big as dogs nuzzle her belly. This river is patient. The river knows every rock she's washed smooth. Forgiving, she pulls everything into that chocolate-milk belly and says like her own mother used to, *Shush. Ain't worth crying over.*

Inez listens, caught between the roar of traffic above, the rush of water below. Before and after. She's waiting for something. She doesn't know what. A ghost to jump out of the water like a fish on a line. A twinge of some feeling in her chest.

Her new shoes are covered in dust. She stands still. And all around there's nothing but the sound of endless, unstoppable movement toward some other place.

Roxie

The halls of Saint Magdalene Preparatory Academy ring with the dulcet tones of well-turned-out girls. On the brink of rarefied womanhood, they leisurely make their way to class. Straightened hair, tidy uniforms. A hum like a content bass line. But beneath it all I can make out a sweet vibrato:

Scheming, backstabbing, and lying.

I like this sound. It's the sound of money.

On this bright and normal Monday morning, Great-Aunt Regina's diamond necklace treasure hunt is fading into the background. I put in a few hours at the restaurant Saturday afternoon, but eventually Uncle Lenny clocked me out early. I'd protested weakly, then dragged myself home, gone to my room, and passed out like a rock.

We haven't talked about the hunt since. I'm happy to let Uncle Lenny and Aunt Lori handle it. They're heading to Montgomery House today, in fact, for a first go. They know how to play the game. They'll find the necklace and we'll all soon be a few million richer. Batty old rich lady gets a final chuckle. Happily ever after without me having to puzzle through that particular poetry again.

Meanwhile, I have plenty to keep me busy.

I wait tables as many weekends and nights as Uncle Lenny

will let me, but my real bread and butter comes from being Saint Magdalene Prep's resident snoop. My forte is finding things. Uncle Lenny doesn't know about this. But I figure he doesn't need to know everything, especially since most of the jobs are not so PG as finding lost puppies. Most involve looking at people's hairy junk on the dark web.

In addition to lost dogs, Saint Maggie's girls need me to find evidence of cheating boyfriends. They need me to find evidence of cheating boyfriends cheating with their best friends. Evidence of cheating boyfriends cheating with their best friends' boyfriends. I'm not choosy. I'll find jewelry, pets, money. But mostly what people need help with are the nudie photos and videos given in earnest to those same cheating boyfriends. Gifts that now need tracking down and obliterating.

What I do isn't rocket science, but it takes a certain skill set that I spent the first half of my life unintentionally developing. That is, "being as sneaky as a greased copperhead," as Pastor once put it.

My phone buzzes in my pocket. It's my best friend, Nina.

Nina: Got a potential new client for you.

Me: Great. Who?

Nina's been a Saint Maggie's girl since kindergarten. She knows everyone and sniffs out a lot of jobs for me.

Nina: Kirsten Montgomery-Wiggins.

I blink at the name.

Nina: Don't kill me.

It takes me a second to find my thumbs. But when I do, my response is swift.

Me: Nope.

Nina: She seems desperate.

Bet you could charge her double. Triple.

I start to restate my position in more colorful terms, but my fingers hesitate.

The problem is that actually I'm not busy at all. Normally I've got back-to-back jobs lined up, but since failing to find Chloe's dog, three potential clients have ghosted me. I can only assume Chloe's to blame. She really should be more grateful. The lost puppy wasn't my first job for her. Freshman year I made a sticky situation with a photo of a grape Popsicle go away. (Literally sticky. Don't ask.) But the loyalty of girls like Chloe is fleeting.

Nina: Sorry, I shouldn't have even asked.

Don't worry about it. It's not worth it. I'll tell her no.

Me: Wait.

I chew the inside of my mouth. Kirsten freaking Montgomery-Wiggins. Am I really that hard up? As I'm staring at my phone, words suddenly float through my mind like a bad jingle: *Around four heads the angels flew. Silent in their keeping.*

I squeeze my eyes shut. Nope. I need a job. Something to keep my mind from Great-Aunt Regina's word games and all their attendant PTSD.

Me: Fine. Triple rates. Up front.

Kirsten owes me at least that much. And she can afford it.

Nina sends a dollar-face emoji and a devil.

Nina: Atta girl. When?

Me: Now. Tell her to meet me at my locker. I've got a free period.

A few minutes later, Nina writes back.

Nina: She's headed your way. She'll be the one who looks like she moisturizes with the tears of underclassmen. Debrief later?

Me: If by that you mean you'll drive me to the Rusty Nail after school, yes, I will take that offer and raise you a basket of okra fries upon delivery.

Nina: Good. I can't wait to hear what she's lost. I hope it's pics of her perfectly groomed muff. I bet it's monogrammed. xox

I pocket my phone and head for my locker with mingled curiosity and dread. Kirsten has to be pretty desperate to stoop so low as to ask for my help. On top of that, she and Chloe are BFFs, and Chloe can't have had anything good to say about my services.

Seriously, couldn't anyone else in the world have lost something?

I have to walk past old class photos on the way to my locker. Usually I avoid looking at my mom, but today I let myself linger in front of the class of 2005. She had short hair then, a dark bob with bangs. Her eyes are bright and she grins like I never remember seeing her grin. I barely recognize her. It's hard to imagine her here among these short tartan skirts and worldly girls.

When the school first offered me a scholarship, I was hesitant. I'd had enough of religious institutions, thanks. But I was curious to see the halls that my mother had walked down as a girl, and after the visit with Uncle Lenny, I'd tentatively agreed. That was four years ago. It hasn't always been peachy, but I like Saint Maggie's. Really the only problem I've ever had here is currently heading straight for my locker, looking like a cross between a shark and a shampoo commercial.

All clear skin and long legs, Kirsten Montgomery-Wiggins somehow manages to make the same uniform we all wear look chic and expensive. How does she do that? Mine always looks like I forgot to take the hanger out. On her way over, Kirsten passes Chloe. Oddly, Kirsten pointedly ignores her. Chloe's face goes red but she doesn't speak.

When Kirsten is a few feet away, I lift my chin and square my shoulders. My aunt Lori calls this a "power posture," and insists that it suffuses you with some sort of mystical universe energy. I would never in a million years admit it to her, but it does sort of seem to work.

"I guess you know why I'm here," Kirsten says. She folds her arms over her chest.

I swallow down my urge to kick her in the kneecaps and run. "Step into my office and tell me more." I indicate the band room, only a few feet from my locker.

The sight of us coming in together raises interest in the girls sitting around fingering their instruments. More than a couple of heads bend together to whisper. I throw open the door of a supply closet at the back of the room and flip on the lights. "Out," I tell the entwined couple, who are also busy fingering each other's instruments.

The girls look up indignantly but shuffle their uniforms back into place and scram. They know better than to argue. I pay rent to the marching band for use of this closet.

I wave to the ancient sofa they've vacated. "Have a seat."

Kirsten's nose wrinkles. "No, thank you."

"Wise," I say. "That was definitely not the worst thing that's happened there." I pull a folding chair out of a corner, drape it with a choir robe, and sit. Make-out seshes tend to not happen on rickety metal chairs, but you never know. I'd hate to be the only virgin at Saint Maggie's with chlamydia.

"I heard your great-aunt died. I'm sorry," Kirsten says, still standing. The sentiment catches me off guard. This is not a side of Kirsten I'm familiar with. I keep my guard up.

"It's okay," I say. "She was old. We weren't exactly close. How do you know about my aunt?"

She tugs at a gold cross on a delicate chain around her neck like it's choking her. "She was my neighbor."

I should have guessed. Regina's wasn't the only multimillion-dollar residence on the block, of course. Biltmore Forest is probably the most exclusive neighborhood in a hundred-mile radius. "So. What can I do for you?"

Kirsten glances at the frosted glass on the door. "Are you sure no one out there is listening?"

I hold up a finger. "Wait for it . . ." A tuba blares, joined by a trumpet and then drums. "I'm sure."

She's forced to come closer to be heard over the noise. After draping another choir robe on the couch, she sits. Her legs are long and lean, sculpted by years of some sport. Probably one involving horses.

"People say you can find things."

"People are correct." I take out my notebook and a pen. "What is it you've lost?"

"I can't tell you."

Opening to a fresh page, I nod. Roughly fifty percent of these conversations start out this way. Zero points for originality, Kirsten. I realize my nerves have settled some. It helps that I'm on the better side of our power dynamic for once.

I trot out my normal spiel: "Listen, I know it might be embarrassing, but believe me, I don't care. Think of me like a doctor, and you're a patient who just needs to get your bum rash sorted out. Whatever you say doesn't leave this closet. Frankly, at this point, you'd have to be pretty creative to shock me."

I wait while Kirsten glowers up at the dim light bulb in the closet. I'm sort of afraid she's going to make it explode out of sheer malice. "I know who has it."

"Sounds like you don't need me. I'm not a repo service. I just find."

"I mean, I know, but I don't *know*-know her."

I take another look at my old nemesis. Is this really the girl who once made me shiver in my sneakers? I almost feel disappointed. "Can you give me just a smidge more to go on?"

Kirsten huffs and takes out her phone. "I don't know her name. All I've got is this." On the screen is a picture of a pretty blond woman. Her eyes are closed. She looks either like she's sleeping, or . . .

I recoil. "She's not dead, is she?"

"No. She's alive. As far as I know."

"Good, because dead girls, while interesting, are probably a bit over my pay grade. Did you take this picture?"

"Yes."

"You didn't, like, do something to her, did you?"

"Of course not." Kirsten's answer is sharp and quick. Too quick. "Can you find her?"

"What can you tell me about her?"

Kirsten hesitates. "She might be a . . . dancer."

"I'm guessing you don't mean ballet?"

"A stripper. Maybe a sex worker."

"Gotcha. Well, that's a start. Age?"

Kirsten shrugs. "Early twenties?"

"This thing of yours that she has—is that what you're really after?"

"It is and it isn't."

Annoyance plucks at me. "It would help if you gave me an idea of what *it* is. Wanna play Bigger Than a Breadbox?"

While Kirsten glowers, I rest my chin on my hands. "I'll

just wait here until you're ready to help me help you. Believe it or not, I'm actually good at this. You're not doing yourself any favors, keeping stuff from me."

For a second I see her waver. "I *know* you're good," she says. "I wouldn't be here if I didn't need you. I have to find this girl. It's important. I know you don't exactly like me, but . . ."

"Like you?" I interrupt. To my own surprise I start to laugh. "You're worried that I don't *like* you? Are you even serious right now?"

I wait but she doesn't reply. She actually has the nerve to look sort of confused. I feel my blood kick up a degree.

"Oh, boy. Okay, let's just get this out of the way." I cap my pen. "Here's the thing: You might not remember this, but I do. From the day I got to this school, you made my life a living hell. A solid year of H-E-double-L. And frankly, that's saying a lot, because between my family getting blown up and me being shuffled through four different foster families, it wasn't the best year to begin with.

"But one thing about you, Kirsten Montgomery-Wiggins, you are determined. You decided to make sure the poor girl who'd crawled out of the holler and dared to sit next to you in class knew her place, and absolutely nothing was going to stand in your way.

"Literally the first day I got to Saint Maggie's, you opened up to page one in *Bullying for Dummies* and started drilling." I tick off on my fingers. "Tripping me in the hallway: check. Spreading rumors of bed-wetting: check. Calling me a, quote, *inbred Jesus freak cross-humper*: check." I can feel my face start to go red, but the words keep pouring from my mouth. I hardly know what I'm saying. I feel like Pastor when he used to get all caught up by the Spirit. "Calling me disgusting in front of the whole class when I got my first period during recess: check. My life was basically *Carrie* without any of the cool telekinesis stuff."

I'm breathing hard. My hands have curled into fists. God, it feels good to be mad. I make myself take in a deep breath. One Jerusalem, two Jerusalem. Push air out through my nose, like I've been taught. When I speak again, my voice is level. "The only reason I'm still at Saint Maggie's at all is that Nina Sanchez finally punched you in the face and ended your reign of terror."

Kirsten looks down, mumbling something I don't catch. The music from the band is getting louder.

"What's that?" I demand.

"I said, I might have deserved that."

"Goddamned right you did." I cross my arms over my chest. "Now. All of that happened years ago. We've both moved on. Do I *like* you? No, not at all. Never will. You're still a bully who gets off on hurting people who can't do anything to stop you." She flinches. "It's fucking sad and you should really get some therapy or something, but frankly, do whatever you want, it probably wouldn't help. People like you don't change."

She clasps her hands in her lap, tight enough to make her knuckles go white. Her fancy manicure can't hide the fact that she's been chewing her cuticles.

"Lucky for you," I say, "none of that matters now. What matters is that I am a professional and you are my client. You will pay me up front and I will bust my ass finding this girl for you. And then we can go back to our normal existence of ignoring each other. Hello, are you even listening to me?"

"You're right," Kirsten whispers. She's staring at her hands. "I'm just like them."

"What?"

She looks up. Her eyes are red. "A phone," she says. "An iPhone with my initials engraved on the back." She stands to go.

"Hold on," I say, thrown by the look on her face. Something I've said has penetrated Kirsten's perfect armor. "I—I have more questions."

"Tonight. You can come to my house."

Outside the closet the band picks up speed. Kirsten fumbles at the doorknob, letting in trumpets.

"I want my fee tonight," I say.

She doesn't deign to acknowledge the band girls' stares as she sails through their midst.

"Do you hear me?" I go to the door to yell after her, making sure I'm heard over the music. "You have to pay. Tonight!"

She waves a hand that says, *Fine.* She doesn't even look back.

"Good," I say, but she's disappeared out the door.

Everyone who's been staring at her now turns to look at me, even as they keep blooting on their brass. A cymbal crashes.

"Show's over," I say, and slam the closet door.

Roxie

"She wants you to find a stripper?" Nina asks. The gossip lights her from within. She tosses her thick black hair over her shoulder. "Is this like some *Pretty Woman*–Cinderella thing? Kirsten's lost the love of her life and wants you to track her down?"

"I think she just wants her phone back."

"The stripper stole her phone?" Nina slings her Ioniq into the parking lot of the Rusty Nail, sending gravel flying. "This gets better and better."

I look up from scrolling dark-web XXX ads to make sure we've run over no small children or animals. Nina always drives like she's just robbed a bank.

Kirsten sent me the photo of the girl she's looking for, but there's no sign of her online, at least not so far. But then again, two-thirds of these ads are just T&A, no face.

I remember something. "Hey, are Kirsten and Chloe on the outs?"

"Oh yeah, totally," Nina says.

"What happened?"

"I heard it from Jin Ae that they were together for a minute this summer, but then Kirsten decided she wasn't into girls after all."

"Interesting. The friendship didn't survive the breakup."

"I don't know if I'd call it a breakup. Sounds like they weren't really, like, together-together, but yeah, that's the gist. What's that have to do with the stripper? Is she part of some love triangle with them?"

I grin. "You'd love that, wouldn't you?"

"God yes. Keep me up on the details."

"You know I don't kiss and tell," I say. "I've told you too much already."

"You're no fun." Nina pouts.

There's already a decent crowd of craft beer drinkers sitting on the patio, basking in the afternoon sun. All will soon want a plate of our signature spicy okra fries.

Asheville is staggeringly different from the not-quite-a-town I grew up in, only a stone's throw up the road. Maybe it's the city's legacy as a turn-of-the-century high-altitude retreat for the wealthy and tuberculotic. Maybe it's something in the spring water. Either way, the town is known to have "good vibes." You can't walk down the street here without tripping over a crystal-Reiki healer. Pride flags jolly up every storefront. New art galleries and craft breweries are constantly popping up like zits. Where the rest of Appalachia struggles, Asheville is a tourist destination, its soft mountains providing adventure, but not *too* much adventure. Not *too* much Appalachia.

In contrast, my birthplace of Zebulon Corners is one of those places tourists drive through on their way to Asheville, and stop in only because they were (mistakenly) informed there might be a gas station.

“Zebulon Corners,” people muse, if the name comes up. “Isn’t that the place where that crazy preacher holed up and killed a bunch of people?”

To which the residents of said town shuffle their feet and say, “Must have been some *other* Zebulon Corners.”

I stuff my phone into my pocket and get out of the car. “Come on. You want your okra fries normal or spicy?”

“Do you even know me at all? Spicy.”

The inside of the Nail is cool and dark. Lazy ceiling fans ruffle the napkins. I want to ask Uncle Len how the treasure hunt went today, but he’s on the phone and doing inventory at the same time. I can hear him uh-huh-ing and yepping as I tie my apron on. Nina installs herself in her usual booth and pulls out her laptop. But let’s get real. She’s not here for study hour. Or even the okra fries.

“Should I see if Marcus will hand-deliver your order?” I ask.

“I haven’t got a clue what you’re talking about,” Nina says airily. She pulls up something that looks like a flyer on her screen. I catch the logo for Saint Magdalene’s Students for Racial Justice group that she’s a founding member of.

One of the reasons I love Nina so much, besides the fact that she punches mean girls for me, is that she’s never afraid to be exactly who she is. Which is a gossip-loving, justice-championing Bond-girl look-alike. She comes by her swagger honestly: Her dad is a trial lawyer and her mom is a former Miss Colombia. Mrs. Sanchez likes to hint that she was once the mistress of a drug lord, and I can never quite decide whether she’s telling the truth or just messing with me. Either way, I like her style.

Boys our age can't handle Nina. She blows their puny little minds. I saw a dude trip and fall into a fountain in the mall once, staring at her. Seriously. He had to have stitches.

Still, Marcus, our head chef, is twenty-four: eight Earth years and about a million life-years older. If they ever hooked up and her parents found out, they would use their not-insignificant fortune to build a dungeon to put Nina in until she turns eighteen. She knows this. I really don't think she'd ever go there.

But Marcus is smoking hot. And as Nina likes to remind me, it doesn't hurt to look.

"Just send me whatever you can manage without putting your ass on the line. Thanks, Hank," I hear my uncle say.

My ears perk up. Hank is Uncle Lenny's buddy from his Bureau days. Sometimes Uncle Len asks him to run checks on potential new employees. "Are we hiring?" I ask.

There are certain types of ex-cons my uncle won't bring into the restaurant. Basically anyone who'd look at his underage niece with less-than-pure designs.

He hangs up the phone. "Maybe."

"So?" I ask. "Are we millionaires?"

"Hardly." My aunt Lori throws herself into Nina's booth. "We must have turned that entire place upside down—visually, that is, because this treasure hunt is strictly *no touching*—and have zilch to show for it."

"Lori, can you get table twelve's order?" Uncle Lenny asks.

"I mean, seriously, we used to play this game as kids," Lori goes on. "It was never this hard."

"Yes it was. We just had Lucille to help us." Uncle Len glances at me, probably afraid I'm going to freak out again.

I busy myself wiping down a nearby table. "Mom was good at it?"

"The best," Lori sighs. She looks like she's about to lie down in the booth and give up. "I'm so *tired*."

"Lori. Table twelve?"

"Ugh, fine. Tyrant."

Uncle Lenny sighs at her retreating back. "I really need to fire her."

Lori lists her occupation as "lifestyle expert." Translation: She spends fifteen hours a day on social media and as little time as possible waiting tables for actual money at the Rusty Nail.

"So," my uncle says, "how was school?"

"*Amazing*," I tell him. "As per the usual."

"She almost got detention for correcting Sister Agnes in religious studies," Nina offers.

"Roxie. Again?"

I shoot Nina a dirty look, then place an earnest hand over my heart. "I could no longer be silent as she denied the significance of Lilith as a key biblical figure, just because she isn't actually *in* the Bible. Even though there are ample historical references to her in primary Hebrew texts, including a little ditty called the Dead Sea Scrolls. And I thought it was important to posit that Lilith's systematic transformation by religious scholars from an independent woman to dirty-minded succubus was instrumental in laying the foundation for thousands of years of Christian patriarchy."

"Preach," Nina says.

Uncle Lenny throws a towel over his shoulder. "Look, I get it, but you need letters of recommendation for college. Can you please keep it civil?"

"I can't help it that my growing up in a cult resulted in a profound distrust of organized religion. Sister Agnes has drunk the Catholic Kool-Aid; she thinks having a vagina is a character flaw. I'll get recommendations, don't worry. Just not from her." I start stuffing bar napkins into the holders. "That history is going to be great for my college essays, by the way. 'Poor backwoods girl escapes fiery death at hands of domestic religious terrorists, becomes national treasure.'"

He grunts, goes back to inventory.

"I need to leave early tonight," I say. "Homework date. Can I take your car?"

"Yeah, sure," Len says, then looks up. "Wait, homework date with a boy?"

"With a girl," I say, wagging my eyebrows. "What did you think all that Lilith talk was about?"

"Oh. Well. Ah . . ."

"Kidding. I mean, she is a girl, but it's not romantic."

"Oh. Right. Well, you know you can always talk to me about, um . . ." He trails off. "I mean, girls, guys, whatever. Whomever. Uh . . ."

I look over at Nina. "He's so cute when he's flustered."

Nina wrinkles her nose. "Adorable." She looks back down at her laptop and her grin disappears. She taps furiously. "Dammit. What's going on? Nononononono!"

“What’s wrong?” I ask.

“My files are gone! I spent hours working on these posters for the march on Saturday and someone on the shared drive has deleted them! Aurgh!” She throws herself back against the booth. “I loathe group work.”

“Here, let me look,” I say, scooting in beside her. I pull her laptop in front of me. “Nothing on the internet is ever truly lost. Especially where shared drives are involved.” I tap and click my way through the first levels of my normal tricks. I’ve done this a few hundred times. Usually I’m recovering and then really, *really* deleting pictures of boobs. It’s not that hard if you know what you’re doing. People act like this stuff is impossible to figure out, but all I did was spend a weekend reading Reddit threads about data recovery.

“Rox, I need a hand over here running drinks!” Uncle Lenny yells.

“Coming!” A few more clicks and then: “Voilà.”

A flashy poster pops back up on Nina’s screen. *March for Racial Justice This Saturday!* She squeals with relief. “Oh my God, you really are a genius. I love you so much.”

“I know.” She reaches out and almost hugs me. Then stops herself. I hop out of the booth and blow her a kiss. “And I know.”

Inez

Inez has a new potential customer.

The first step is to message, make sure he's not a bot. Then a phone call, long enough to pick up on psycho-killer vibes. He passes the test. It's not a high bar, but he does surprisingly well. So well that she wonders if she should worry. Has he done too well? Psychopath-well?

But she decides to move on to step three. If she's going to continue in this line of work, she can't afford to be picky *and* paranoid.

Step three is new. Step three is a date. She suggests mid-level hotel bars. Places where her customers won't run into their wives. She's found that some guys like going on the "date." They like pretending that what they're doing is more than simply an old-as-time transaction with an inevitable end. But some men are too nervous. They're still afraid of being seen, of word getting around. Some never show for the meet. Some whine and wonder why she won't just come to their homes, like other girls do. She's lost clients. So be it. These days there's always a face-to-face before a body-to-body.

She tells herself she'll see it—that something violent simmering in their eyes. The devil, her mother would have called it. Inez doesn't believe in the devil. Humans are evil enough without supernatural help. But *something* will be there, flashing like a signal. She'll see it and this time she'll be able to stop the ride and get off before the car slides from the tracks.

She meets the new guy for lunch at a place called the Rusty Nail. His suggestion. His name is Marcus. She is shocked at how good-looking he is, and almost turns around and leaves. In her experience, good-looking guys are not to be trusted.

Marcus orders okra fries and soft drinks for them. Inez doesn't drink alcohol while working, and she watches the glass go from the bartender's hand to the soda fountain to the bar top before them.

"You don't seem like the kind of guy who'd have trouble getting a date," she says, after taking a sip. Better to be frank about this sort of thing.

"This is easier," Marcus says, shrugging amiably.

He's young, Black with hazel eyes. Nice smile, a dimple high on his left cheek; strong shoulders. At least three women at the bar are eyeing him. Touching their hair, laughing loudly. All the signals.

"Relationships are complicated," Marcus tells her. "I don't need complicated right now."

"Fair enough."

It turns out Marcus actually works at the Rusty Nail. This is good news. She figures a psycho-killer wouldn't take a potential victim to his place of work.

They talk about his job (chef), where he's from (Asheville, born and raised), a TV show they both like about rescue dogs. They don't talk about her job, or even where she's from. He seems to know better than to ask.

The time goes by quickly, and soon he's standing up, apologizing for having to leave. He pays for her drink. "See you Wednesday?" Normally she's content to go straight home with the guy after a reasonably successful date. But Marcus wasn't planning on this and has already committed to going to the grocery for his grandmother before his shift starts. She'll go to his place Wednesday. Eight o'clock.

And she can't help it. She should be immune to this by now. She shouldn't even have it in her anymore. But when he kisses her cheek goodbye, a tingle spreads from his lips all the way down her throat. Something twitches inside, like it wants to unfurl. *He's going to buy groceries for his grandmother.*

She realizes she's looking forward to seeing him again.

—

Inez has just gotten home when the message comes from Buddy. A regular. Not his real name. She thinks of him as Buddy because that's what he and his friends all call each other. Can she come over later? Six p.m. He's so horny. Eggplant emoji. Eggplant emoji. Peach emoji. He gives her an address, not his dorm or frat house, somewhere she's never been before.

She sighs. She wants to say no. After the date with Marcus (not a *real* date, she reminds herself sternly), the last thing she wants to do is go service Buddy.

But Buddy always pays cash and doesn't quibble over the price. He might have an eensy coke habit, but he's never been violent or out of control.

She looks at the pile of unpaid bills on her counter.

It's a date, she writes. Wink emoji. Kiss emoji. Her face stays flat. Modern romance. Thank god for emojis.

By the time she arrives at the new address a few hours later, Marcus has been banished from her mind.

So this is where Buddy lives. She should have known he was a rich boy. Filthy rich. Oddly enough, the house is actually right next door to the mansion she cleaned at yesterday. Small world.

Before she gets out of the car, she checks her hair and makeup in the rearview mirror. She puts on lipstick, adjusts her fake eyelashes. She shoos away the part of her that is weak and small. She imagines her skin turning diamond hard. She tests her come-hither face. Her reflection is convincing.

As she's walking to the front door in her four-inch heels, she looks up. The sky is clear but she can feel it in her bones. It's going to rain.

Roxie

It starts to pour on the way to Kirsten's house. One second it's drizzly and the next it's purple-black, and by the time I get to the address Kirsten has given me, it's coming down so hard that I shoot past the driveway, missing the tasteful (read: tiny) house number on the gate. Also I was distracted by the fact that the next driveway leads to Montgomery House. I thought Kirsten just meant they lived in the same hood, but she and Great-Aunt Regina were literally next-door neighbors.

I brake, back up, and am about to pull in and announce myself at the call box when the gate opens on its own. A sporty gray Porsche barrels out. It barely slows to swerve around me and is gone.

"Rude," I tell whoever is hidden behind the car's tinted windows.

As I pull in, it occurs to me: Regina Montgomery. Kirsten Montgomery-Wiggins. Are they related? I chide myself for being too caught up in my own drama to think about it. Kirsten didn't mention anything, but it's a weird coincidence if not, especially with them being neighbors. I make a mental note to ask.

I park in front of a brightly lit mansion that is as enormous as it is unattractive. Fake columns line the portico like a plantation house. Shrubbery has been shaved into submission. The grass is an unnatural shade of green, like they've had it painted. It is a picture of upper-class normalcy and pretty much exactly the sort of place I'd expect to find Kirsten.

The only thing strange is the front door. It's wide open.

I park and make a dash through the downpour to the house. I'm drenched in an instant. On the porch I stop before crossing the welcome mat. Something's wrong. This isn't the sort of house where you leave the front door open. Air-conditioning pumps out. I stand shivering at the threshold, a puddle of rainwater forming at my feet.

"Hello?"

I press the doorbell. Unlike our doorbell's screech, brassy tones echo through the house. This place even *sounds* expensive.

There's no answer.

I wipe my feet and go in.

"Kirsten? It's Roxie. Hello?"

A grandfather clock bongs the hour a few feet away and I jump. "Pull it together, woman," I mutter to myself.

Where is she? The feeling of wrongness deepens. Why was that car hauling ass out of here? Maybe I should call the cops. This is the point in the movie when you're yelling at the main character to turn her ass around and do just that. That's what a smart person would do.

Me, I keep going.

I creep past a dining room wallpapered in blue and white like a china tea set. Past a cavernous living room with real art. It's not Montgomery House, but this place isn't too far from it. There are oil paintings of landscapes and a grand piano. I've stopped calling Kirsten's name by now. I don't like the way my voice echoes.

At the doorway to the kitchen I stop. It is cotton-wool-in-the-ears quiet.

"Kirsten?"

I'm about to turn around and do what my primordial brain has been telling me to do for a while now. *Go.*

But then I catch sight of something on the floor. It's subtle, just a little bit of something puddled behind the kitchen island. Wine maybe. And yet I still don't turn my ass around and get the hell out of there. Of course I don't. Because I'm an idiot. Because I've never been able to walk away. Because I've got to see the whole picture, every detail. I have to know.

There's a ferrous smell in the air, and below it a note of something else familiar I can't place. I walk forward, step-by-step, my stomach dipping lower and lower, until I can no longer deny what's before me. First her perfect hair, and then her perfect face, and then her long, perfect limbs.

Kirsten Montgomery-Wiggins, pale and dead in a puddle of blood and iced tea.

Inez

More pucking blood. On the hem of her dress this time. Is she going to be cleaning it up forever? Sometimes she wonders if she's imagining it. Is this how her psyche is dealing? *Out, damned spot.*

Yes, she's read Shakespeare, thank you very much.

She brews green tea.

Hell is empty,

And all the devils are here.

Damn straight.

Ghosts and devils. Her mother had believed in both. Not Inez.

Not until last night, anyway.

Fair is foul, and foul is fair.

If only Lady Macbeth had had access to industrial cleaning products. Latex gloves. A pot of tea. It might have been a very different story.

Roxie

"I still don't understand what it is you were doing here," the officer says, not for the first time.

I dig my knuckles into my eyes, then yank them away. They smell like blood. I washed my hands, but it's still there. My stomach rolls. "I told you, Kirsten invited me over."

"Uh-huh. But you say you weren't friends." Officer Lamb has an accent like he crawled fully formed out of the deepest, darkest holler in all Appalachia. He's young and shaved completely bald. It's distracting the way the lights reflect off his head.

"I mean, no, not exactly."

"Not exactly as in you were . . . what? Enemies? Lovers?"

Uncle Lenny leans in. "Officer Lamb," he says, "I think you've got everything from my niece you need. It's late. She's had a rough night, and we'd like to get home before midnight."

"Duly noted, but I'll decide when we're done here, *sir*." Officer Lamb looks over my shoulder, signals to someone.

I can sense that Uncle Lenny is physically restraining himself from reaching over and smacking the officer's silly bald head. If he were still an agent, he could pull rank, but he's not. He's Lenny Hunt, the *former* FBI agent. Most cops wouldn't have liked him in the first place on principle because cops are as territorial as tomcats, but with Uncle Lenny it's worse. They actually know him. He's that guy who turned his back on the system entirely, that asshole restaurant owner who thinks he's so great because he hires convicted criminals and *don't come crying to us when they rob your ass*.

To be fair, good cops like him. But bad cops are cynical bastards who would love to see Uncle Lenny fail. I can't tell yet which category Officer Cue Ball fits into.

After finding Kirsten, I called my uncle and 911, in that order. "I'm getting an Uber," he'd said before I was even done talking. "I'll be there in twelve minutes. Don't move. Don't touch anything."

I wanted to tell my uncle, *Duh, I'm not stupid*, but I was having trouble getting my mouth to work after blurting out that I'd stumbled onto a murder scene. Plus, I *am* stupid. I'd already walked through the blood and tea to check Kirsten for a pulse, even though it was obvious I wouldn't find one. It was clear from across the room that she was gone. A gunshot wound had opened her chest.

My uncle made sure to arrive before the cops so he'd be harder to get rid of. I know my rights, what I'm obliged to do and what I'm not; Uncle Lenny's drilled me. Still, this isn't the kind of thing I want to do alone. Lenny's been glued to my side since he got here. He isn't about to let Officer Lamb get any funny ideas about my involvement.

We're currently sitting under a police tent in the Montgomery-Wiggins driveway. It's stopped raining, but you could wring the air out like a sponge. Techs in white space suits do crime-scene stuff inside the house. There's an electricity in the air. This thing's going to be big and they know it. The ambulance left half an hour ago with Kirsten's body. I wonder where her parents are.

"Agent Hunt?"

Uncle Lenny and I turn to see a tall older man walking toward us, leaning on a cane.

"Mr. Montgomery," Uncle Lenny says, and stands up. He doesn't correct the older man about his agent status, only says stiffly, "I'm very sorry for your loss."

Mr. Montgomery acknowledges Uncle Lenny with a nod, and then his attention shifts to me. "I'm Kirsten's grandfather. I understand you found her."

I glance at Lamb, surprised he's allowing this.

Mr. Montgomery's face is lined and what little hair he has left is whispery silver. But his eyes are clear, sharp. A pale piercing blue.

"Yes," I say. "I'm very sorry, too, Mr. Montgomery. Kirsten was a . . ." *Narcissist. Bully. Snob.* "Classmate."

"Thank you for helping with the investigation," Kirsten's grandfather says. "Officer Lamb tells us you saw someone leaving the scene?"

I look at Lamb again. "Yes," I say. "I didn't get a good look at the driver, though. It was a gray Porsche, tinted windows. There are cameras along the drive, right? I'm sure they caught it."

"Let's hope so. You're at Saint Magdalene's?"

"Yes, sir." I hesitate. "Kirsten actually wanted my help finding someone. That's why I came over."

Uncle Lenny and Officer Lamb swivel to look at me.

"You didn't think to mention this before?" Lamb asks.

"Who was she looking for?" Mr. Montgomery interjects, as if Lamb hasn't spoken.

"I—I'm not sure. A girl. A woman, I guess. She was going to tell me more when I got here."

Kirsten's grandfather comes closer. Lamb finds a folding chair for him. He sits so we're almost knee to knee. He wears a cashmere sweater against the night's chill. A heavy gold signet ring lolls on his hand. Yale.

"It's a thing I do," I say. "Find stuff for people."

I should show them the photograph of the blond girl that Kirsten sent me. I should tell them about the phone that was stolen from his granddaughter. But for some dumb reason I don't.

I hear Pastor's voice shaking the little clapboard chapel:

Who shall we put our faith in? Who shall we trust? "Take ye heed every one of his neighbor, and trust ye not in any brother . . . They have taught their tongues to speak lies; they weary themselves committing iniquity."

He had looked straight at Mama when he spoke. She knew exactly what brother he was talking about.

And in the end, he was sort of right, wasn't he?

I see blue lights flashing in the infinite dark. I watch the windows blow out on our trailer, the fire so hot it melted the fillings in Mama's teeth.

"Interesting coincidence," Lamb says. "Her asking you to come over at exactly the time she's murdered."

Uncle Lenny starts to stand. "Like I said, I think we're done here."

"Please." Mr. Montgomery puts a hand out to stay us. "Roxanne, did my granddaughter say anything else about this girl? A name? Anything?"

I shake my head. "I'm sorry." Maybe I'll tell him more later. But not now, in front of Lamb.

"Can you let us know if you think of anything?"

"Yeah, sure."

Kirsten's grandfather watches me for a few seconds. "You find things for people?"

I nod, avoiding my uncle's eye.

"That's why you were here." He looks at Officer Lamb. "Can she see it?"

Lamb hesitates, then hands Mr. Montgomery a plastic evidence bag with a wrinkled piece of paper inside. The older man holds it carefully in his hands and says, "The officers found this in her pocket." He turns it so I can see the page. "Does it mean anything to you?"

The paper is creased and has a bloodstain on it. I look, then reel back, horrified. "What the hell?"

I look from the words on the paper to Mr. Montgomery to Uncle Lenny. My uncle looks as shocked as me.

Mr. Montgomery leans in, eager. "What is it? What does it mean?"

I open my mouth, but nothing comes out.

Lenny puts a hand out to stop me. "Don't answer that, Roxanne. Officer Lamb, if you have any further questions, we're happy to help, but tomorrow. At the station. With our lawyer." He's gone pale, but his voice is firm.

Lamb glances at Mr. Montgomery, who gives him a tiny nod. Lamb says, "You're free to go, Miss Hunt."

Uncle Lenny steers me to the car.

I get into the passenger seat, and it's not until I close the door that I realize that every muscle in my body is rigid. I stare at the lines of water running down the windshield.

"Why the hell did she have that?" I whisper.

"I was hoping you knew," Uncle Lenny says.

I look back out through the glass. So much blood, everywhere. Like a small lake on that kitchen floor, Kirsten's body an island. Little shards of broken crockery.

Uncle Lenny starts the car. I manage to put my seat belt on and then reach into my pocket for my lighter, clutch it in my hand. I roll the wheel, but its scratch gives me no comfort. We speed away.

In my mind, the words on the paper dance and mock.

Around four heads the angels flew
Silent in their keeping
Vanity thy name is mine
And paint masked all the weeping

Roxie

AGE SIX

The woman and the little girl are making the long trek home up the mountain. Sav-Mor groceries sit on the back seat of the car, their plastic sacks shivering in the wind. The car's air-conditioning doesn't work, but the little girl doesn't know to miss it. She is six. She likes riding in the car with her mama, with the windows down. She turns her skinny arm into an airplane wing.

Her mother knows to miss air-conditioning. She misses air-conditioning very much, thanks. Guiltily, in secret. It's why she lingered at the Sav-Mor this afternoon, long past when she'd collected her thirty dollars' worth of groceries. She had put the little girl in the cart and pushed her down each aisle twice, savoring her goose bumps. The girl had been uncharacteristically quiet, eyes full of the rainbow parade of products towering on each side. Things she knew better than to ask for.

In the back seat now, the little girl's sleeves are rolled up. She's hiked the ankle-length skirt up past her tiny knobby knees. She makes a *veee-ooo* noise under her breath as her arm slices humid mountain air, hits the occasional bug.

Her mother looks at her in the rearview mirror. "Have you figured it out yet?"

The little girl frowns. "I'm thinking. Tell me again."

The game always starts the same way, with the words the woman learned as a child: *"And I will give thee the treasures of darkness, and hidden riches of secret places, that thou mayest—"*

The little girl interrupts. "Yeah, I know that part. Tell me the rest. *My arms* . . ." She frowns. "You say it. I can't remember."

Her mother says:

When you take my arms
And dance with me
I'm as tipsy as can be
One foot spins
Two elbows resting
Heavy loads I'll be besting

The little girl's scowl deepens as she mouths the words silently to herself. She's kicked off her shoes, too, and now she rests a heel on the open window. Her mother's smile falters. The naked foot makes her uneasy. She should tell her to put it down.

"Can we have hot dogs tonight?" the girl asks.

"Are you thinking about it? What gets tipsy when you dance with it?"

"I'm thinking! Can we?"

"We'll ask Pastor when we get home." The woman pushes strings of hair behind her ears. Her aunt had laughed when she started wearing the long dresses, pulling her hair into a braid. "You look like a Mennonite. Is he a Mennonite?"

It had been one of their last conversations.

They pass the general store in the curve, long since out of business, but with the Coca-Cola fridge still on the front porch. The old man who used to tend the store lifts a hand to them from his vegetable patch. A couple of black hens strut at his feet. The little girl waves exuberantly, but the woman hesitates, then lifts her hand too late, when he's already out of sight. Her husband never waves back when they drive past the old man. Her husband doesn't wave at anyone.

They start up the big hill. The woman's keeping an eye on the car's temperature gauge. It's in the red zone. She downshifts, presses the accelerator, and cajoles the ancient vehicle with a mix of promises and curses under her breath until they reach the turnoff for home. The teenage boys who live down the road have knocked over their mailbox again. Pastor will have to go out and fix it.

"Is it Benjamin?" the little girl asks.

"Now, where on that horse could I hide a piece of candy? You know Benjamin's sweet tooth."

"Yeah, and Benjamin isn't tipsy. But he does carry heavy stuff."

"Think about the elbows."

The little girl leans her head back against the seat, frowning.

The woman can picture her husband coming down the road to examine the damaged mailbox, swinging his pickax, a post-hole digger on his broad shoulder. His eyes shaded by his hat brim, mouth hidden by his black beard, he will mull a sermon as he works. He's been preaching lately about Babylon. *We would have healed Babylon, but she is not healed: forsake her and let us go every one into his own country.*

They're definitely in their own country out here. She reaches into her purse and fishes out a roll of Tums. Chews one against the ulcer in her belly. It always gets worse at the turnoff.

She wishes to God she could smoke a cigarette. Sometimes she goes for a walk in the woods and, when she's sure she's alone, she picks up a twig of about the right size and puts it in her mouth. Takes out her old lighter, flicks it, even though there's no butane in it. She takes a deep inhale around the stick, pretends to fill her lungs.

It's not the same.

The gravel road to their home is shady and dark, rutted. She has to go slow so the car doesn't scrape. As she chews her Tums, the chores she hasn't done yet start to flutter in, roost in her brain. Dinner, feeding the humans and then the animals. There's laundry to take in off the lines, and she's left the beans too long in the garden. They need picking; they'll be getting tough. She wonders if she'll have time this evening. Probably depends on how long vespers go. They're reading Jeremiah. Again. *Thus shall Babylon sink, and shall not rise from the evil that I will bring upon her: And they shall be weary.*

You said it, Jerry. She is weary and ulcerous and would be tempted to sell her soul for a night of HBO in an air-conditioned hotel.

The little girl sits up straight. "I think I know what it is."

"Put your foot down," her mother tells her. "Straighten your dress."

They bump into the clearing. The woman doesn't see anyone around. She feels her chest ease a little. She parks in front of their trailer, the most attractive of the five. She tries to keep it nice. Tidy. Flowers in the boxes that hang off the porch. Sister Kathleen keeps their place clean and orderly, but she thinks flowers are a vanity.

The little girl throws herself out of the car and takes off for the barn at a sprint. Her mother smiles after her. Clever girl. She's figured it out. "Come get the rest of these bags and bring them in after you find it!" she yells.

The woman carries the sacks up to the trailer and fumbles with the screen door, finally manages to get it open without dropping anything. It's dark inside. She heads to the tiny galley kitchen, thinking she'll put the groceries up and then go back out into the cooling evening to get the beans before she has to put supper on.

"Where have you been?"

Her heart jumps like a startled bird. The bags slip from her hands and land on the linoleum.

She glances over her shoulder. He's sitting at the dining table in the gloom, silent and still as a mountain. The good book is open in front of him.

She swallows, mouth dry. "I—I was at the Sav-Mor," she says. She stoops to pick up the bags. "Groceries."

He licks a finger, turns a page. "It's been three hours. I called you a dozen times."

She winces. Her phone is still in her purse. She hasn't looked at it since they went into the store.

"I'm sorry," she says. She keeps her tone calm, neutral. "I didn't hear it."

He doesn't answer. She can feel him. He fills every space in the room. She sees his chest rising and falling from the corner of her eye.

She keeps slowly taking things out of the bags, putting them away. Small movements. Her hands shake. Cornmeal, Crisco, hot dogs, sugar, flour. Buttermilk and toilet paper. Things they can't grow at home. Mark-downs and Sav-Mor brand specials. She pulls the receipt out of the last bag, smooths it, and places it on the counter. He will want to check it. She takes the change out of her pocket, eighty-five cents, and puts it down next to the receipt.

"Give me your phone."

She finds it in her purse and hands it over. Her palm is sweating. She goes back to the kitchen. He flips the phone open, looks through her call history, his frown deepening even though there is nothing there but his own name. He pockets it, watching her. She sees, but doesn't protest.

The air in the trailer is hot and torpid. She feels like the stained ceiling is pressing down on her.

"There was traffic," she says. "School was letting out and—"

He slaps a hand down on the table. She jumps. Tastes blood in her mouth. She's bitten her lip.

She knows better than to look at him. She pulls a frying pan down. She'll get started on dinner. A bowl to mix the cornbread in. She takes a knife out of the drawer, sets it on the cutting board. It's old but she keeps it sharp.

His voice rumbles out of the darkness. *"For Adam was first formed, then Eve. And Adam was not deceived, but the woman being deceived was in the transgression."*

He stands up.

Her breath quickens. Her bladder feels very full all of a sudden. She edges closer to the knife.

Her husband is a big man, dark hair, dark eyes, old Scots-Irish stock. Raised chopping wood and mending machinery with his hands. Arms like tree roots. She marvels sometimes at how crazy she once was for him. He inspired a lust that would creep over her like a rash. A lust that wasn't even in the spitting range of proper. She would watch him from the front pew, burning, feeling like every time he glanced her way he could see straight through her dress, past her ribs, into the heat of her sinful desire. Fighting it only made it worse.

He said God sent her to him that day she first stepped into his orbit. Actually it had been a hangover. There was a trail to a waterfall that led past the church, and she'd been hiking with two girlfriends from her dorm, all of them trying to stave off the effects of last night's frat party with some fresh morning air. They had heard the commotion coming from the clapboard building and gotten a fit of the giggles, daring each other to go into the snake-handling, poison-swilling, talking-in-tongues church. She was the wildest of the three, and so she did it. She went through the doors and sat down. And there he'd been, like a goddamned young Moses, like Charlton Heston up there behind the pulpit.

They'd gotten married three weeks later. She quit school. She'd been pregnant by the time they'd known each other a fortnight.

He walks toward her, languid as a cat.

She continues her charade of dinner prep.

There is no lust left in her veins, but sometimes the fear feels exactly the same. Like touching a live wire and losing all control. She can feel his breath on the back of her neck.

"For if a man know not how to rule his own house . . ."

He wraps his calloused hand around the front of her neck. Her fingers flutter toward the knife, but she is too far away. And he knows that if it came down to it, she would never be able to do it. She's not a killer.

He presses up against her and she can feel him through his clothes, her thin dress.

". . . how shall he take care of the church of God?"

"Please . . ." she rasps.

The side of her head explodes in pain. Black bursting with bright stars, and then she's surprised to find herself sitting on the floor.

He watches her blink and look from the blood that is dripping down from her hair into her lap, up to the edge of the oak cabinets he built and installed himself the first year of their marriage, when carpentry felt like love. One of her hairs hangs there.

"Get up," he says.

She tries, but she's too slow, and he picks her up by her braid, by the hair he used to bury his face in when they were first married. He'd been tucked in between her hair and her neck when he'd said, "I think I love you more than God," and before she could figure out what to say to that, he threw himself out of their bed with a strangled sort of yelp, grabbed his belt, and went out to the barn. He returned later with welts across his back and a new look in his eyes.

It's this look he gives her now. He takes hold of her thin arm in one hand, starts to undo his belt with the other.

"Please," she says again, and feels something loose in her mouth, a molar come unstuck.

"Mama?"

The adults both go still, turn to look at the tiny silhouette in the door.

She is small enough that the plastic bags she carries drag the ground. She hefts them up over the doorsill, takes a tentative step inside.

The woman swallows blood, clears her throat. "It's okay, honey."

The girl looks at the drops of blood on the floor. Looks at her mother's face. Her lip starts to tremble.

Pastor lets go of his wife. He steps toward the little girl. "Out."

She doesn't move. "Mama?"

His hand curls into a fist.

Her mama staggers forward, nearly falls, laughs at herself—"So clumsy!"—comes around Pastor and takes the groceries out of her daughter's tiny hands. She smooths her child's fine hair. "Did you find it?" she asks quietly.

The little girl glances at her father. He isn't supposed to know about their game. It's blasphemous. "It was in the wheelbarrow," she whispers. She clutches the plastic-wrapped candy in her dress pocket.

"Smart girl." Her mother kisses her daughter's forehead. Her lips leave a smudge of blood. Seeing it, her smile fades. Her eyes go dull. "Go out and play."

"But—"

"Go," her mother says. "I'm fine, I just tripped," and then she's pushing her out the door. The little girl resists, tries to slip past her, but she sees her father coming up behind her mother. His eyes are pricks of light in the dim room, and she doesn't see him, but an animal in a cave, a beast. She freezes. And then her mother is closing the door in her face, locking it.

The girl can hear noises inside after that, unidentifiable. Thumps and snarls. The noises of a beast.

She bangs on the door for a long time, but no one lets her in.

Eventually she takes the candy out of her pocket and throws it as hard as she can, away into the growing darkness.

Roxie

"You don't have to go to school today," Uncle Lenny says. He sets a cup of coffee and a bowl of granola in front of me at the kitchen table. "You can just stay here and rest. Watch bad TV."

I poke at my breakfast. "Tempting."

He pretends not to monitor me out of the corner of his eye as he goes about his business, banging things loudly, making one of his disgusting green smoothies.

"Uncle Len?"

He's back at the table in an instant.

"I want to come with you next time," I say. "To Montgomery House."

His brow furrows. "Rox . . ."

"I'm good at the treasure hunt game."

"I don't doubt it. That's not what I'm worried about."

I shift in my seat. "I know I freaked out at the restaurant before. But I'm okay now."

"Roxanne," he says gently, "you found your classmate murdered last night. It's okay to not be okay."

I stir my granola. I have zero appetite.

Uncle Lenny is looking at me like I'm something delicate and potentially explosive. A land mine. "You told Officer Lamb that you 'find things' for people. What did you mean by that?"

Damn. Here we go. I blow steam off my coffee, stalling. "Girls at school sometimes ask me to help them find things they've lost," I say carefully.

"Like what?"

Pictures of boobs.

"Oh, jewelry. Pets. Sometimes files."

"Files?"

"Computer files."

"Yes, I'm familiar with the concept. What *kind* of files?"

I gesture vaguely. "Stuff that gets accidentally deleted . . . You know, homework and stuff."

Dirty pics. Mostly photos of people's hoo-hoos.

"Why you?"

"I'm good at it?"

Uncle Lenny's brow puckers further. "It sounds like it could be potentially dangerous."

"Dangerous? Not necessarily."

"*Roxanne.* What's that mean?"

"It means I am very careful."

"Rox, a girl who wanted you to find someone for her got murdered last night. That sounds dangerous to me."

My stomach goes cold. I push my untouched granola away. "That had nothing to do with finding stuff," I say.

"It could have had everything to do with it."

"Listen, can I do the treasure hunt with you, or not?"

Uncle Lenny doesn't reply. He just keeps staring at me. I stare back.

I don't know how to explain out loud the feeling I woke up with. I just know I can't pretend like I didn't see those words scribbled on the note in Kirsten's pocket. The part of me that needs to know *why why why* is not going to let it go. That part of me is a physical thing. I've always had it. Mama used to call it curiosity. Pastor called it disobedience. My psychiatrist might have come close when he said maybe we should explore the idea of compulsiveness; an unbearable feeling like something is "just not right."

To me, it's like this: When I was seven, a family of squirrels took up residence in the space between the ceiling and the roof of our trailer. For weeks they'd squeak and scrabble over our heads on their little clawed feet and you couldn't help but feel like they were about to come dropping down on you, chittering and scratching. None of us could sleep or eat or think straight while they were there. Eventually Pastor tore half the roof off to get to them. I know it sounds dumb, but that's what it feels like now. Like squirrels. Like there's something skritching around on my insides that won't leave me alone. Sometimes rolling the wheel on Mama's lighter helps. For a while. But the only way to make that feeling go away is to satisfy it. To expose it. To tear the roof off. To see it and understand.

My uncle reaches out to hold my hand. I want to let him. I really do. But I can't help it. I pull my own back.

He puts his hand in his lap. His face is hard to read. He's not upset; it's something else. "Okay," he says finally. "You can come with us. We'll go this afternoon."

—

Uncle Lenny drops me off at school. As soon as I walk through the doors, I regret my decision to be here. I'm met with whispers and red-eyed stares. Bad news travels fast.

Nina's waiting for me at my locker. "Congratulations," she says. "You're the hottest gossip since Tricia Hensley hooked up with that K-pop star. Well, you and Kirsten, obviously."

A puddle of blood and shattered crockery looms behind my eyeballs. I try to think of some witty repartee but can't make my brain get past the sight.

"Rox? You okay?"

I make a show of messing around in my locker, taking books out and putting them back in. "I'm fine."

"You wanna talk?"

"No."

Hurt flashes in Nina's eyes. I lower my voice. "How does everyone know I was there anyway? My name's not in the news."

Nina shakes her head. "Maybe Kirsten's parents told someone else's parents?"

I hadn't seen her mom or dad last night. God, they must be a wreck. I wonder why her grandfather was there and not them.

"I saw the murderer," I say.

Nina creeps closer. "You did?"

"I saw a car, anyway, leaving the house. Not who was driving it, though."

"Holy shit. You could have walked in on them killing her. You didn't see the driver?"

"No. It was raining pretty hard and the car windows were tinted. They had security cameras on the driveway, though.

They'll run the plates and figure out who it was." I edge closer. "But listen, there's something else. You know the whole treasure hunt thing I was telling you about? Great-Aunt Regina and her diamonds?"

I tell her about the poem they found in Kirsten's pocket. Nina's eyes go wide as I speak. "But . . . How? Why?"

"They were neighbors. Maybe Great-Aunt Regina gave her the poem also?"

Nina frowns. "Like she wanted her to find the diamonds, too?"

"I don't know, it doesn't make sense to me either. But maybe if I do the hunt and find the necklace, it will."

"What about the dancer Kirsten was trying to find? Kirsten's phone?" Nina asks. "What did the police say about that?"

"Um," I say, not meeting my friend's eye, "I might not have told them about the stolen phone."

"What?" Nina asks. "Why not?"

Trust issues—cough—with cops.

I shrug. Nina gives me a long look. But she doesn't push. "Come on," she says. "We're going to be late for class."

As we walk down the hall, she glares ferociously at the people watching us until they drop their eyes, cowed.

My best friend Nina is a fairy-tale queen.

Not a blond Disney princess. Nina's the old-school kind. An off-with-their-heads queen. One who is gorgeous and terrifying. One who'd make her enemies dance in red-hot iron shoes until they fell down dead.

It's good to be friends with the queen.

—

I keep checking the news all day between classes, but either the police haven't identified the Porsche and its driver yet or they're playing their cards close to their chests.

Kirsten's death becomes a bigger and bigger news story. By the time I check after lunch, it's even been picked up nationally. Of course it has. People love this sort of thing. Young, pretty rich girl gets slashed. Murderer on the loose. Meanwhile war, famine, etc. . . . yawn, who cares.

People are the worst.

I've tucked myself into a corner table in the library with my laptop. The news outlets have found Montgomery-Wiggins family photos somewhere, and they keep flashing the same one: happier times on a powerboat. Parents: trim and athletic. Kirsten and her big brother, Mitch: paragons of vitality, smiling like someone asked to count their teeth.

I know I should have told Officer Lamb and Mr. Montgomery everything about the girl and the phone Kirsten wanted me to find. I'm not stupid. I know I should tell them and back away. Lamb's the cop. I'm the sixteen-year-old. But I don't. I find myself staring at Kirsten's blond dancer's photo. Who is she? Why did Kirsten want to find her? Kirsten had a new phone by the time we talked. I mean, she could have bought a hundred new phones a hundred times over. Why did she want *this* one back? Was it personal? And the million-dollar question: Did the dancer have something to do with Kirsten's death?

It only takes a quick search to find Kirsten's family's social media pages. I start with her mom. The photo of the boat outing is on her pages. I assume that's where all the news outlets got it. Sculpted, polished, Carol Montgomery-Wiggins's profile picture is a practiced smile, good enough for public, but there's something fragile underneath it. The longer I look, the more it looks like a grimace. It's like she's bracing herself. Like she knows something bad is just over the horizon. Am I reading into it too much? Sometimes I find myself wondering how people could have looked at my mother back then and not *known*. It was written all over her. Why didn't they say something? Why didn't they ask? Where's the line between minding your own business and ignoring something because you just don't want to get involved?

I shake thoughts of my mother out of my head and send Kirsten's mom a message.

Mrs. Montgomery-Wiggins,
This is Roxanne Hunt. You probably know who I am by now. I am so sorry for your loss. If there's anything I can do, please let me know.

I'm dubious she'll read it, even more so that she'll respond. Who checks their social media at a time like this? But I add my phone number, just in case. I search online and find that Kirsten's mother works for her father William Montgomery's vaguely named company, SouthEast Holdings. There's not much on the internet about them. They don't seem to even have a website.

I don't find a social media page for Kirsten's dad, but her brother, Mitch, is on a couple of different sites. Like his mom, his accounts aren't yet set to private. That will happen soon, once the media requests and the crazies get to be too much. Mitch is a freshman at Miramont College, a very good and stupidly expensive private university in Asheville.

He hasn't posted anything since Kirsten's death, and his old posts are mostly about major-league sports rivalries, partying with friends, or his red Jeep Wrangler, which he seems to be in a serious relationship with. The most interesting thing he's posted is what looks like a missing-person poster. It's pinned to come up first on his profiles. "HAVE YOU SEEN EVAN?" it asks, displaying a headshot of a fratty-looking guy and a phone number.

While I'm in my account, I glance through my notifications and messages, but I'm set to private, so there's not much to see. No requests for interviews. No dredging up of my sordid little family history and connecting it to this newest bloody twist. Not yet, anyway.

I feel a tap on my shoulder and slam my laptop lid shut. I swivel to find Chloe Hamilton staring at me with big, mascara-streaked eyes.

"Can I sit?" she asks, nodding at the empty chair beside me.

I make room, trying to mask my surprise, and she perches carefully, like her limbs are made of glass.

Chloe shudders a breath. "You found her?"

I nod.

"At least you found something."

I don't answer. Chloe isn't exactly a bitch, but she sure could play one on TV. She's a ballet dancer. Book smart. Pretty enough, in a white-bread sort of way. I wonder if her dad's bought her a new dog yet.

She lets out a long, careful exhale. I recognize the measured way she does it. A therapist made her practice in front of them. "What sort of asshole would do something like that?"

I shake my head.

"Why were *you* there?" Chloe hears the way this sounds—jealous—and blushes, but doesn't back down.

I hesitate. Kirsten never specifically said not to talk to her friends—or ex-friends—about what she wanted me to find. I weigh the pros and cons. On the one hand, Chloe might know who the girl is. On the other, everyone's a suspect at this point. It could have been Chloe behind the wheel of that Porsche last night. She could be here talking to me as a fishing trip, trying to see what I know.

"She asked me to come over," I say finally.

Chloe's face twitches. "But why? You guys, like, hated each other."

"We didn't *hate* each other."

Chloe gives me a look.

"Okay, maybe I hated her, but I was way beneath the mental effort it would have taken for Kirsten to hate me."

Understanding dawns on Chloe's face. "She asked you to find something, didn't she?"

I don't answer. "Was there anything strange going on with Kirsten recently?"

“Other than her being a complete bitch to me for the last month?” Chloe takes a second to adjust her posture and compose herself. “I’m sure you heard the gossip. We were . . . together.”

She looks past me. Past the study carrels and heavy oak bookshelves, toward the stone-framed windows where you can gaze onto the green lawn, soft and even as a pelt.

“And then you weren’t?” I ask.

She glares back at me, her hurt and anger clearly looking for a target. She quivers with the intensity of it for a second, and then deflates all in a rush. “I think . . . I think she was seeing somebody else she didn’t want me to know about. A guy.”

“Who?”

“I don’t know. She wouldn’t admit to it.”

“What makes you think she was seeing someone, then?”

Chloe considers me. “I saw her out with him once, at night, downtown. They looked . . . intimate.”

I see it in her guilty sideways glance. Chloe was following Kirsten.

“Did you ask her about him?”

“She denied it, freaked out, and called me a stalker.” Chloe brushes roughly under her eyes. “Please. It’s not like I don’t know my best friend when I see her. After that she stopped talking to me completely. Wouldn’t answer my texts or calls.”

“And you’d never seen him before? The guy she was with?”

“I think he was from her dad’s office.”

“Why do you think that?”

“Her dad hires law students over the summer. They’re

always hot. And she was working there part-time. He was older. Put two and two together."

"Would you recognize him again if you saw him?" I ask.

"Maybe . . . I only saw him for a second. Short brown hair, tall." She looks up. "You don't think it was him who . . . ?"

I lift my shoulders. "Maybe."

"Her mom said it was some rando."

"She did?" I can't keep the surprise out of my voice. Why would she say that? Is that what she really thinks? Is that what the cops told her? That it was a botched robbery or something?

"I had a bad feeling about that guy," Chloe says darkly.

"Why?"

"Just . . . he looked, I don't know, sketchy? Definitely too old for her. Probably some sort of pervert. When I saw them, she seemed upset. She was telling him something. Like, pouring her heart out." Chloe's face twitches with the effort of holding back tears.

I want to tell her to just go ahead and cry, but I'm afraid she might scratch my eyes out.

"What do you think they were talking about?"

"I don't know, do I? She didn't want to confide in her *stalker*."

The bell rings for the end of the period, and Chloe shakes herself. She stands up, straightens her skirt, runs a tissue under her lashes. Her back elongates and her feet turn out into what I think is second position. She doesn't even seem to realize she's doing it. She makes it look like a fighting stance.

"Did you find what Kirsten was looking for?" she asks. Her voice is moderated.

"No."

She snorts, like she's not surprised. "If that guy I saw did this to her—they had better nail his ass. Fuck a trial. I'd like to see him dragged out in the road and shot."

The unvarnished words crawl up my spine. Something ugly twists Chloe's pretty face. I think again about her and her new boyfriend circling in her car, waiting for me to lead them to their prey. I want to ask where she was the night Kirsten was murdered. But I'll find out some other way. I'm not sure I want to get on Chloe Hamilton's bad side.

Inez

The death of Kirsten Montgomery-Wiggins is all over the news.

Inez sits in the blue light of the television. She waits for the reporter to say something about a suspect. A car leaving the scene. Inez is pretty sure the Porsche's windows were tinted enough, but still. Where had that girl come from? There wasn't supposed to be anyone home until late.

No leads, the reporter says. Anyone with information should call this number.

Should she be worried? Is a SWAT team about to burst through the door of her trailer? Should she run? Hide? But where would she go? She has no money for a hotel, no one she can think of to stay with. And frankly she doesn't have the energy.

The news segment ends and another begins. A new plan to revitalize an old neighborhood. People are protesting. Their signs say *Urban Renewal Means Black Removal*.

There is still nothing about a man's body being found.

She lifts the remote, turns the TV off. She's left in a vacuum of night and wraps her quilt tighter around her shoulders. Sometimes she can still catch a whiff of her mother in the fabric. Through the open windows, the September evening is cooling. The last of the summer insects drone. They grow quieter every night. Soon it will be too cold to leave the windows open.

Bits and pieces from that night are coming back to her. The sound of laughter, the shape of an ear, too close to her face. Chunky gold rings on old-man fingers. The boy in the pink shirt's neck, young and sunburned, dripping sweat. Mixed in are things she knows aren't real. A man with the face of a wolf. A claw raking down her arms. She squeezes her eyes shut until the pictures flare and fade. Who needs to remember something like that? It's not like she could ever explain any of it, if it came down to it. It's not like she can tell the police. They'd be on her in a second with solicitation charges.

On top of . . . well. Murder.

Roxie

"Don't touch, dear. It's rococo."

I pull my hand away from the gilded frame. "It's ro-diculous," I mutter.

Uncle Lenny gives me a warning look, which I pretend not to notice. Painted on the cabinet's doors is a lady on a swing, her baby-blue dress foofing in the wind, sunbonnet about to fly off. Flower garlands are dangled by cherubs in claustrophobic swoops. The whole thing makes my sinuses ache.

Aunt Lori comes up behind me. "Do you think this is it? Look! Angels!" She scans the words of the poem she's scribbled onto a piece of paper. "And it's painted!"

Around four heads the angels flew
Silent in their keeping
Vanity thy name is mine
And paint masked all the weeping

"No. Where are the four heads?" I say. "Plus, none of the rest of the poem fits. Plus, that thing is butt-ass ugly, rococo or no-co."

"Language," Uncle Lenny grunts.

"It's not ugly," Lori says, licking her lips. "It's *expensive*."

The housekeeper, Ms. Claverhill, sniffs disapprovingly. I've always liked Ms. Claverhill. I appreciate her razor-sharp sense of order. The first thing she did when we arrived at Montgomery House today was remind us of the ground rules of the treasure hunt. Number one was wipe your feet before entering. Number two was no touching. Everything she says seems to take on particular gravity, too, because she says it in a British accent. (Uncle Lenny: "Of *course* Aunt Regina's housekeeper is British. Typical.")

Ms. Claverhill explained for my benefit that the next clue would be hidden inside an object somewhere on the grounds. We were to choose something, guided by the first clue-poem. It was just like I used to play with Mama, except instead of a piece of candy as our prize, we'd find a new clue inside the object. That clue would lead us to another object and so on until we finally found the diamonds.

"The chifforobe *is* valuable," Ms. Claverhill tells Lori. "But if it does not contain the next clue, you may not keep it."

Oh yeah, that's the other thing. If we guess correctly, the objects we pick are ours to keep. Or sell to the highest bidder, if I know my aunt at all.

Lori's not the only one who's mentally appraising the wares. I've already noted a Miró and a Chagall on the walls, and we've barely made it past the foyer. I'm reminded that the diamond necklace was hardly the most valuable thing in the house. I wonder why Great-Aunt Regina chose it as the prize.

"Shall we make our way to the library?" Ms. Claverhill asks. "Inez has put the tea service out for us."

She leads the way and Uncle Lenny drops back to my side. "You okay?"

I give him a thumbs-up. Yes, I quietly hyperventilated in the back seat of the car on the way over here, but I'm good now. The memory of Kirsten's corpse is pushing me on. Maybe her murder had nothing to do with the clue-poem found in her pocket, but I still want to know why she had it. I need to know. All I can do is play the game, hope it leads me to some sort of answer that will soothe these goddamn squirrels running around in my bones.

"Where did you guys look when you were here before?" I ask.

"Everywhere," he says. "We just couldn't ever convince ourselves we had the right thing."

"I'm still partial to the Alfa Romeo," Lori says over her shoulder.

Uncle Lenny sighs.

Ms. Claverhill leads us through a room with twelve-foot ceilings and end tables displaying ceramic figurines—shepherdesses mostly—as delicate as spun sugar. I remember being told on my first visit that this room was off-limits. I had a history of colossal destruction, so, fair.

Great-Aunt Regina's mansion shares a property line with the Biltmore Estate, the famous home of the Vanderbilts. It was built around the same time and is also historically landmarked.

The first time I came here was with Uncle Lenny at Christmas, a couple of months after the adoption was finalized. My parents had been in the ground for over a year. I was spit-shined and polished, on a variety of prescribed drugs meant to medicate the feral out of me. I had stopped setting fires. That night I had even consented to wear a dress (fine, Uncle Lenny had paid me ten bucks). Not that this effort ingratiated me to Great-Aunt Regina's guests, a who's who of Asheville's small but powerful tribe of real estate moguls, golf-course owners, and retired investment bankers. Great-Aunt Regina had filled them in on my sordid history and they treated me like a rescue dog. Cute, but probably full of worms. A biter.

So I was surprised when Great-Aunt Regina suddenly appeared at my elbow while I was staring at the ceiling-scraping tree, trying to distract myself from thinking about my last Christmas Eve with my parents. That one I'd spent shivering by the creek, a campout that Pastor had decided would help us fully appreciate how Jesus had been born in a barn. The night had been cold enough to curl rhododendron leaves. Still, it was one of my better memories. I had huddled in Mama's lap, even though I was too big for that sort of thing. Covered in a scratchy wool army blanket, I had relished the rare opportunity to be close to her without Pastor giving me that look and telling me to stop acting like a baby.

"Having fun?" Great-Aunt Regina asked. She was wearing purple velvet and fox fur, jewels on knobbed fingers that clutched the head of an ebony cane. The famous necklace was slung around her neck as casually as Mardi Gras beads.

"Yes, ma'am."

She arched an imperial eyebrow. "No, you're not. Don't lie to a liar." Looking around, she added, "I'm bored stiff. These things just haven't been the same since the doctors took away my bourbon."

I looked at her out of the corner of my eye, curious despite myself.

"You should have been here back when I was young and gorgeous. Lord, we had to roll some of these old farts out in wheelbarrows the next morning. The dancing! The sex! The drugs!" Her eyes shone with a thousand reflected twinkle lights.

She snapped her fingers at a passing waiter. "You. Give us two of those. Don't just stand there with your mouth open. Who's cutting your checks?"

Great-Aunt Regina downed the glass of eggnog he had handed over and smacked her lips. "That's better."

I sniffed mine before taking a sip. My eyes watered. "You know I'm twelve, right?"

She dabbed cream from the corners of her mouth and shrugged. "I know you're Lucille's child. The orphan."

"I prefer to go by Roxie."

"Roxanne Hunt. Snake charmer. Poison drinker." Her mouth twisted in a smile. "Girl pulled from the wreckage."

Seeing the blood rise in my cheeks, she laughed. "Don't take it the wrong way, child. I'm a survivor, too. All the best of us are."

I didn't know what to say to that, so I just took a great big gulp of my drink. I choked, but managed to keep it down. Great-Aunt Regina nodded approvingly. "I prefer my bourbon straight, but at this point I'd drink bathtub gin. It's the only way I'm going to make it through an evening with these fools."

Eventually Uncle Lenny swooped in to chastise his aunt and relieve me of my beverage. (Uncle Lenny: "She's a kid!" Great-Aunt Regina: "Never too late to start.")

We pass through a sitting room with tall windows looking out onto the yard. Or maybe this is a parlor. There are more rooms in this house than I have names for. Through the glass the Blue Ridge Mountains are on display above an autumn flower garden: late roses, zinnias, and bright blobs of dahlias.

At the end of the garden lies a hedge maze (yes—a hand-to-god *hedge maze*), at the heart of which is a small family cemetery. You really have to wonder about people who'd put their graves in the middle of a maze. Is it some sort of elaborate metaphor? A joke? Like, congratulations for making it through, you probably hoped for a fountain because you're likely very thirsty, but instead here's some dead people. The stone obelisks of their monuments poke up from the center of the groomed boxwoods like giant pointy heads.

"You may sit on the furniture," Ms. Claverhill says, ushering us into the library. "But please remember not to touch anything else."

"Bottoms only," I say. "Got it."

A woman in a maid's uniform is leaving the room as we enter. "Thank you, Inez—you can go back to polishing," Ms. Claverhill tells her.

A silver tea service waits for us in front of a cold fireplace, along with one of those blue tins of stale cookies old people always have hanging around their houses.

I grab a cookie and walk to the shelves. I scan the volumes, but nothing jumps out at me. I'd searched, but couldn't find any trace of the clue-poem online. Maybe it's by some obscure poet in one of these books? Maybe the necklace is hidden in a hollowed-out cavity? That has a very Agatha Christie feel to it.

But then again it seems too easy, and besides, nothing about the poem says "book."

"Is that gold?" Lori asks, pointing at some sort of nautical-looking instrument on a rolltop desk.

"No," Ms. Claverhill says, enough scorn in the one-syllable word that a lesser flower would wilt.

Lori doesn't seem to notice. She peers into a vase. "Is this a Ming?"

The housekeeper looks pained. *"No."*

"How long have you been the housekeeper here, Ms. Claverhill?" I ask.

She takes a second to straighten her already perfect posture. She doesn't wear a uniform, just a simple navy skirt, a white blouse, and a sweater with small pearl buttons. Reading glasses hang on a chain around her neck, no jewelry. "Thirty-two years." There's pride in her voice.

"You knew Aunt Regina better than anyone," Uncle Lenny says.

She tilts her head. "I knew her." Ms. Claverhill apparently has feelings about how well staff should "know" their employers.

"She wasn't easy, was she?" Aunt Lori asks.

Ms. Claverhill doesn't answer directly. Instead she walks to a portrait on the wall of a young Great-Aunt Regina. "Mrs. Montgomery had a certain . . . magnetism. People flocked to her. So many parties took place under this roof. She loathed boredom above all else." Ms. Claverhill's cheeks go pink, like she's said too much.

I walk over to study the portrait.

"Bevies of suitors wooed her after her divorce," Lori says, coming to stand beside me. "She was still young. But she said the divorce was the best thing that ever happened to her and she wasn't interested in shackling herself all over again."

Great-Aunt Regina wasn't a normal sort of pretty. She was striking, like David Bowie or one of those high-fashion models who looks weird in real life but photographs well. In the portrait she wears a low-cut dress that showcases a creamy expanse of skin, across which her diamond necklace is draped. Her swept-back hair is dark brown, almost black. I've seen the portrait before, but looking at it today, I notice something: Her face is flushed and her pewter-gray eyes burn with mischief. Great-Aunt Regina is watching us from wherever she is now and *loving* this.

"Did you help her set up the treasure hunt, Ms. Claverhill?" Uncle Lenny asks.

I have to hide my smile. My uncle might act like he hates all this, but he can't help slipping back into FBI investigator mode.

"She wouldn't have been able to get around very easily," he muses. "She was in a wheelchair for the last two years. She must have had help."

Ms. Claverhill doesn't answer. Her poker face is *good*.

We wind our way through the mansion, and with every new room a new argument erupts about what to choose.

Lori's pick: a painting of four nudes at a table, in a room where the ceiling is painted in fluffy clouds. "Look, that one on the end looks like he's weeping."

"We've been through this, Lori. There are no angels."

"Maybe it's just the *idea* of angels."

"I want to get out of here with more than the *idea* of a diamond necklace."

Uncle Lenny's choice: the La Cornue stove in the kitchen. "Sometimes the eyes are called heads. *Around four heads the angels flew*?"

"Lenny. Just stop. You're not even trying."

"But it's a really nice stove. I even like the color."

In a sudden flash of inspiration, I insist we all tromp out to the cemetery in the middle of the hedge maze. "There are four graves out there! The original Montgomery family! *Four heads . . . Vanity thy name is mine.* What's more vain than a giant death monument? Maybe there are angels on the tombstones."

But after twenty minutes of tromping and back-tromping, we emerge sweating into the center of the maze to find nary an angel among the obelisk gravestones of the first Montgomerys to live in the mansion: Theodore and Hope and their adult children, Katherine and Henry. The obelisks are decorated with birds.

Two fruitless hours later, my aunt flings herself onto a divan. Her carefully mussed blond waves have dissolved into frizz, and her makeup is wearing at the seams. We're in what I can only describe as a boudoir. Ms. Claverhill, who has followed us silently from room to room on our trek, must feel sorry for Lori, because she doesn't even tell her not to touch the furniture.

We were originally drawn into the room by an enormous painting of a flamingo throwing up a wing, thinking it might be our angels. We lingered because Lori was then drawn to the closets full of designer vintage dresses. "The Valentino," she'd crooned, like a penitent murmuring the name of her saint.

I eye a Grecian bust wearing ropes of sparkle. Maybe Great-Aunt Regina just hung the diamonds in among the costume stuff, out in plain sight? But then again, there's only one head, no angels, and a quick survey confirms the necklace isn't among the baubles. There is something weird about the bust's face, though. Finally it clicks into place.

It's modeled on Great-Aunt Regina. Talk about *Vanity thy name is mine.*

I plop onto a stool in front of a dressing table. Agitation crawls all over me. Why is this so hard? Is it because there's so much more stuff? When I was little, the search had to be limited to our trailer and a barn that was on our property. The options were limited.

"Do you remember when we were kids and we did this?" Lori asks, shading her eyes like her head hurts.

"Of course," Lenny says. He snorts. "Half the time we didn't know if we even wanted to find the prize."

I look over. "What do you mean?"

"For the most part she'd hide good stuff. Candy bars. Toys. But sometimes she'd . . ." He frowns. "The woman had a weird sense of humor."

"One time it was a dead mouse in a trap." Lori shudders.

"And once it was a piece of broken glass." Lenny rubs his hand.

And I will give thee the treasures of darkness

"At least this time we know what to expect," I say.

"Not that it's helping us right now," Lori mutters.

I look back around the room. The dressing table I'm sitting at has about a million little drawers. A couple of carved naked ladies with long, strategically placed tresses hold up a central mirror. Two side mirrors let me look at my exhausted face from all angles.

four heads
angels

What the hell are we going to pick? I check my watch. It's getting late. Somehow I thought it would be obvious once we were here. But now I'm wondering if we've walked past the thing we're looking for a hundred times.

Think, Roxie, think. You were good at this once.

Think hard, Rox, I hear my mother's voice say. *It's all there. Everything you need to solve the mystery.* I try to push her out of my brain.

The sun is just above the horizon, and the light has gone a hazy bronze. I can see the hedge maze out the windows from where I'm sitting, all its whorls and dead ends. It feels apropos. I look back at my face in the mirror. I have deep-set, dark eyes like my father's. My mother's stubborn mouth.

I scowl at myself. *Think harder.*

I take a deep breath, let it out slowly. If this was one of my finder jobs for a girl at school, I would start with the people involved. Who were they? What did they want? What do I know about Great-Aunt Regina? What was important to her? What did she care about? What would her gaze have lingered on as a worthy place to hide something? I close my eyes. Clear my thoughts. Let the poem run through my head.

Around four heads the angels flew
Silent in their keeping
Vanity thy name is mine
And paint masked all the weeping

I hear Great-Aunt Regina's voice:

Don't lie to a liar.

You should have been here back when I was young and gorgeous.

I'm a survivor, too. All the best of us are.

I open my eyes. The flamingo in the painting reflected behind me raises its pink wing.

And I see it.

I sit up, reach out, and move one of the side mirrors. Adjust the other one slightly. Light hits my face.

I count. "I'll be goddamned."

"No touching, please."

"Language."

"This is it." I spin to the three of them. "Ms. Claverhill, we choose the vanity."

Roxie

Aunt Lori sits up straight. "A *vanity* table. God, of course. But where are the angels? Those carved things are just nudes. And the four heads?"

Uncle Lenny looks skeptical, too.

"Look," I say, jumping up and waving him over. "Sit. Now look in the mirror."

He obeys. "What am I supposed to be seeing besides a handsomely careworn man? Intelligent brow, piercing eyes—"

"Shh." I cut him off, adjust the mirror so that the sculpted bust of Great-Aunt Regina is reflected in the glass. I bounce on my heels. "How many Great-Aunt Regina heads do you see?"

He frowns, checks the reflections. "One, two, three . . ." His eyes light up. "*Four.*"

"And look at how the flamingo wings hit the carved nudes."

They appear to have hot-pink wings. And they hover around Regina's four marble heads.

His face splits into a grin. "I'll be damned."

"*Around four heads the angels flew. Silent in their keeping,*" I pronounce.

Lori hip-checks her brother. "Let me see." She takes his place and her mouth pops open. "*Vanity thy name is mine. And paint masked all the weeping*! Makeup!"

"Exactly," I say. "This has got to be it." I look to Ms. Claverhill, sure that now I'll get some hint from her about whether I'm right. The woman is as carved in marble as Great-Aunt Regina's bust. Does she practice while she's lying in bed at night?

"Uncle Lenny?" I ask.

"Fine by me."

"Lori?"

She chews her lip, then nods. "It beats an oven."

I rub my hands together like some sort of crazy villain. "Can we look inside?" I ask Ms. Claverhill.

Before she's even done nodding her permission, I've wrenched the top drawer open. Something sparkles, exposed. I grab, but it's just a rhinestone hair clip. Lori opens other drawers. We riffle through combs and soft brushes; costume jewelry; handkerchiefs and ribbons; makeup in compacts, desiccated and hard. Perfume gone scentless. Everything you'd expect to find in a rich lady's dressing table that hasn't been used since the mid-eighties.

Everything except a clue.

I pull out the last drawer, holding my breath, and raise something that appears to be an instrument of torture. I look to Ms. Claverhill for explanation.

"A girdle," she says.

I sit back on my heels, disbelief thick in my throat. "I don't get it. Where's the clue?"

Aunt Lori slaps a compact down on the dressing table. "It's not here. Goddamned riddles!"

Uncle Lenny puts a hand on my shoulder. "It was a really clever guess, Roxie."

I twist away. "I'm telling you, I'm right. We've looked everywhere. This is it."

I pull more things out of the drawers. A hairbrush. A glass nail file. Am I wrong? I'm not. I know it. I'm a fucking champ at this sort of thing. I take a drawer and shake it. Lipsticks and brushes jumble and jump out. They bounce across the carpet. Ms. Claverhill clears her throat. I stare into the empty drawer.

Maybe I'm wrong.

I feel a familiar heat start to creep into my neck.

Prideful.

I squeeze my eyes shut.

Arrogant.

"Roxanne?" Uncle Lenny asks gently. "Listen, don't worry about the necklace. It was a long shot to begin with. We don't care, do we, Lori?"

Lori stutters, "N-no, of course not."

Can't you see that God is trying to tell you something?

I resist the urge to put my fingers in my ears.

In the mouth of the foolish is a rod of pride . . .

Years of therapy, dozens of "strategies," hundreds of hours of mindful breathing, and still, Pastor can just wander into my brain and provide commentary anytime he wants.

No, I tell myself.

I hold very still and breathe in and out. One Jerusalem, two Jerusalem, three Jerusalem . . . *Get out of my head.* I hold tight and count.

"Rox?"

I blink and find Uncle Lenny in front of me, worry all over his face. His hands are out, hovering. I'm hot, sweaty. My ears are ringing. I step back, away from him. I can't look at his face right now. I keep breathing in and out, in and out.

"Is she having a . . . you know, a thing?" I hear Lori whisper.

"Just give her a second . . ."

Slowly, very slowly, I come back to myself. The empty drawer comes into focus. I'm still holding it.

I stare at it, seeing nothing. And then I'm staring at it and seeing nothing, but something about the nothing is bothering me. It's wrong. But I don't know why.

"I wonder if the Arts Foundation would notice if I just took one dress?" Lori is asking. "Since we didn't find the diamonds . . . ?"

"It's wrong," I say softly.

"I know, but . . ."

"Not that," I tell my aunt.

"What, Rox?" Uncle Lenny asks. He edges toward me again.

"This drawer is lined." I lick my lips, concentrate. "In newsprint."

"So?" Lori asks dully.

The woolly feeling starts to fade. "So newsprint is too pedestrian for this fancy piece of furniture, this fancy woman." My throat feels raw.

You're fine. You're good. You didn't lose it, I tell myself. *You cast the devil out. Now focus.*

"It's wrong," I say again, louder. "The drawers should be lined in silk. Hundred-dollar bills."

Uncle Lenny frowns. "Do you want to sit down, Rox?"

I blow a layer of powder out of the drawer. There's nothing obviously remarkable about the page that's lining it. It's the front of the *Asheville Citizen* from May 28, 1960: "Mayor's Office Reveals Massive Urban Renewal Plans." But in the back corner, an edge of the paper is curling away.

Gently, I tease it up and pull. It comes away easily, the glue brittle. And underneath, carved into the wood in rough capitals, I find the words:

BIRD MARTIN

"What is it?" Lori asks, crowding in to look. "What does that mean?"

I feel Uncle Lenny tense beside me.

"What?" I ask him.

The words mean something to him. But his mouth clamps into a firm line.

"Are any of the other drawers lined?" Lori asks.

We make quick work of checking and find one other. The rest are bare. When I pull the second newsprint liner away, my breath catches.

Five stanzas are written in fresh black ink on the walnut.

We lean in to read.

"Holy shit," I say. And no one corrects my language.

The Robber Bridegroom

Part I

Around four heads the angels flew
Silent in their keeping
Vanity thy name is mine
And paint masked all the weeping

Come in, come in, they called to her
Their goblin fruits to offer
To the bold dark maid who dared to rave
"I am this mountain's daughter"

Man golden tongued and high red cheeked
Girl lovely as a posy
Petting her and fêting her
Until the dawn spread rosy

Drunk of wine and velvet nap
Lust seen for affection
"Oh maiden brave," crooned crooked knave,
"Yon meadow thine reflection"

Clue:

The room was deep, the air was still
The worms, they did their part
To scour and hide the red blood tide
A witness: the tell-tale heart

Inez

"You're early," Ms. Claverhill says when she opens the door.

Inez hitches her bag up on her shoulder. It's her second day working at Montgomery House. Ms. Claverhill called the agency yesterday and asked for her again. Inez feels a sort of pride in this. Plus she likes being here. A mansion sure beats the hell out of dorm bathrooms.

"Bad habit. Can't seem to break it. Should I come back later?"

"No, no, of course not. Come in," Ms. Claverhill says. "There's plenty to do. Whole rooms still to be cataloged before the Arts Foundation takes the keys." She ushers Inez into Montgomery House. "I wish we'd found you sooner. So many of your predecessors seemed to find time a flexible notion." She marches through the empty, echoing rooms.

Inez's mom had been one of those. Always late for everything. Maybe Inez is subconsciously making up for it. She watches the movement of Ms. Claverhill's sturdy, purposeful calves. Inez wishes she'd found this place sooner, too, before the rich lady who lived here had died. Maybe she could have turned it into a full-time job. How different would things have been if she had?

"You can start in here," Ms. Claverhill announces at the door to a room full of big dead animals. Zebras and antelope. Their faces are unnerving; all seem to be caught in a moment of terror. She can't imagine who would have commissioned their hunting trophies to look like that. The whole room is charged with their panicked energy.

Fortunately she is tasked not with cataloging dead animals but with polishing and dusting. Ms. Claverhill will come along behind with tags and her clipboard. Inez starts with a large brass vase, trying to ignore the sense that she's being watched by predators. In the convex surface her face is stretched. For some reason it makes her look like her younger self. A little girl.

Sweet girl, her mother used to call her.

Nice girl. Good girl. It was all her mother had ever asked of Inez. Be kind. Be good. Inez wasn't sure if it was because she didn't have the imagination to ask for anything more, or if she just didn't want Inez to get her hopes up at being something other than a girl from the trailer park. The good grades Inez brought home without much thought or effort seemed to amuse her mother. *How did you get so smart? Not from me. Certainly not from Paul.*

Paul was her father. Inez had been the result of a brief romance, but Paul had a wife, three kids, and a trailer of his own in Bryson City and wanted nothing to do with her. Inez had made her peace with that after a poorly-thought-out ambush at the gas station where he worked. She had been sixteen and going through *a thing* (as her mother put it). She introduced herself over the counter, and after he pulled himself together, Paul gave her the entirety of his fifteen-minute smoke break. He checked the time on his phone twelve times (Inez counted) while they stood on the stained concrete pad behind the station and he chain-smoked three cigarettes. When she asked if she could come by sometime, meet his kids (her siblings!), he said, *I ain't so sure the wife would like that.* Inez took the hint. They hadn't spoken since.

She was over it. She knew a therapist would probably have a field day with her. Daddy issues. Mommy issues. Nice girl insecurities. Sex work because she craved the male attention she'd been denied. She could self-diagnose with the best of them. She'd watched *Dr. Phil* with her mom; she wasn't a moron.

Sorry, Mama, I didn't turn out to be much of a nice girl.

Does she even know any nice girls? She went to elementary school with some. Girls who completely vanished from her memory until they showed up in her social media, asking to be friends. Girls who dream about their wedding dresses and baby names and fear God and decorate with inspirational quotes. Girls who make her eyes glaze over.

Not a very nice thing to think, Inez.

Inez had never been a *bad* girl. She wasn't perfect, but she wasn't bad. And it wasn't that she liked sex and got into doing it for money because, hey, why not? It was surprising, actually, how many girls did it for just that reason. *Because I'm good at it,* they'd say. Which was fine and dandy as long as you could be picky about who you did it with. As long as you didn't have to do the rapid mental calculations while keeping a flirty smile on your face, trying to decide if you could make rent without having to put some pimply frat boy's junk in your mouth.

The first time she'd done it, she'd spent the entire time in a state of shock. *Really? Am I really doing this?* She hadn't been a virgin, but she still could've counted the number of guys she'd been with on one hand and had fingers left over. The boys from the dorms never even considered that she would say no. They'd found her while she was cleaning the common room. Just walked right up and propositioned her. She'd been more shocked than anyone to find herself saying yes. Had they mistaken her for someone else? Had they seen some scenario like this on a porn site? Their sense of entitlement was breathtaking.

Even as it was happening, she knew she was more like the college girls down the hall than the women who hung out on Peace Street. She should have been one of those college girls, sitting around in her pajamas, painting her toenails and drinking rum and Sprite out of a coffee mug. She was the same age. Could have gone to college herself if a million little things had happened differently.

Instead she found herself taking four shit-faced boys, still jiggling with baby fat, one by one into a suite bathroom and letting them bend her over like a mule. Only two of them actually finished, quick and jolting. Of the other two, one lost his nerve and they spent an excruciating five minutes sitting in silence until he figured it was safe to go back out again, grinning and pumping his fist. The other one was drunk and couldn't keep an erection. He ended up pushing her away with a slurred "Dumb fucking bitch," before falling down in a corner and passing out, a condom still half covering his shriveled penis. She'd taken two twenties out of his wallet because, well, *puck him*.

Later, as she sat in her car, staring at the wad of cash in her hand, all she could think was *That wasn't so bad.* She'd made them wear condoms and pay in advance, like she'd had a secret hooker living inside her the whole time, somebody who knew the rules.

Payment first. Condoms. She still lived by those rules. She soon learned that these boys were the kind who'd haggle. They were the kind who would say she didn't deserve four pucks' worth of payment, that they should get some sort of group discount. The kind who'd threaten to kick her in her dumb pucking cunt. She made it a rule to never bargain. She got payment first, and if payment in its entirety was refused, she peaced out. Making it any more complicated than that wasn't worth it.

She thought she was being smart and safe. She knew there were risks, but she really thought she had done everything she could to protect herself. And it wasn't like she was naive. She knew that bad things could happen to good people, even people who were careful.

But still, when it happened to her, she wasn't ready. Is anyone ever ready? No, of course not. Because when it happens, you realize that being smart and careful is a joke. You can take all the precautions in the world and still end up passed out in the back of your car, aching between your legs, with the taste of chewed-up aspirin in your mouth.

With absolutely no idea what had happened to the last eight hours.

Roxie

"What time are we going back to Montgomery House?" I ask Uncle Lenny on the drive to school the next morning. I know perfectly well, but he won't stop sneaking little glances at me, and I'm afraid he's going to bring up my feelings again. Diamond necklaces are safer territory.

"Lori will pick you up after the funeral," he says, slurping coffee.

We stopped by our regular coffee shop on the way to school and both ordered Red Eyes, our usual, which is a double shot of espresso with coffee on top. Elixir of the gods. His black, mine with plenty of cream and sugar. He's long since given up trying to get me to cut back, worried about stunted growth or my heart exploding.

Today I will cut anyone who tries to get between me and my caffeine. I spent way too many hours after getting home from Montgomery House researching the new clue-poem. I'd been all for staying and trying to figure it out, but Uncle Lenny had been resolute. He was done for the day. He'd already had to find someone to open the restaurant for him and had needed to get back to take over.

The part labeled CLUE makes it pretty clear that we need to move our search subterranean.

The room was deep, the air was still
The worms, they did their part
To scour and hide the red blood tide
A witness: the tell-tale heart

Montgomery House has a massive cellar, and that's where we'll start this afternoon.

Sure, I could have left it at that, gone to bed and gotten a good night's sleep, but no. Instead I kept searching and ended up in a warren of internet rabbit holes. I'd like to think it's because I am thorough. Not obsessed.

I heard Uncle Lenny come in around one in the morning, at which time I was learning that "The Robber Bridegroom" is a Brothers Grimm fairy tale. A particularly gruesome one, even for those dudes. The short version is that a girl goes to her wealthy fiancé's house and spies her Prince Charming cannibalizing another young woman. She only escapes because his servant hides her.

"Goblin fruits" could be from a poem written in 1859 by Christina Rossetti called "Goblin Market" about two sisters being tempted by said goblins and their drug-laced fruits. (The poem also might be a repressed lesbian sexual awakening thing? The internet has many opinions on this that, while fascinating, were far too varied and most likely irrelevant for me to dig into.)

"I am this mountain's daughter" is intriguing because it sounds very specific. Maybe it's even a direct quote, but I couldn't find anything about it online.

And of course, there's the "tell-tale heart." In the story by the same name by Edgar Allan Poe, our antihero kills a man, chops him up, and buries him in the floor. Like that was ever going to end well.

Right before falling asleep on my laptop (and later waking up in a puddle of my own drool), I'd searched for "Bird Martin." All that came up were pictures of a dapper little swallow. I'm not sure what, if anything, the family *Hirundinidae* has to do with the necklace.

Even less what any of this has to do with Kirsten Montgomery-Wiggins.

I still have no idea why she would have Great-Aunt Regina's clue in her pocket. My great-aunt must have given it to her, but why? Was Kirsten trying to find the necklace, too? Maybe that was all part of the game. Maybe we were unwittingly competing against her. But in that case, why would Great-Aunt Regina not tell us? What good is a competition if you don't know you're competing?

There are no new developments on Kirsten's murder. Without anything to report, the networks and gossip sites are focusing on the Montgomery-Wiggins family, cataloging their riches (vast) and digging up dirt on Mitch's DUIs and Kirsten's mom's wild socialite days. Interesting, but not useful as far as I can see.

At school the veil of mourning is still pulled tight. Kirsten's funeral is at noon, and afternoon classes have been canceled. Everyone will go. It's going to be the social event of the season.

In the meantime, someone has been handing out black silk flower pins, which perch over our hearts on our white blouses. I try not to roll my eyes when I'm given one. Even Kirsten's death feels *extra*.

Every period begins with a teacher giving a little prepared speech about remembering Kirsten's shining light, topped off with a choice Bible verse (*Thy rod and thy staff they comfort me*, etc., being a favorite). They remind us that it's okay to grieve, and urge us to use the school counselor. Poor Ms. Wilson had a line twenty girls deep outside her office when I walked past this morning, so good luck with that.

I don't think the teachers have any clue how to handle this. I guess they're doing the best they can, saying all the stuff that sounds right, but clearly Saint Magdalene's has never had a student die in such an incomprehensible way. They're out of their depth.

When the state took custody of me—after the event that left seven people, an acre of forest, and three trailers a charred mess—I had to go to counseling. Go figure. The child psychologist, Dr. Richard, was nice enough, but soft. He liked to use weird, anatomically correct dolls. He was underprepared for my raging ringworm and lice, my hair down to my butt. My ability to quote entire books of the Old Testament. My strange way of sitting as still as a wild animal and how I'd snarl if he moved too quickly. He did not like it when I ripped the heads off his dolls.

Dr. Richard did his duty but cleared me through the system as fast as he could, five sessions in his airless little office where he talked more than I did. Of course, when I started setting fires in my foster families' homes, I had to go back. When I finally agreed to start the adoption process with Uncle Lenny, I told him I would cut out the fires, but I wouldn't go to therapy anymore. I was done with Dr. Richard trying to peel away my exterior like a hard-boiled egg to get at the thoughts in my head. *I don't think anyone really wants to know what's in there,* I said.

I do, Uncle Lenny had countered. *And sorry, but therapy's nonnegotiable. But we'll find someone else.* He really must have felt guilty about what had happened that day when my whole world went up in flames, because we went through six different therapists until I finally found one I could tolerate. The only one who didn't want me to give up Mama's lighter. I still see Dr. Adams once a month. We talk a lot about guilt. Mine. Uncle Lenny's. Dr. Adams thinks he still feels a lot of it. *That's not why I wanted to adopt you,* Uncle Lenny protested when I presented this information to him. *We're family.* I shrugged. Guilt was part of it. His and mine. I was doing therapy, after all. I should know.

By second-period study hall my caffeine buzz is gone, replaced by the beginnings of a headache. I eschew the library for the band room closet, where I can't feel eyes on me. I drape a robe on the couch, plop down and pull out my laptop.

I start with Chloe Hamilton's alibi.

And yes, I have a million other things I should be focusing on, a massive load of AP classes and homework not least among them, but the sight of my biology textbook makes me want to throw it at the oboe player who sounds like she's strangling a duck.

Chloe's social media tells me that she was at ballet class at the time of the murder, as she is most nights from four to seven. It will be easy to confirm with the dozen or so other ballerina witnesses.

I move on to Kirsten's possible secret law-intern boyfriend.

Montgomery, Leach, and Wiggins, Attorneys at Law, has a website. Under "About Us" I find touched-up headshots and bios of all the partners, including a little homage to William Montgomery (retired partner, founder, CEO of SouthEast Holdings). The current partners include Ron Montgomery-Wiggins, Kirsten's dad. He has the same dark hair and eyes as Kirsten, but where she's severe, he looks practically jolly. Less like someone who's going to win your case than bake you muffins. I scroll past junior partners, associates, administrative assistants . . . until, bada boom, summer interns. There are no photos, just names: Evan Fowley, Kelly Graham, Mitch Montgomery-Wiggins, and Kirsten Montgomery-Wiggins.

Kelly Graham doesn't at all match Chloe's description of the dark-haired guy she saw Kirsten with, but I check her out anyway. Her social media shows a blond who works hard and plays harder. She's summa cum everything, and also likes to take selfies at the club with her "beyatches" at 3:00 a.m. pretty much every night of the week. (She's better about her privacy settings than most, but not good enough to give me much trouble.)

Next up for scrutiny is Evan Fowley. The photo that comes up sends a spark of recognition through me, and after staring at it for a second, I realize why. I go back to Mitch Montgomery-Wiggins's social media. Evan Fowley is *the* Evan. The missing Evan from Mitch's posts. Mitch has reposted something from Evan's sister since the last time I checked his page.

> *Please please please I'm begging anyone who might know where my big brother Evan is to contact me!!! He was last seen leaving the Smoky Mountain Brewery on Haywood Avenue on September 13 at around 12:30 AM and if you've heard from him or have any idea where he might be please let me know!!!! We are VERY WORRIED! The police are not taking this seriously they say he's probably just gone somewhere to blow off steam but Evan promised he would never disappear like that again and I just want to know he is OK. PLEASE, Evan if you're reading this call me or Mom or Dad!!!!!!! We love you so much!!!!!!!*

The post is followed by a lot of responses telling Evan's sister to stay strong, etc., but no one offers any leads on where her brother might be. One person writes, *Recovery can take a long time! Don't lose heart!*

I take a closer look at the law student. He's handsome in a helmet-hair-and-dimples sort of way. Nothing about these photos says user. But it's social media, so who knows. No one posts photos of themselves passed out drunk on a dirty mattress.

Is Chloe right? Was Evan Kirsten's secret boyfriend? He went missing about a week before Kirsten's murder. It seems like if Kirsten was worried, it would be *him* she'd ask me to hunt down, not some girl.

I dig a little deeper into Evan's online life. His selling points: He majored in poli-sci, was a member of the men's Ultimate Frisbee team, and pledged Delta Kappa Epsilon. His social media is dull: a smattering of right-leaning news posts, but nothing psycho. Sports. I don't see anything linking him to Kirsten, but that's not too surprising either. It's not wise to let word get around that you're dating a sixteen-year-old. Especially if said sixteen-year-old is the boss's daughter at a firm where you're interning.

Is he in trouble? Or just holed up somewhere with a bottle and/or a pharmacopoeia, hiding from the world?

I craft a subtle message and send it, hoping to flush him out:

Me: I know who you bonked this summer.

I go back to Kirsten's social media. Since her death, people have posted countless condolences on her walls. Cheesy song lyrics, bad original poetry, and approximately five million crying-face emojis. Half of them are girls from Saint Maggie's whose names Kirsten probably didn't even know, people she didn't give two hot shits about. But the girls of Saint Maggie's can't seem to help themselves. Death this close up is intoxicating and they're ready to guzzle it like pilfered liquor.

I'm so deep in my research that it takes several seconds to

realize my phone is buzzing with an incoming call. The number on the screen is one I don't recognize.

"Hello?"

"Is this Roxanne Hunt?" It's a woman's voice.

Outside the room a cymbal crashes. I press the phone closer to my ear. "Yes, who is this?"

The voice quavers. "Carol Montgomery-Wiggins. Kirsten's mother."

"Mrs. Montgomery-Wiggins!" I close my laptop and put it to the side. "How are you?" I wince. "I mean . . . I'm sorry. That's a dumb thing to ask."

"It's all right. Thank you, Roxanne."

An awkward silence blooms in the space between us. *So . . . about how I found your daughter's dead body . . .*

"You're the girl who . . ."

"Yes," I say quickly. "I just . . . I'm sorry."

"Thank you." She clears her throat. "I don't really know how to ask this. I only got to see her after they'd taken her to the . . . Could you tell . . . I need to know . . . Do you think she suffered?"

Mrs. Montgomery-Wiggins's voice is sluggish, but the pain in the question travels right through the phone, burrows into my ear.

"I don't think so," I say. Honestly, I have no idea. But it's not like I'm going to say that. "I think it must have happened very quickly."

"I see." A shaky exhale. "Officer Lamb said you maybe saw the person who did this." She speaks slowly, carefully. I'm beginning to think she might be medicated.

"I saw a gray Porsche leaving as I was coming in the gate. I didn't get a look at the driver, though. Do you know who it might have been?"

"No, I don't."

"I'm sure the police will be able to find them," I say. "Your security cameras must have caught the car. They'll be able to track down the plate numbers."

"The footage was erased."

"What?"

"Someone must have hacked into our account and gotten rid of it. Not an easy thing to do, I'm told. But everything from six p.m. is gone. The footage from the gates, the driveway, the front and back doors, all of it."

I swallow. That's not good. Not only does it mean that they can't trace the car, but it throws into question everything I told the cops. I'm the only person they know was definitely there, at the scene, blood on my hands.

Fantastic.

"Well," I say, "maybe they'll find fingerprints? The gun?"

"Maybe. They've searched the house and the grounds and haven't come up with much that's useful yet. Did you see anything else, Roxanne?"

"No. I really wish I could be more helpful."

On the other end of the line Mrs. Montgomery-Wiggins makes no comment. She's either contemplating what I've said or slipped into a coma.

"There is one thing," I say. "I talked to Kirsten's friend Chloe. She thinks Kirsten had a boyfriend."

"A boyfriend? No, I don't think so."

"Chloe thought he might have been a secret. Maybe a law student interning for your husband?"

"I'm sure I'd know if my own daughter was seeing someone. Especially if it was one of them—someone older. It's not like her to keep secrets."

Parents. Bless their naive little hearts. And if she's not interested in entertaining the idea of a boyfriend, I wonder if she even has any clue about Kirsten and Chloe's brief whatever-it-was. I consider mentioning it, but hesitate. I won't out that little secret just yet. The cops will look into all Kirsten's close relationships, and the rumors around Chloe and Kirsten will come up soon enough.

"It could be nothing," I say. "Chloe didn't know for sure. You know how talk gets started." The silence I'm getting back is starting to unnerve me. "Mrs. Montgomery-Wiggins, do you know anything about a girl Kirsten was looking for?"

More silence.

"Mrs. Montgomery-Wiggins?"

"I should go," Kirsten's mom murmurs. She sounds very far away. "I have to get ready for the service."

I search for something to say. Nothing comes to me. I can only tell her again, "I really am sorry."

She doesn't reply. I'm not sure she even heard me. Only dead air fills the space between us. She's gone.

Roxie

The funeral service is held at the chapel on campus. Over lunch the Prada and Balmain blacks have been unzipped from their garment bags. The more adventurous are wearing hats and veils. We look like a convention of well-heeled witches.

Nina, dressed in an ebony corset dress that I'm sure cost more than a semester's tuition, meets me out front. The service is standing room only, so we find a spot in the back. We have a good view of the room from here.

I haven't spent much time in churches since I was a kid—for obvious reasons they make me twitchy—but fortunately our school's Catholic chapel is modern and undemanding. The cream walls and abstract stained glass don't leave much room for gory crucifixes. There is a small altar to the Virgin Mary and one to Saint Magdalene. Both preside over flocks of candles with little electric switches on the bottom that you can turn on if you want to send up a prayer. No matches. Missing also are the locked boxes with air holes drilled in the sides sitting ominously under the altar. The air smells like perfume and cleaning supplies. Not a whiff of righteous sweat anywhere on the premises.

Officer Lamb walks in. He takes off his hat so the stained glass reflects off his head and makes his way to the back, on the opposite side of the chapel. His roving eyes settle on me for a moment, a frown of suspicion flicking over his face. I restrain myself from cocking a pistol finger at him.

Nina elbows me and nods to the door. The whispering kicks up a notch as Kirsten's parents and brother file in and make their way to the front. I crane my neck to see. Kirsten's mother clings to her husband's arm. They're followed by Kirsten's grandfather, Mr. Montgomery. At one point he puts a hand on Kirsten's mom's shoulder, but she shrugs her father off. Interesting.

One by one the family members take their turns at Kirsten's open coffin. Kirsten is wearing a high-necked dress that doesn't look like something she'd approve of at all, but I guess they had to hide the damage to her chest. Mitch looks down at her, radiating anger. When it's Kirsten's mother's turn, she places a perfect pink rose inside the coffin and stands limply by her husband, watching him tuck in a stuffed rabbit. He strokes his dead daughter's cheek before helping his wife to the pew.

The touch makes my skin crawl. I look around to see if anyone else finds this action as weird as me, but all I see are sad red eyes. For a moment I'm brought back to my mother's memorial. There hadn't been enough left of her to bury, much less touch.

Just then I see a familiar figure slip in the door.

Aunt Lori? What's she doing here?

But before I can catch her eye, she's tucked into the crowd at the back of the room. The organ strikes up and the collective grieving begins.

—

I find Lori later at the grave site as the mourners gather around Kirsten's casket. More pink roses, incongruously perky for the event.

"I didn't know you knew Kirsten," I say quietly. We're standing near the back of the huge crowd and can barely hear the words the priest is saying.

"I didn't," Lori whispers back. "I'm here for her mother."

We both watch Carol Montgomery-Wiggins. She's sitting as still as one of the stone memorials in their family plot, eyes hidden behind big black sunglasses. Her son has his arm around her.

I look at Lori curiously.

"Even if she wants nothing to do with me." Lori sighs dramatically.

"What do you mean?"

"We were close growing up, but after all that business with the estate borders . . ."

"Estate borders? What borders?"

Lori blinks false-eyelashed eyes. "Between the Montgomery House estate and Kirsten's grandfather's property. It was divided during the divorce, but later on it was contested. It got ugly."

She sees that I'm still not following.

"That's Aunt Regina's ex-husband, William Montgomery."

"*What?*"

Lori nods, her cheeks flushing with the pleasure of good gossip. "You didn't know? Oh, it was a huge scandal. He got Kirsten's grandmother pregnant while he was still married to

Aunt Regina. They only got married after Regina tossed him out on his ear."

My jaw drops. "How has no one told me this?"

"I thought you knew, silly. That's how Regina managed to hang on to Montgomery House. William Montgomery is richer than God, and you can imagine his connections, but apparently the judge in their case was some sort of Baptist puritan who felt it was his duty to punish adultery. I think he lost his seat on the bench after the case was over." She lowers her voice even more. "The land that Kirsten's parents' house sits on used to be part of the Montgomery House estate. That's all the judge let him keep. Well. That and some millions."

I stare at Kirsten's family. Had Kirsten known about our connection?

"When she was younger, Carol was a bit of a rebel," Lori continues. "I didn't realize she was really only friends with me to spite her father. Not until she grew up and decided she liked her father's money more than she liked her friends."

As the two things that have been forefront in my mind—Kirsten's death and Great-Aunt Regina's treasure hunt—begin to bleed into each other, something hits me like a truck.

I gasp loud enough that a few of my fellow mourners turn to frown at me.

I know her.

I know the woman Kirsten was looking for.

Roxie

I can barely contain myself for the rest of the service. I'm desperate to get to Montgomery House to see if my suspicions are right. As soon as the priest says the final amen, I nudge Aunt Lori in the ribs. "Let's go."

"Wait, I just want to talk to a few people first."

I groan. "Seriously? It's not a cocktail party."

Aunt Lori's already walking toward a group of mourners. "Behave yourself. Go ahead to the car, I'll be there in a few minutes."

I'm nudging my way through the mourners, still reeling from what I've figured out, when I feel a hand grip my elbow and start pulling me to the side.

My heart takes off. "Hey!" I wrench my arm away, glaring at the person attached to the hand. It takes me a second to place him.

"Why are you contacting Evan?"

It's Mitch, Kirsten's brother. Up close the resemblance to his sister is striking, even down to the curl of their lips.

"I was trying to get in touch with him about your sister, actually."

He glares at me, looks around at the crowd. "Can we talk?"

He doesn't wait for an answer, just slips away into the forest of closely laid monuments.

I hesitate for a second, then follow.

I find him standing with his hands shoved into his pockets between a stone statue of a veiled woman and the entrance to a small mausoleum. Trees in various stages of turning red and gold shade the old stonework of the turn-of-the-century grave markers. Leaves skate across the path.

"My sister and Evan weren't *bonking*, if that's what you were insinuating."

I wince. How was I supposed to know the dead girl's brother was monitoring his missing friend's account?

"Where did you even get that idea?" he asks.

"Chloe Hamilton," I say. "She thinks they might have been seeing each other."

"Chloe doesn't know what the hell she's talking about." Mitch takes his hands out of his pockets, runs them over his face. "Look, I know you found my sister and that this is all probably rough on you, too, but my family would really appreciate it if you left the investigation to the police."

"Yes, but—"

His eyes spark. "Frankly, it's none of your business." He starts to turn back to the people he's left by the graveside.

"Actually, it *is* my business," I say, blocking his path. "I'm the only person the police know for sure was at your house that night. I told them about the car I saw driving away, but your mother said the security footage that would have captured it was deleted."

And your sister had that damn clue in her pocket. Definitely my business. But I leave that out of the conversation.

Mitch doesn't speak. His mouth is still a hard line of suspicion.

"I'm not trying to get in the way," I say. "I want to help."

I see Kirsten's body on the kitchen floor. Her white limbs in such strong contrast to the puddle of blood. Mrs. Montgomery-Wiggins's question echoes in my head: *Do you think she suffered?*

"I don't want anyone thinking I killed your sister," I say. "Are you sure Kirsten and Evan didn't have something going on? On the sly?"

"No. Evan's a friend. I would have known."

It's the same thing his mother said. Is it true, or are they just naive?

"You didn't see who was driving the car?" Mitch asks.

"No. It was raining too hard. The car's windows were tinted. Do you have any idea who it might have been?"

He doesn't reply immediately. "I don't remember Kirsten ever mentioning you. Were you friends?"

"Not exactly. She wanted my help finding someone. Do you know who that car belongs to?"

"The police mentioned that. She was looking for some girl?"

He knows who the car belongs to. But I won't get him to tell me if I don't give him something in return.

"Kirsten thought she might have been an exotic dancer," I say carefully, watching for his reaction. I take out my phone and show him the photo Kirsten sent me of the blond girl's face.

His eyes widen. "A dancer? Why would my sister want to find a dancer?"

"I don't know. She never mentioned anything about her to you?"

"No. Nothing." He looks past me, back to the grave site. "I have to go."

"Wait, what about the car, do you know it?"

He doesn't answer. He starts back toward the mourners. I see his mother step out of the sea of black, toward us. She looks from him to me. After a few steps, Mitch stops. "Please, Roxanne, can you just leave it alone? We're all barely hanging on over here."

I watch him go, his shoulders hunched. I get that I should feel sorry for him, but I'm too frustrated. He knows something about the car. I'm sure of it. I try to reassure myself that this is a good thing. If he knows, then surely he's told the police.

The day has gone chilly. More leaves spin to the ground. I see Aunt Lori peel off from the mourners, start toward the parking lot. I cross my arms over my chest and follow.

Roxie

When Ms. Claverhill answers the door at Montgomery House, I feel the emptiness behind her like a vacuum. Corners fade into dusky silence. It's getting harder and harder to imagine anyone ever lived here.

I'm the first one in, peering around for any sign of the maid.

Because what I realized at the funeral was that the young woman who served us cookies and tea in Great-Aunt Regina's library and the person Kirsten wanted me to find are, in fact, one and the same. I think I heard Ms. Claverhill call her Inez. I'm extremely annoyed with myself for taking so long to figure this out. I must have been too focused on the treasure hunt at the time. I only saw her for a second, but I'm almost positive it's her. I just need to take another good look at her face to confirm I'm right.

"Good afternoon," Ms. Claverhill greets us.

There's no immediate sign of Inez. As Ms. Claverhill ushers everyone inside, it occurs to me to wonder if the housekeeper even knows about the gory murder that took place on the other side of the woods. I wonder how much she knows about Inez. I don't think I'd ever seen her at Montgomery House before. Maybe she was a recent hire.

Did Kirsten know Inez from here? Because they were neighbors? But in that case, why would she have trouble finding her?

I keep my eyes and ears open as we follow Ms. Claverhill through the house, but it's dead quiet. "Where would you like to look first today?" she asks.

"Cellars. Right, Rox?" Uncle Lenny says.

It takes me a second to focus. "Cellars. Uh . . . yes."

As we pass through the empty kitchen, Ms. Claverhill says, "I'll put the kettle on for tea. I'm the only staff today, I'm afraid."

I almost curse out loud. No Inez. Now what? Do I ask Ms. Claverhill for her phone number?

The housekeeper leads us to the back of the kitchen, where there's a massive oak door and a corridor leading to what looks like a staff break room.

As she unlocks the oak door, I casually peer into the break area. There's a shabby sofa and a TV, a calendar on the wall, and what might be a list of names and phone numbers. Bingo. Staff schedule. Inez's name and number should be there. No need to alert Ms. Claverhill to what I'm doing. It's just a matter of getting in and snapping a quick photo.

"Roxanne?" I look up. Ms. Claverhill is holding the cellar door open for me. Everyone else is already on their way down.

"Coming."

I plunge down into a clammy darkness. The light from the bare bulbs is feeble, and it takes some imagination to decide where the stairs are. We go down and down and down some more.

"The cellars are quite large, as you can see," Ms. Claverhill tells us, ever the docent.

The room's boundaries are lost in the pitch dark. The air smells musty-minerally. Shapes stagger and loom out of the shadows as we raise our phone flashlights: furniture under dusty sheets.

"At one point the Montgomerys had one of the largest wine collections in the United States. They did an enormous amount of entertaining. Prominent guests from across the country—the globe, even—were always visiting. Dignitaries, heads of state and industry. Celebrities."

"*Drunk of wine and velvet . . .*" Lori frowns, trying to remember the rest.

"*Velvet nap,*" I supply, and shiver. I'm still in my funeral clothes. I wish I'd brought my hoodie.

"We don't have much occasion to come down here," Ms. Claverhill says. "Most of these things are Mr. Montgomery's. Mrs. Montgomery had it all moved down here after the divorce. And of course, there are the excess hunting trophies."

She waves the flashlight beam at a monstrous figure draped in cloth. A moose? On one wall is a huge deer head, half covered by a sheet. And could that possibly be a gorilla? That's not legal.

"Mr. Montgomery didn't take his things with him?" Uncle Lenny asks.

I glance up, hearing the interest in his voice. He looks almost perky all of a sudden.

"He tried, but Mrs. Montgomery managed to bar him from reentering the home after he was ejected."

"This is impossible," Lori says, waving her flashlight around. "Look at all this junk! Where do we start? Half of it we can't even see. What if she just lifted a sheet corner and stuck the necklace in something?"

"Aunt Regina wouldn't hide it like that," Uncle Lenny says. "She would have considered it cheating. Against the spirit of the game."

"We have to think about the clue," I say. I recite it:

The room was deep, the air was still
The worms, they did their part
To scour and hide the red blood tide
A witness: the tell-tale heart

Goose bumps rise on my own arms. It's one thing to read the poem in the daylight, academically. It's another to be down in a lightless hole in the ground, thinking about worms and a red blood tide. I half expect a heart to start thumping under my feet.

A distant shriek makes Lori jump.

"The kettle. I'll be right back," Ms. Claverhill says, and she turns to mount the stairs. "I can trust you to follow the rules?"

"No touching anything," Uncle Lenny confirms in his law-enforcement voice.

I begin exploring, winding through the indistinct contours of a bygone life. I'm not sure what I'm looking for exactly. Signs of a dead body? Worms?

Uncle Lenny takes off in another direction.

"Wait for me," Aunt Lori says, hurrying in my wake of broken spiderwebs. She hugs her elbows. "This place gives me the heebie-jeebies. I'm getting a strong negative aura. Very red-brown. You know I'm sensitive to these things."

I wedge my way around a stack of crates and hear something small scurry away. "In Poe's story 'The Tell-Tale Heart,' the dead body is hidden under the floorboards."

"The floor is stone," Lori says, looking at her manicure. "Do we need to dig? Please don't say we need to dig."

"Maybe there's some sort of trapdoor? Uncle Lenny? What do you think? Uncle Lenny?" I peer around a tower of boxes and find him shining his light into a file cabinet, flipping through papers. "What are you *doing*, sir?"

He jerks away guiltily.

"What happened to *no touching*, Agent By-the-Book?"

"Sorry, what did you say?" He shuts the drawer.

"I said what do you think?"

Uncle Lenny looks around the room as if he's just noticed it. "I have no idea."

"Tell-tale heart." I spin in a slow circle. "Look for something with a heart on it. A painting, a carving, something like that."

We spread back out again, the only sound our shoes on the gritty floor.

The sure feeling I had coming down here quickly fades. Lori's right. This place is crammed full of stuff we can't even see. How are we supposed to find anything? Maybe I'm wrong and the clue isn't down here at all.

I bump into a box and it clatters to the floor. What look like bones spill out in an eruption of dust. Lori gasps. I bend down and shine my light on them. "Just deer antlers," I say. More trophies.

I feel itching frustration start to spread through my limbs. My fingers creep to the spark wheel of my lighter in my pocket for reassurance. "Tell-tale heart. Tell-tale heart. Heart. *Heart. Hart.*"

Lori rubs her temples. "Just saying the words over and over again isn't going to summon the necklace to us, Roxie."

I shush her. "A *hart*. Isn't that a deer?"

"What are you talking about?"

"It is," I say, my chest thumping. I thread my way to the opposite wall, where the enormous stag head hovers. Only the left side of its head is covered by the sheet, and antlers spike menacingly toward the ceiling. The layers of dust aren't as thick on the draped cover.

Like someone has recently moved it.

"Rox?"

Up close the deer is gargantuan. Bigger than any of the deer we have around here. Its pelt is the color of dried blood.

A tell-tale *hart*. I look into its glass eye, dark and shining. In the gloom the deer looks alive. I edge closer.

"Okay, lay it on me, dude. What did you witness? Tell your tale."

We stare each other down.

Still being careful not to touch, I shine my flashlight all over the deer's head. Its muzzle is slightly parted. And there, between sharp white teeth, I see what I'm looking for: a tiny furl of paper. A message.

Ladies and gentlemen, a clue.

Roxie

The deer *is* a hart. Specifically, a red hart from New Zealand. Ms. Claverhill informs us of this when I sprint up to the kitchen to announce our choice. I watch her face for signs that I'm on the right track, but she merely says, "A fine specimen."

With permission granted to touch it, Uncle Lenny and I wrangle the head up the stairs—no mean feat with all those wicked antlers—and place it in the middle of the kitchen island like some sort of gothic main course.

Under the bright lights the hart shows its age. Its pelt is dusty, bald in places like mice have stolen bits of fur to line their nests. Still, it's impressive, so big it seems prehistoric.

With careful fingers I tweeze the bit of paper from the deer's mouth. Teeth scrape my knuckles and send a shiver up my back. If this thing was alive, it would snap my finger off like a carrot.

The paper is rolled into a tight cylinder, the poem handwritten like the first. I read out loud.

The Robber Bridegroom

Part II

A gift to give, a gem to see
Of wonder beyond measure
Descend the stair with your night-black hair
To view a nobleman's treasure

A-spy mine eye could scarce believe
My love in hand with maiden
I crept to follow, stone heart's hollow
A nook to hide and wait in

Ringed her neck with stars made plain
Twas a noose of cunning making
A net of dreams of finer things
A thirst beyond all slaking

Clue:
The knowing gaze in knowledge hung
Once charming, proud and foolish
In death my jest, most bitter rest
Games played rough and ghoulish

Uneasy silence fills the air.

The poem's darkness settles down around us. I think of the "Robber Bridegroom" story again. A woman seeing her love bring another woman down into the dark. And eat her.

"Any ideas?" I finally ask.

"A *jest . . . Games played rough and ghoulish,*" Lori says. "There's a game room, right? We should look there."

I shake myself. "Let's go."

As we're filing out, Uncle Lenny's phone rings.

"It's the restaurant." He nods toward the garden, visible through the window. "Can I take the call outside? I'll catch up."

Aunt Lori leads the way back toward the main part of the house, refreshed now that she's out of the dungeon and we're a step closer to being millionaires. "I've got a good feeling about this," she tells Ms. Claverhill. "Like I'm being pulled toward the necklace. Diamonds have a very strong energy, you know . . ."

We're nearly to the foyer when I jerk to a stop. "Hang on. I forgot my jacket," I say. "I'll catch up, too. And I promise I won't touch anything!"

I trot away before Ms. Claverhill can protest, backtracking through the kitchen, past my jacket, which I stuffed into a chair under the table earlier. I can hear Uncle Lenny's muffled voice outside as I dart to the staff room.

The list of names and phone numbers is pinned by the calendar. Inez's name isn't there, though. There *is* a number for "Quali-Clean." Maybe she's a temp? I snap a photo. I'm about to go when I hear the kitchen door open and Uncle Lenny's low voice.

"Yeah, tons," he says. "File cabinets, boxes. Going back God knows how long."

I slide behind the staff room door, out of sight. Who is he talking to? Definitely not Marcus at the Nail.

"No, I had no idea it was all here. . . . I don't think so. That warrant was only for his home and office. By that point he wasn't living at Montgomery House. . . . Well, that's the thing, isn't it? Of course he wouldn't point us in this direction. And of course my aunt wouldn't make things simple on me by telling me his stuff was down there."

There's an edge in Uncle Lenny's voice. Something urgent. Like he's excited. Or worried. Maybe both.

"Yeah, keep me posted. I'll call you later. Thanks, Hank."

I hear his footsteps fade, the kitchen door creak as it opens and shuts again.

Hank. At the Bureau. What the hell was all that about? I give my uncle a few seconds' head start, grab my jacket, and follow him out. Files and boxes? Did he mean the stuff downstairs that he was looking at, William Montgomery's old things? What does he think is there? Whatever it is, it's got him more excited than even the prospect of diamonds.

I find everyone in the game room, which, in addition to a billiard table, a roulette wheel, and a fully stocked bar, is inhabited by the primary collection of stuffed and mounted animals. A small zoo's worth.

"This is where the boys' club met?" I ask.

"Actually, this was Mrs. Montgomery's domain," Ms. Claverhill says.

"She did love games," Uncle Lenny concurs. He peers into a glass cabinet on the wall, where several wicked-looking knives are on display. "Loved *game*. Hunting. Africa mostly."

"Great-Aunt Regina killed all these animals?" I ask.

Uncle Lenny looks around. The animals do not look happy to be here. They snarl and grimace. "Yep."

"Disturbing. Okay, so this clue starts, *The knowing gaze in knowledge hung . . .*" I look around at all the animals. "A gaze. Knowing eyes."

"A hunting trophy again?" Lori asks.

I take stock of the critters: There's a gazelle, a zebra, a lion, several iridescent birds, and what I'm pretty sure is an endangered puffin. "It would make sense, but I don't know. Would she really put the next clue in another trophy?"

Uncle Lenny frowns. He's looking at something on his phone. "Yeah, I don't think so. Not clever enough. She's going for something else."

"Well, maybe we should look at the rest of the poem," Lori says, clearly frustrated. She comes back to peer over my shoulder at the piece of paper. "*Descend the stair with your night-black hair . . . A nook to hide and wait in.* Maybe it's in the cellar again."

"No." I shake my head. "It's something to do with the part labeled *Clue*."

"Well, you're so smart, you figure it out!" Lori snaps. She stalks off toward a zebra.

I stand in the middle of the room, waiting for revelation. "Uncle Lenny? What do you think?"

"Hmm?"

"Stop playing with your phone and help us!"

"Sorry." He stuffs it in his pocket. "Let's hear the clue again?"

Exasperated, I speed-read the poem for the second time as Uncle Lenny stares into space. I'm about to go shake him when his face splits into a grin.

"What?" I demand.

"We're looking in the wrong room," he says. "Follow me."

Inez

We need to talk. Can we meet?

Inez reads the text with a frown but doesn't reply. She'll deal with that later.

She looks back up at the house she's parked outside of. She wasn't sure what she was expecting, but it wasn't a cute little green cottage with pinwheels in the flower boxes.

But she's already double-checked the address Marcus has given her. It matches the number on the mailbox. There's a *Black Lives Matter* sign in their front yard, and one that says *Emancipation from Gentrification*, like the ones she saw on the news the other night.

The house sits on a leafy green road with a hodgepodge of old and new homes. Nothing big or fancy, but the street has a nice feel to it. In a park across the street kids shout and run around in the barely-dusk. Birds sing in the hedges. People are out. They're on front porches enjoying the evening, sitting on the hoods of parked cars, laughing. A couple of moms chat while they push kids on the park swing set.

Does Marcus really live here? She'd imagined an apartment. Something less . . . domestic.

She gets out of the car, tugging the hem of her skirt. Her legs are long and the snakeskin-print mini is short. She's wondering whether she should call or knock when the front door opens and Marcus appears.

"Hi." He's wearing a button-up shirt, and there are little wet spots on his shoulders like he just got out of the shower.

"Hi," she says, swallowing past butterflies that have risen annoyingly in her throat. "I wasn't sure I was at the right place."

He glances around: The front porch with the floral-cushioned glider. The marigolds in neat planters. "It's my grandmother's house," he says, walking down the stairs and coming to stand in front of her.

She can smell him. Spice and fabric softener. She finds herself tempted to touch those wet spots on his shirt. She imagines he'd be very warm.

"She's lived here her whole life. One of the only original houses in the neighborhood still left." Marcus rubs a hand over his hair and little droplets spring from it. "I'm around back. This way."

For a moment she thinks she sees a curious face peeking through the curtains, but then it's gone. She suddenly feels embarrassed by who she is and what she's here for. She misses her mother with gut-punch force. She almost doesn't follow Marcus. She wants to keep standing in the driveway, soaking in all the normalcy of this quiet neighborhood. The smell of mown grass. She wants to eat dinner at a dining room table, watch a sitcom on TV afterward.

"How are you?" Marcus asks, and she realizes he's nervous.

She shakes herself. The mood between them isn't right. Someone's going to have to take control of the situation or it's all going to go downhill fast. It's hard to get a hard-on when you can hear kids playing T-ball in the park and your granny is sitting in the front room knitting.

"I'm great," Inez says, and gives him a lazy smile.

He relaxes, takes her hand. He leads her past a vegetable garden and toward what appears to be a converted garage, his apartment.

"I'm glad to see you," she says.

She realizes only after it's popped out of her mouth that it's not just a line. It's true.

"Me, too." The look he gives her isn't so much lust as longing, and for a second Inez is terrified she's going to burst into tears.

For puck's sake. Pull it together.

Marcus opens the door for Inez. They go inside.

Roxie

Regina Montgomery stares down at us.

“She’s very pleased with herself, isn’t she?” Aunt Lori asks.

Uncle Lenny nods. “*The knowing gaze in knowledge hung.*”

“I see what you did there,” I tell Great-Aunt Regina. “Knowledge. The library. The knowing gaze is *your* knowing gaze. The game is *your* game.”

I reach for the portrait. We’ve confirmed our choice with Ms. Claverhill. “Help me take her down.”

“If we’re lucky, there’s a safe back there,” Lori says, coming to my aid.

I grunt, taking Great Aunt Regina’s weight. In her gilded frame she’s heavier than she looks.

“Damn,” Lori says when we uncover only a square of unfaded wallpaper. I look at the back of the painting. Blank too. I shake it, but can’t hear any necklaces rattling around on the inside.

Behind us Uncle Lenny’s phone rings. “Hello?”

“We’re going to have to do some surgery,” I say. “The poem must be inside.”

“She is,” Uncle Lenny says to the caller. “Is it absolutely necessary?”

“Who’s got a knife?” Lori asks.

"I can probably find one in the kitchen if you wish," Ms. Claverhill says.

"Nope." Uncle Lenny hangs up his phone and tells us, "It's going to have to wait."

"What?" I demand.

"Why?" Lori echoes. "We're getting really close!"

"That was Officer Lamb. He wants to talk to Roxie. *Pronto*, as he put it."

"No, Uncle Lenny. Not now. He can wait."

"Sorry, but I told him we were on our way."

"But—"

"Roxanne, no. Don't worry. We've gotten two clues today. That's good. The next one will hold for a bit longer." He eyes the portrait. "Should we bring the old girl with us?"

"It's just like Aunt Regina to make us cart home her memento mori to hang in the living room," Lori says. "*Your* living room. She doesn't go at all with my decor."

"We'll put her next to Bart," I grumble.

It's okay, I tell myself. A quick detour and then we'll get back to work. A bad feeling curdles in my stomach just the same. What does Lamb want to talk with me about?

"Bart?" Lori asks.

"That's what I'm naming the deer," I say. "Bart the Hart."

"Come on," Uncle Lenny says. "Grab your dead animal and your dead aunt and let's get moving."

At the police station, Officer Lamb takes us into one of those windowless interrogation rooms you always see on cop shows. The kind that's lit with fluorescents, smells like coffee that was brewed in a boot, and is designed to mess with your head. Chairs with one leg too short. A ticking noise that you can never quite find the source of. I've been here before. Not in this particular room; another one down the hall, where they debriefed me for hours after the raid on our compound. I wonder if Lamb knows this. As soon as he shuts the door, closing us in, a vein starts pulsing behind my eyeball.

I. Want. Out.

"Have a seat," Lamb tells us. "I'll try to make this brief."

I perch on the edge of a chair and start bouncing my leg. Uncle Lenny gives it a look. I manage to make it be still for about three seconds.

"We got a call about an abandoned vehicle," Lamb says, "so we went out to check." He takes a small stack of photographs from a file and slides them toward me.

I sit up. It's the gray Porsche.

"That's it," I say. "That's the car I saw leaving the Montgomery-Wiggins house."

Officer Lamb watches me. "You're sure."

I look carefully at the three photographs on the table before me. Front, side, and rear views of the car, which is parked on a dirt road in front of a wall of kudzu vine. Meaning it could be anywhere. "I mean, it's a gray Porsche. How many gray Porsches can there be in Asheville? Mitch knows who it belongs to. Did he tell you?"

"You've been talking to the deceased's brother?"

"At the funeral today." I hold up my hands in innocence. "He's the one who approached me."

Officer Lamb motions for me to give the photos back and I reluctantly push them across the table. He taps them into a neat pile. "Does the name Evan Fowley mean anything to you?"

"Yeah," I say, my pulse kicking up. "I know Evan. I mean, I know of him. He and Kirsten worked together over the summer at her dad's law firm. He's missing. Is that *his* car?"

"Any idea why he might have been at your friend's house that night?"

"She wasn't my friend," I say before I can stop myself.

Officer Lamb raises an eyebrow.

Uncle Lenny clears his throat. "Do you think this young man was involved in the murder, Officer?"

"If your niece is telling the truth about seeing the car, then possibly."

"I *am* telling the truth. Why would I lie?"

The officer doesn't answer. He leans back in his chair, smiles faintly. He seems relaxed, but I can tell from the twitch in the lines around his eyes that he's watching my every move like a hawk. He's wide awake and waiting for me to slip up.

I realize my leg has started bouncing again. I force it to stop. "Are you looking for him?" I ask. "Have you checked his credit cards, airlines, stuff like that?"

"This ain't my first rodeo, Miss Hunt. A large withdrawal was made from his account the day of Kirsten Montgomery-Wiggins's murder. And that's curious. But what's even more curious to me are two things that involve you. First, your reaction to that piece of paper we found in her pocket."

I go cold all over. "It's . . ."

"It's the same poem my aunt gave us in her will," Uncle Lenny interrupts, coming to my rescue. "It's a clue." He explains in the briefest detail possible the treasure hunt my great-aunt has set up for us. "And before you ask, we have no idea why Kirsten had a copy of it on her," he finishes.

"Huh," Officer Lamb says, and shakes his head like, *Weird-ass rich people*. He takes some notes on his pad. "We might come back to that in a minute, but first, the other thing I'm curious about is your relationship with the deceased. The morning of Kirsten's murder, did you two have an argument?"

Sweat starts to prickle out under my hair.

"Hang on a second," Uncle Lenny says. "This has gone far enough. You didn't say anything about questioning my niece when you asked us to come in today."

"What are you talking about?" I ask Lamb.

"Roxie," Uncle Lenny warns.

Lamb turns to a page in his file. "Direct quote from a Miss Heather Beauregard, third-chair tuba: *They were shouting at each other. She [Kirsten] left the room in a huff and Roxanne yelled after her, 'You have to pay.'*"

"But that was—"

"Heather seemed to think that you and Miss Montgomery-Wiggins were not on the best terms. That she used to bully you. Is that true?"

I open my mouth, but Uncle Lenny puts a hand out to stop me. "Officer Lamb, this has been interesting, but I think we'll be going now. I was under the impression we were here for a friendly chat. My mistake. I guess I should have asked my lawyer to come in after all."

Lamb doesn't take his eyes off me. "We're all friends here, Agent Hunt."

"It's just Mr. Hunt now."

"Whatever you say." And with an accommodating smile, Officer Lamb gets up to show us out.

—

In the car Uncle Lenny buckles up and goes on full offense.

"He's just trying to shake you up, Roxie. There's nothing to be worried about."

I nod. My hands are still trembling. "Sure."

"He wants to throw this bullshit at you and see what you do. It's a stupid cop trick."

"I know."

"If they actually had any evidence—"

"Uncle Lenny," I interrupt, "don't worry. It's fine. I'm fine."

"You don't seem fine."

"It's just . . . you know." I suck in a deep breath and try to let it out slowly. "Cops. Being back there at the station."

Uncle Lenny clenches his jaw, looks ahead out the window. He knows all too well what I mean. He was there with me when

I was a scared eleven-year-old. Finally he says, "Was Kirsten one of the girls who used to . . . ?"

"Call me an inbred Jesus freak? Yeah, that's her. She was a real charmer." My uncle starts to speak but I interrupt him again. "We were twelve. Girls are bitchy at twelve."

He drums his fingers on the steering wheel. "*Did* you have an argument with her that morning?"

"No," I say. "All that was taken out of context. I was just telling her my rates."

I remember the shocked look on Kirsten's face when Nina punched her that one time. That memory used to give me life in my darkest hours.

I might have deserved that.

"She actually sort of apologized that morning," I say. "Or at least came as close to it as I think she was capable."

My uncle lets out a long breath, starts the car. "There's nothing to worry about," he says again. I can't tell whether he's talking to me or himself.

I don't answer. If Lamb gets it in his head to make my life a misery, he can. I know it. Uncle Lenny knows it.

Meanwhile, though, Lamb has given me some new information to work with. I now know Evan Fowley was behind the wheel of that Porsche. He was there that night. Which means he's murder suspect number one.

Now I just need to find him.

Roxie

AGE ELEVEN

The FBI agent approached us at the town park. Technically, he approached Mama. I wasn't normally allowed to go to the park, but Mama had finished the weekly grocery shopping in a hurry and hustled us there. She sent me off to the swings and sat on a bench, ramrod straight. After a few minutes, a dad-aged man came and sat beside her. Not too close. He wore a baseball hat and was eating from a box of raisins. He spoke to her. Mama did not speak to strangers. I expected her to get up and move to another bench, but to my surprise, she spoke back.

I decided to investigate. I had just crept up behind them when I heard, "Does he have guns?"

Mama nodded. I slipped behind a tree, made myself small.

"A lot?"

She nodded again.

The man was looking out in the direction of the kids playing in the sandbox, but I could tell he wasn't seeing them. "Anything else?"

Mama hesitated. "There's a locked box, a big metal chest in the back room of our trailer. I don't know what all's in it."

"Can you find out?"

She rubbed her arms like she was cold, even though it was a warm spring day.

He added, "Only if it doesn't put you in any danger."

"I can try to unscrew the hinges on the back," she said.

The man lowered his voice, so I only caught half of his next question. ". . . a target?"

Mama shook her head. "I told you, it's the men who make all the plans. Him and Brother Roger and Brother Mark. I'm not allowed in the meetings. But . . ." She trailed off.

I could tell the man wanted to push her to talk, but he held himself back. Smart move. Mama scared like a cat. One step too close and she'd be off in a flash.

Finally she shook her head. "I don't know anything else." She stood up. "I need to go find my daughter." She started off across the playground, shoulders hunched.

I edged my way back around the tree so that only the man could see me.

He looked up. "Well, hello. How long have you been there?"

I didn't respond immediately. I kept my eyes on Mama. "She's not lyin'. They don't let women talk about that stuff."

He kept his gaze steady on Mama, too, waiting.

"I know where they're aiming for, though."

"Do you, now?"

I nodded. "They're gonna get the baby-killer doctors. In Charlotte. I heard Pastor say it."

He shook his raisin box, peered inside. "Is that right?"

"They're fixin' to blow 'em up, ain't they?"

He didn't answer, but beads of sweat began to glisten on his brow. "Any idea when?"

"No. But I can find out." It was easy to crawl under the trailer and listen through the paper-thin floor.

At this he finally looked at me. "You're Roxanne?"

I nodded.

"I'm your uncle, your mom's brother. You didn't know you had an uncle, did you?"

My eyes grew wide. "You're the policeman?"

"Sort of. I work for the FBI. It's like the police. Now, let's get straight about something. Your mama and I are talking about some real serious stuff. Grown-up stuff. Stuff you don't need to get involved in."

I crossed my arms over my chest. "Grown-up stuff, huh? Bullshit."

That got his attention.

"You think I got a choice? I'm involved same as her." I jutted my chin at Mama, who was peering up into the tube slide, looking for me. "If she's your sister, then you know. She's a good person. She don't want to kill nobody. But she ain't got a choice either." He opened his mouth to speak. I cut him off. "She's not gonna help you. She says she will, but she's too scared of getting caught."

"She thinks he'll hurt her?"

"Worse."

"We can protect her. I promise, we can protect both of you."

I gave him a withering look. "No. You can't."

"We can take you out of there, take you someplace safe."

I dropped to my haunches and picked up a stick. I was starting to lose interest in my uncle. If he even was my uncle. Maybe it was a trick. I started drawing circles in the dirt. "Ain't nowhere safe."

The man started to speak again, then stopped. He rubbed the back of his neck. "We're gonna put him in jail for a long, long time, Roxanne."

I glared up at him. "And then? A long, long time ain't forever. What about when he gets out and comes looking for us?"

My uncle frowned, and I saw the resemblance then. Maybe they really were brother and sister. If so, where the hell had he been all this time? "How old are you, Roxanne?"

"Eleven."

He looked back at my mother. Maybe he was thinking about how he should have had this conversation long before now, before it got to this point. Maybe he was thinking about what a shitty uncle he'd been up to this moment. Maybe, like me, he was thinking about his priorities. What did he need? What was most important?

"She can't help you," I said. "But I can. I can find out his plan. Who, when, where, how bad. I can get her phone. I can call you."

He opened his mouth to protest.

"And I'll erase the call history. I'm not an idiot."

Mama was making a slow circuit of the playground. She raised a thin arm to shade her eyes, still searching for me. Our long dresses made us look silly. The other mothers on the playground wore cargo pants and blouses. The other kids wore shorts and T-shirts. Mama and I looked like we'd stepped out of time. But I wasn't laughing. I'd seen the new bruises as she put the dress over her head that morning. The old scars. I saw the slight limp in her step that had been there for years now.

"I don't want to always be worrying," I said. "I don't want *her* to always be worrying he's going to come after us. You understand what I'm saying, *Uncle*?" I straightened my back, feeling my own scars stretch. Feeling my own fresh wounds pulse in anger. *"And children will rise up against their parents . . . And the stars of heaven shall fall . . ."*

"Excuse me?" he said.

"I *said*, do we got a deal?"

Roxie

Uncle Lenny drops me and Great-Aunt Regina's portrait off at home and heads to the Nail. I have grudgingly sworn to Lori that I won't rip into Regina's portrait until she and Uncle Lenny are there, so I leave my dead aunt sitting propped up on the couch with a nice view of the TV and head upstairs to my room.

I tried to get Uncle Lenny to take me along to the Nail, but he said, "Not tonight." He circled the air in front of my face with a finger. "This is going to scare customers. Go do your homework. Get some rest."

(Uncle Lenny on prior occasions: "Sweetie, the way you're looking at them, the patrons think you're one of the ex-cons. The kind who chopped up her entire family into itty-bitty pieces with a hatchet and fed them to her pet raccoon.")

Great-Aunt Regina's vanity table waits for me in my room like an overdressed, uninvited party guest. There's nowhere else in our two-bedroom bungalow to put it. My reflection in its mirrors confirms Uncle Lenny's assessment. My dark hair hangs heavy around my face. I've got purple circles under my eyes. I sigh. All I need is an ax. And a raccoon.

The carved naked ladies framing the mirror regard me with pity. *Maybe if you tried a little blush, darling . . .*

Uncle Lenny and I used to work on my range of expressions in the car in the months after the adoption, when all I did was scowl. "Surprised face!" he'd throw at me. "Happy face!" "Constipated face!" I got a quarter for every passable emotion. I did not get rich this way.

I sit down at the vanity and take Mama's lighter out of my pocket. It's a cheap one from the gas station showing a doleful black bear climbing a tree next to the fading words *The Great Smoky Mountains!* I flick it. Spark but no flame.

I found the lighter in the dirt next to the rabbit hutch, along with a bunch of other burning crap that had launched out in a five-hundred-foot radius from our trailer. The Bic had been mysteriously untouched. I put it in my pocket in the seconds before the SWAT guys picked me up under my armpits and threw me into the back of a car. A cop tried to take it off me, but I bit him.

I pull out my computer and check for fresh news about Evan. Nothing's changed. He's still in the wind. He went missing five days before Kirsten's murder, but then shows up at her house. Did he murder her and then abandon his car? Is he hiding out? Who else can I talk to that would know where he might be? His family doesn't know. Mitch doesn't. Other friends? I go back to my list of people associated with Kirsten and pause on Kelly Graham, the other law intern. Maybe she's got some ideas. Maybe she saw things. A romance between Evan and Kirsten that went sour, perhaps? I message her, asking to talk.

Next I try calling the number for Quali-Clean I got at Montgomery House to see if I can track Inez down. A bubbly female voice tells me that I've reached Asheville's premier cleaning service and that while office hours are eight to five, I should be sure to leave a message and someone will be right back with me. I hang up.

I'm thinking about forcing myself to do some homework when my computer pings: *Video chat request from Kelly Graham.*

I click it open to see Kelly peering curiously at me. Her hair is held back with a towel and her face looks freshly scrubbed, like she just got out of the shower. "Mitch told me you might get in touch," she says by way of hello. "Who are you, some sort of Nancy Drew wannabe?"

"I lean more toward Philip Marlowe, actually."

She grins. "You know it's bad manners to poke your nose into other people's business."

"My manners are pretty bad. I grieve over them in the long winter evenings."

Now she laughs. "Well, shake your business up and pour it. I don't have all night. And the quote's '*during* the long winter evenings.' "

"Touché," I say. "And the quote's 'I don't have all *day*.' "

She is bustling around as she talks, walking from room to room. "Look, we can quote *The Big Sleep* to each other, or you can ask me questions I may or may not answer." She narrows her brown eyes. "You're not making a podcast or something, are you?"

"God no."

"Too bad. I love a good romp down a true crime rabbit hole. Listen, I'm late to meet some friends. Do you mind if I do my makeup while we talk?" She sets the phone down, waves an eyeliner pencil like a magic wand.

"Go for it."

"Kirsten and I weren't close," she says, setting to work on her face in an off-screen mirror. "I'm not sure how much I can really tell you. We ate lunch sometimes. I guess looking back I'd say Kirsten seemed . . . lost?"

Lost. It isn't the description I'm expecting. Stuck-up, yes. The pain-in-the-ass boss's daughter who you have to be nice to, yup. But certainly not *lost*. "What do you mean?"

Kelly pulls the skin of her eye taut and draws a perfect line mere millimeters from her eyeball. "Not at first," she says. "When I started my internship, I pegged her as classic type A. Always dropping her credentials into conversation. Volunteering for everything. Overcompensating maybe, because she was so much younger than the rest of us and the boss's daughter." Kelly switches eyes. "But then about halfway through the summer . . . it's like she was a windup toy that just stopped."

"Stopped? Why?"

"No idea."

"But there wasn't anything that caused it?"

She picks up a tiny box. "Might have been. If so, she didn't confide in me about it." Kelly begins attaching false eyelashes, eyes wide.

"This happened about midsummer?"

She blinks at herself in the mirror, her eyes suddenly anime-big. "Yeah. I think so. It was after the lake weekend."

"Lake weekend?"

"The firm rents out a bunch of condos on Fontana Lake and everyone comes with their families. Corporate bonding bullshit. Insanely boring. I only went because I needed to network. And there was free booze." She rolls lipstick out from a tube.

"Did something happen?"

"Yeah, a lot of tedious chitchat with the wives happened while the menfolk drunk-drove powerboats. That's about it." She pauses to slick red on her lips. "Cheap bastards. You'd think they'd at least splurge for a weekend at the beach. Fontana is so redneck."

"*Something* must have happened," I say.

She caps the lipstick. "I mean, there was this thing that happened Saturday night . . . Honestly, I'd sort of forgotten about it."

My skin prickles. I wait.

"I was coming back to my condo to go to bed," Kelly says. "It was late. I'd been hobnobbing with some of the wives. Mainlining white wine, hearing stuff about their husbands I really didn't need to know. Anyway, I was walking back around midnight when I saw Kirsten. She was on the path heading toward her place."

"Coming from where?"

"I have no idea. But she was kind of stumbling. I figured she was drunk. Actually, I wasn't sure she was going to make it up the path to the front door. I was about to go over, see if she needed some help, but then I saw she was crying."

"You didn't say anything to her?"

"I didn't want to embarrass her. I don't think she ever knew I was there. She made it to her door and went in and that was the end of it."

"And you have no idea why she might have been upset?"

"Nope."

"You never asked her about it later?"

"In the morning she seemed fine. And we all left that day. There wasn't a lot of time to talk. By Monday it didn't seem worth mentioning. And, I mean, like I said, we weren't close like that. It would have been awkward."

"But she seemed different after?"

"Yeah. I guess the timing lines up."

"Different how?"

She thinks for a second. "Distracted? Sometimes her dad would ask her to photocopy something, or pull a file, and she'd just stare at him, like he was speaking a foreign language. Other times she'd be all jumpy."

Kelly runs a blush brush along her cheekbone absently, thinking. "You know, there was this one other time . . . I mean, maybe it's nothing."

"What?"

"A couple of weeks after the lake weekend, I went down to the basement to file some stuff. All the old hard copies are on these big shelves and it's dark and you can't really see much. Anyway, Kirsten was down there looking at a file. I came up on her—she must not have heard me—and when I said her name, she jumped about a foot in the air."

The hair on the back of my neck stands up. "She was looking at a file?"

"Yeah. When I startled her, she dropped it; papers went everywhere. I tried to help her pick it up, but it seemed almost like she didn't want me to see what she was looking at. She kept grabbing stuff out of my hands, telling me not to worry about it."

"But you did see?"

"Just bits and pieces, enough to know it was old, some case from the sixties. Real estate thing."

I wait for her to go on. "And?"

She shrugs. "And that's it."

"You just saw that it was a real estate thing? No names?"

"No, but all the files are organized by the client's last name, and she was in the *M*'s."

M. The first name that pops into my head is Montgomery. Something to do with Kirsten's family? Her grandfather? *A real estate thing.* Something about the feud between William Montgomery and Great-Aunt Regina?

"So is that it for the interrogation?" Kelly asks. "I need to shake a tail feather."

"Just one more thing," I say. "Do you know if Kirsten and Evan were seeing each other?"

Kelly blinks. "Evan? Evan Fowley? No. I mean, I don't think so. What makes you ask that?"

"One of Kirsten's friends thinks she was seeing somebody in secret. She thought it might have been someone who worked at the firm."

"I guess they could have been. They certainly didn't let on at work."

"Do you think that whatever happened to Kirsten that night at the lake could have involved him?"

She cocks her head. "I don't know. I guess it's possible. I didn't see him after dinner that night. He was at some invitation-only thing with the partners. People with penises only." She pauses. "I hope Kirsten and Evan weren't seeing each other."

"Why?"

Kelly considers her nails. They're fake, smooth and shiny as blobs of hard candy. "He's missing, you know."

"I know. Any idea where he could be?"

"Nope. He's not returned any of my messages. Dropped off the face of the earth."

She doesn't sound that broken up about it. Should I tell her he was there the night of Kirsten's murder? But I only ask, "Why do you hope Kirsten wasn't seeing him?"

"Because with that boy, *the streets are dark with something more than night*." And with a little bye-bye wiggle of her fingers, the screen goes dark.

Inez

Sometimes Inez does parties. Most of the time they're fine. And sometimes they're not.

It started with sloppy college boys at frat houses, which left her feeling so dirty and degraded that she came up with a ritual. After the night was wrapped up, tips counted, she would go home and shower until the hot water ran out. Then she would put on her oldest, baggiest sweatpants and sweatshirt and, while it was still dark, drive up onto the Blue Ridge Parkway. She would pack a thermos of coffee and microwaved strawberry Pop-Tarts, wrapping them in tinfoil and putting them in an insulated lunch box so that when she opened it, a warm, sweet breath of childhood puffed out.

She would drive to the Craggy Gardens overlook and sit on the hood of her car while the engine ticked and complained about the long ascent. She would loosen her still-wet hair from its tie and let the rising sun dry it. She would drink coffee and eat artificially flavored icing and tilt her face to the light and let the UV rays burn away everything foul that remained.

After a while she added grown-up parties to her repertoire. Or that's how she thought of them. The college kids were boys.

These were men. A certain type. Rich. Too busy for affairs. Used to everything being a fair-market exchange of goods and services, sex included. For a while they seemed better, generally. Not the men themselves, but the parties. They were smaller, the men paid like grown-ups, and the action tended to wrap up by midnight. They liked pinup blondes. One friend would tell another friend, and that one would tell a guy he went golfing with and so on.

The party she went to that warm night in late June was at a vacation home. A new client. As she walked to the front door, Inez told herself, *This isn't forever.* A few more times, and then she'd have enough saved. She'd find something better. She'd been looking at nursing programs online. She was smart enough. The bedpans and vomit wouldn't bother her; she'd seen worse. Her mother would like her becoming a nurse. The ones from hospice had been kind to Mama those last days. Competent hands. Reading the lights on the machines like modern auguries. They looked death in the eye without blinking. There was a nursing program in Oregon that looked amazing. But it was expensive. And in Oregon.

The vacation home was really nice. That was fine. That was good. That meant decent tips. The front door had opened. A guy stood there, youngish, like one of the college boys she serviced. He wore a baby-pink polo shirt and his face was sunburned. Inez couldn't help but notice how good-looking he was. Behind him was a room full of men. Adults. Boys. Dressed in a rainbow of polos and loafers like they were all getting ready to hit the links. Some sort of intergenerational male-bonding thing. Her body, their rental toy. How charming.

The boy looked her up and down, quality-controlling the merchandise. He was close enough that she could smell his aftershave. He gave her an approving smile. “Hello, gorgeous.”

Inez was a professional. She smiled back. “Hello yourself.”

Roxie

"Wait," Lori says, holding out her hand. "Give it to me. I want to cut her."

I turn the knife over and back away. "You know, there are people you can talk to about these sorts of impulses."

It's the next morning after my call with Kelly. Talking with her left me unsettled, and I didn't sleep much. But what else is new. I yawn lavishly. We're in our living room, finally ready to see what's behind Great-Aunt Regina's smirk. Between the restaurant and school, now is the only time we can all be here to do this.

Now being the ungodly hour of six thirty a.m.

Uncle Lenny and I watch as Lori wrestles the portrait into position. She inspects the backing and then jabs the box cutter in with a grunt of pleasure.

Uncle Lenny leans toward me. "See that she doesn't get any more coffee, would you?"

"Oh, you didn't like her any more than I did," Aunt Lori huffs, dragging a crooked incision down one side. "After all the runaround she gave you, I'd think you'd be first in line to do this."

"Runaround?" I ask.

Uncle Lenny and his sister exchange a quick look. But

then Lori is peeling away a corner, squealing in excitement. "Look! Look!"

We huddle in close (well, as close as I'm willing to get to Lori and a sharp object) as she hacks, revealing stanzas written in the same spindly slant as the other poems we've found.

"Careful!" I say.

We peel the backing away, and I can't help feeling a little queasy, like the canvas is Great-Aunt Regina's skin.

When the lines are finally free, I read aloud to the room:

The Robber Bridegroom

Part III

Thirteen times they knotted round
The load post, castle bearing
And struck with belt till boil and welt
Upon her breast 'twas flaring

My once true love gray noble man
Cast goat-slit eye upon I
Saw me not, or with her lot
My life worth cubic zirconia

Scores of years, a thousand tears
Since bones became my altar
Around her neck a gem, a wreck
That bold young mountain's daughter

Clue:

A kingdom ripped in half by fools
A corpse in need of hiding
A nest for the prize 'neath the blind owl's eyes
A Bird in Hope abiding

The words sink in for an uneasy minute.

"*A corpse in need of hiding*? Like a corpse-corpse?" Lori asks.

We both look at Uncle Lenny. "I'm sure it's just a metaphorical corpse," he says unconvincingly. "She's being dramatic. Poetic license."

"*Struck with belt till boil and welt / Upon her breast 'twas flaring*?" I ask. "What sort of metaphor is that?"

Uncle Lenny doesn't answer. "Go get ready for school."

—

I bike to Saint Magdalene's, hoping the ride will help me think. We'll go back to Montgomery House on Saturday—Uncle Lenny can't go until then because Thursday and Friday are our busy nights at the Nail—and I need to figure out where to start looking.

As I dodge cars and puff my way up and down hills, I let the poem run through my brain, trying to distill it into something tangible. *Around her neck a gem, a wreck.* Is that a reference to the diamonds? *A corpse in need of hiding . . . A nest for the prize 'neath the blind owl's eyes.*

A Bird in Hope abiding.

Bird.

Hope.

A corpse.

The image of Kirsten's body, bloody on the floor, floats to the surface of my mind. I squeeze my eyes shut, trying to get rid of it, but that's not the best idea when you're riding a bike in rush-hour traffic, so instead I try to remember if I've seen any paintings or sculptures of owls at Montgomery House.

But I find myself coming back to what Kelly Graham said last night. Kirsten changed over the summer. Something happened to her at the lake. She was shaken and crying, stumbling around in the dark. Had someone hurt her? Evan? What had Kelly meant when she'd said, *With that boy, the streets are dark with something more than night*?

Who would know what happened? Kirsten's brother, Mitch? He was there, too. Might be time to call old Mitchell up, convince him to talk to me. I can see if he has any news on Evan's whereabouts.

And then there's still the mysterious housekeeper / exotic dancer to track down. Inez. Her, at least, I've got a lead on. I try the number for Quali-Clean again as I'm locking my bike up at school.

A decidedly chipper voice answers, "Good morning, Quali-Clean! This is Amber, how may I help make your day sparkle?"

I stifle the urge to gag. "Good morning, Amber!" I say, matching her enthusiastic drawl. "I'm calling because my dear girlfriend Linda told me about this marvelous gal she had come clean for her and I was hoping I could book the same person? I believe her name is Inez?"

"Oh gosh, well, I am so sorry, ma'am, but we don't actually take requests for specific cleaners unless you're already a customer?" Amber sounds genuinely distraught. "It's company policy."

"Oh darn," I say. "That is very disappointing. Do you think you might fudge it just this once? I would be so appreciative. Believe me, Linda is impossible to please when it comes to her cleaning ladies, and if she was impressed, then this one must be the best. Pretty please?"

"I'm so sorry," Amber says. "But I can set you up with another of our fabulous staff. All of our cleaners are top-notch. If you'll just give me a few details and tell me your availability for the next week or so—"

I hang up.

Dammit. Now what? I didn't even find out if Inez actually works at Quali-Clean.

When I walk into school, I find Nina at a table in the lobby, stumping for Students for Racial Justice. I plop down in the chair next to her. "They found the gray Porsche I saw at Kirsten's house that night."

"Thanks for signing up, Becca! Love your necklace. What? Seriously?"

"Guess who it belongs to."

"Who?"

"Evan Fowley." I wait for her shocked reaction.

"Who?" Nina asks. She smiles at Mei Trang, who's just come to the table. "Your name and email, please. We've got our first action of the year on Saturday, if you can make it: protesting the razing of Asheville's oldest Black neighborhood to make way for luxury condos."

"He was an intern who was working at Kirsten's dad's law firm. He went missing a week before her murder. But he—or at least his car—was there at her house the night she was murdered."

Nina keeps her smile focused on Mei until she walks away. "So he did it. And bailed."

"It's looking that way."

"Wow. Well, good, they'll track him down and that's that. Gina! Over here!"

Is she even listening to me? "You're busy. I'll take my musings elsewhere."

Nina sighs. "Actually, yes, I *am* busy. I know you're going through some shit, and I do want to talk about it, but this is really important, too. Hey, G! Thanks! See you Saturday! Wear good marching shoes!" She turns back to me. "People are about to be pushed out of their homes. I need to recruit ten more girls for the protest before first period starts. I promised the organizers a good turnout."

I check Nina's list. "You've already signed up forty people."

Nina flicks her hair. "I want a solid fifty girls there in pearls and Saint Maggie's T-shirts, ready to chain themselves to bulldozers."

"Sounds fun."

"Good, because I've signed you up. Hey, Anna! Coming to the march on Saturday?"

I watch the comings and goings of Saint Maggie's, a sea of white shirts and tartan green. Many of the girls are still wearing their black silk flower pins in memory of Kirsten, but it's clear that the murder is starting to settle into the background. We've put Kirsten to rest, but life hasn't stopped. There are still grades to worry about, college applications, cross-country meets, crushes.

"Am I obsessing?" I ask.

Nina winces. "A teeny bit?"

I bite my thumbnail. Is she right? Why is it so hard to know when you've gone from charming kook to ax-murderer-with-a-pet-raccoon? I mean, I don't have a raccoon. Yet.

"Officer Lamb thinks I did it," I say. "He heard that Kirsten and I had old beef. And I was there with blood on my hands. That's means, motive, and opportunity."

Nina is quiet. She even lets a few potential marchers slide by. "They've got nothing on you. Your uncle Lenny will never let them press charges. He'll fight it. He'll burn that station to the ground first. I will, too."

I give her a look.

"Sorry. Poor choice of words. Listen. You want my two cents? Forget Kirsten. Put your super-finder powers to work scratching up some diamonds."

"You're right," I say. "As per." I rub my temples.

"As per," she agrees.

I don't remind her that actually, I haven't forgotten the diamonds. They're connected. Kirsten had the clue in her possession the night she was murdered. Inez was working at Montgomery

House. It's all tangled somehow. Last night I dreamed I saw Kirsten and Mama in the Montgomery House garden. The mansion was on fire behind them. They were dressed all in white. Kirsten reached out and put something in my hands. When I opened them, I found a mass of wriggling worms.

"And I know I sound like a parent right now," Nina goes on, "but do your homework. Please? You can't lose your scholarship. Maggie's would be *so* boring without you. Come to study hall with me this afternoon. We've got that test coming up in precalc Friday."

"Nah, I'm good," I say.

Nina raises an eyebrow. I'm not. She knows it.

"Maybe I'm obsessed, but I found Kirsten *dead*, Nina. On the ground in a pool of blood and fucking iced tea. It's not something that happens to you every day. I feel *responsible*."

"Rox. The person who did that to Kirsten is still out there. What if they come after you for snooping around?"

"Seriously, you did not just say *snooping around*."

"I did. You are. Don't change the subject."

"Changing it." I shift my position and put on a brilliant smile as a batch of potential allies approaches. "Ladies! I love your nail art. Ready to help dismantle the dominant paradigm?"

Roxie

"Good morning! Can I have everyone's attention? Before we head out, I want to make sure we're all clear on what we're protesting." Nina hands Anna Johnson a sign that reads *No Gentrification without Representation*. "Nobody's going to say Saint Maggie's girls don't do their homework."

I was surprised to find that our meeting point for the march is only a couple of blocks away from where I "lost" Chloe Hamilton's dog. The Saint Maggie's group is gathered on the sidewalk next to the park, among a slow but steady trickle of protesters arriving in the early-Saturday-morning mist, drinking coffee from paper cups and fist-bumping. I'm pretty sure I saw Man-bun in the crowd, he of my porpoise-saving days. The organizers have told Nina that Saint Maggie's girls will swell the ranks to a couple hundred protesters.

"We are standing in the heart of what was historically known as the East End," Nina says in her I-mean-business voice, not pausing as she directs Becky Lawson to take a sign (*Blue Ridge Developers: Your hands are RED*). "Once a struggling but dynamic Black community, much of the East End was leveled in the late sixties, early seventies, along with Stumptown, Southside, and several other predominantly Black neighborhoods, all in the name of economic progress, aka urban renewal. The city said the substandard housing was a blight—Abigail! Yael! Over here!

"Most of the people who lived here were convinced to move into new public housing. Highways were then strategically laid out to separate that public housing from white neighborhoods. As you'll note, we are sitting a mere stone's throw from the breweries and restaurants of downtown Asheville. In a city where housing prices have quadrupled in the last fifteen years, this neighborhood is prime real estate. Developers would like to take the street we're standing on along with three others, wipe them clean, and put in a new luxury subdevelopment." She waves some more Saint Maggie's girls over. "Grab a sign, y'all.

"Blue Ridge Developers have bought out most of the residents, at what they say are fair market rates. The only 'problems' are the holdouts: twelve families, seven of which are headed by women over sixty-five. Shockingly, they aren't interested in being turfed out of the homes they've lived in their entire lives, or losing the neighborhood they've worked so hard to keep together.

"We're marching today from here to City Hall, where the CEO of Blue Ridge Developers, Laurence Hamilton, is meeting with the city council in a special session. He's going to be pushing for the city to take this land by eminent domain and sell it back to him in the name of economic development. To be clear, that's what we're here to protest today. People—predominantly white men—with lots of money shitting on people of color with less money. That's what we're trying to change. Questions? No? Good. Let's get ready, people. We start marching at nine on the dot."

I sip my coffee, wait for the girls to go back to their preparations, then ask Nina, "So the fact that Marcus lives in one of these homes has nothing to do with your interest?"

She arches a regal brow at me, indicating that answering would be beneath her dignity. Marcus, provider of my morning brew, is serving coffee to all the protesters off his front porch, flanked by a tiny old woman in a lawn chair who I think is his grandmother. She chats with people as they caffeinate.

"I was protesting the development long before I knew Marcus lived here, thank you."

"But it doesn't hurt, does it?"

Nina's mouth twitches. "It is possible to be a voice for racial justice and, at the same time, appreciate beauty where I see it. Please don't underestimate me."

"Never."

Just then I notice a familiar face near the back of the crowd. "Huh. What's Hank doing here?"

"Who?"

"Uncle Lenny's friend from the Bureau." I wave at him.

Nina frowns. "As in the Federal Bureau?"

"Of Investigation, yep."

"Late-twenties guy with the black baseball hat?"

"Yeah, Uncle Lenny's protégé before he left. Didn't realize Hank was down with the struggle." I wave harder. Either the agent doesn't see me or I've got heretofore unknown powers of invisibility.

Nina rolls her eyes, waiting for me to catch on. I put my hand down. "Oh wait, he's here to infiltrate our ranks, isn't he? That's why he's pretending not to know me."

"Bingo was his name-o." Nina touches up the lettering on her sign with a Sharpie. "The organizers told me that lately they've been getting a few plainclothes cops in the mix at protests. They're easy to spot. Crew cuts. Pleated pants. The FBI is a step up. Probably says we're doing something right. Getting noticed."

A screech of feedback cuts through the air. The march organizer, a young Black woman with long dreadlocks and a bright yellow T-shirt reading *Asheville for All*, raises her hand for attention. She lifts a bullhorn.

"Good morning, everybody, and welcome! We're glad so many people have made it out to speak up for this critical issue. This isn't the first time they've tried to dismantle Asheville's historically Black neighborhoods, but we're here to make sure it's the last!"

As the protesters cheer, my mind wanders. I know I owe it to Nina to be fully present, and no, of course I don't want Marcus's grandma to be pushed out of her home, but other things keep barging into my brain. Diamonds and murder, mostly. I assuage my guilt at being a bad friend / privileged white girl by making a promise that we'll make a hefty donation to Asheville for All when we find the necklace.

Uncle Lenny and Lori are picking me up from City Hall at eleven to go back to Great-Aunt Regina's and have a stab at the next clue: *A nest for the prize 'neath the blind owl's eyes.* I spent a good part of last night lying awake in bed, trying to figure out where we should start looking, but only ended up giving myself more bad dreams. This time of owl attacks.

"I need more coffee," I tell Nina, peering into my empty cup.

"Hurry, we're about to move out."

"The revolution must be caffeinated," I say, and beeline to Marcus's cistern.

As I stir sugar into my brew, a voice says, "You're Leonard's girl." I look up to find Marcus's grandmother eyeing me. "I'm Marcus's grandmother, Geraldine Martin," she says. "We appreciate you coming out."

I feel my cheeks go hot. I'd still be in bed if Nina hadn't organized all this. "Um, you're welcome." I sip my coffee. "You've lived here your whole life?"

"My mama and daddy built this house," she says. "Back when owning a home was almost impossible for a Black family around here. They ran the funeral parlor that used to sit on Elm Street. Next to the church and Goody's General." She points at an empty stretch of grass. "Daddy dropped dead of a heart attack the day after they tore his business down."

"During urban renewal?" I'm grateful for Nina's impromptu history lesson.

She grunts. "Urban *removal*. It was the same thing back then. They came in and told us what was good for us, and when we said thank you but no thank you, they did what they wanted anyway. All our protesting didn't do a lick of good. Those men up there in City Hall wanted to rub us out, and they damn near did it." She shakes her head. "Daddy died, and Mama followed not long after. Sis and I fought tooth and nail to keep this place, and it's only by the grace of God our house still stands. I don't aim to let them take it from me now."

I look back up the street, for the first time really seeing it, trying to imagine it full of houses, businesses, people. "Does your sister still live around here, too?"

A shadow passes across the old woman's face. "No, our Birdie flew 'round about the same time the dozers rolled in, back in nineteen and seventy. Hand me that picture album, I'll show you."

Something in my mind prickles as I pick up the cracked-spine album from the side table where it's been propped for people to look through. Marcus's grandmother holds it in her lap and with arthritic fingers turns pages of family snapshots and photos of the old neighborhood. She finds what she's looking for and points. "That was us in sixty-eight. Daddy, Mama, Birdie, and me."

The family squints into the sun next to the crisply lettered sign on the wall, *Martin Funeral Home*. "Birdie was one of the organizers of those protests back then. Got all the high school students involved, just like now. I helped, but it was mostly her."

The young woman Ms. Martin points to looks fierce. A round face and bright eyes like her sister, a crooked smile like she knows a good secret.

"Why did she move away?"

"She didn't move. She disappeared. They say she ran off, but I don't believe it."

"You think something happened to her?"

Ms. Martin presses her lips together. "She was so involved in the protests, the demonstrations. Was always saying she belonged to this mountain and they'd never run her off. And they tried, believe you me. Calls in the middle of the night to our house from fellas saying nasty things about her. Men riding in cars down the street, pumpin' shotguns. She'd laugh at 'em, standing right here on this porch. Lordy, she was brave. Wild, they called her, and worse. Much worse. They got names for a woman so presumptuous as to know herself, her body and her mind."

The prickling feeling suddenly takes clear shape. "Her name was Birdie?"

"Bernadette. But Birdie's what everyone called her."

Birdie.

Martin.

Bird Martin?

The words etched into Great-Aunt Regina's vanity. My brain begins to whir. I feel bits and pieces lining up like dominoes. Not a bird but a person. But why would Great-Aunt Regina have her name written in her vanity, a woman who went missing decades ago, along with a gothic treasure hunt poem? Cold seeps into me. Is there a connection between the girl in the poem and Birdie Martin?

A missing girl.

A corpse in need of hiding.

"Time to go, Granny."

I start out of my thoughts. Marcus has appeared at the bottom of the stairs with a wheelchair.

"You're marching?" I ask Ms. Martin.

"'Course I am. It's my house, isn't it?"

"Roxie!" Nina is waving at me to come on.

I want to ask Ms. Martin about a million more questions, but the marchers are moving out. I start to hurry off to catch up with Nina, but then turn back. "I hope the protests work this time," I tell Ms. Martin. "It's not right, rich old white dudes trying to make you leave your home."

She smiles. "Honey, you're preaching to the choir."

We spend the next hour marching slowly to Pack Square Park. We set up facing City Hall, its Art Deco facade towering above us. Tourists en route from coffee shops stop and stare. Journalists and local TV news outlets flutter eagerly at our edges. Nina is pleased.

At some point a small band of counterprotesters appear, mostly bearded white guys with Confederate-flag T-shirts who don't seem entirely sure what it is we're protesting, but dislike it nonetheless.

Around ten thirty, someone shouts, "Here they come!"

The cry electrifies our crowd and we all turn to watch two men in suits hurrying toward the entrance, doing their best to pretend the hundreds-strong crowd doesn't exist.

I blink. "Is that Kirsten's dad?"

Nina has to raise her voice over the chants of "Hell no, we won't go!" to be heard. "Yeah, he's their lawyer." She points. "And the guy beside him is Chloe Hamilton's dad. He's the CEO of Blue Ridge Developers. Did you not read the materials I emailed you?"

I shake my head in disbelief. "I'll be damned. Small world. Look, Chloe's here, too."

She sits on a far park bench, big sunglasses hiding most of her face, arms crossed grumpily over her chest.

Nina's eyes sparkle. "You think we could get her to join us? Now, *that* would be a good photo op: 'CEO's Daughter Joins Protest.' "

I briefly consider the Popsicle-photo-related dirt I have on Chloe and wonder if I could blackmail her. But no. My client-snoop privileges are sacrosanct. I'd be pretty quickly out of gigs if it got around that I wasn't discreet. "I'll go see if I can convince her," I say. I have zero hope of doing any such thing, but I do want to ask if Evan Fowley was the guy she saw Kirsten canoodling with over the summer.

Leaving the riled-up crowd, I come around the back side of the bench and plop down next to Kirsten's ex–best friend. "Good morning!"

Chloe jumps. "You're with them?" she asks once she's regained her composure.

"I'm on the side of not forcing little old ladies out of their homes, yes."

Chloe snorts and lifts an enormous to-go cup to her lips. I smell sweet mocha spice. "Daddy's offering fair compensation, a lot more than those houses are worth. They'd never get as much on the market. And there are plenty of assisted-living facilities that are perfectly adequate."

"Wow, it sounds fabulous when you put it like that."

"Whatever. Protesting doesn't do anything. All these people are only out here because it's cool to be revolutionary right now. The city's on Daddy's side. They'll approve eminent domain because that's what's good for everybody. These people will realize that eventually, once they've got checks in their hands." She sips her coffee.

For a moment I consider taking her cup and dumping its mocha spice contents on her head, but I decide a lawsuit is the last thing I need to add to my plate right now.

Instead I pull out my phone. "Is this the guy you saw Kirsten with?" I ask, showing her a picture of Evan.

She lifts her sunglasses. I'm surprised to see how tired she looks. "No."

"You're sure?"

"Definitely. Wait. Isn't that the guy they pulled out of the river?"

"Huh? What are you talking about?"

Chloe flips through her own phone and shows me a headline: "Search for Missing Law Student Ends in Tragedy." There's a photo of Evan under the byline.

My stomach turns over. "No way," I breathe. "And you're sure it wasn't him with Kirsten?"

"I'm sure I'm sure," Chloe snaps.

I pull up the story on my own phone and have just begun to skim when I hear my name. I look up to find Uncle Lenny waving at me from a parking spot kitty-corner to City Hall. He's standing with Hank next to his car.

"Coming!" I shout, and stand. I'm stopped by Chloe's grip on my arm.

"What the hell is this?" she asks.

"What is what?"

She rips her sunglasses off, peers around, eyes blazing. "Are you trying to mess with me to get at my dad? Is it you who's been following me?"

"Chloe, I have no idea what you're talking about. Seriously."

"Right," she sneers. "And you just happened to throw some dead guy in my face when you know perfectly well it's *that* guy Kirsten was with? If you're trying to screw with my head, it's not working."

I try to make sense of what she's saying. "You mean Hank?"

"Him." She stabs a pink fingernail in the agent's direction. "The one who's talking to your uncle. *That's* who I saw Kirsten with." She sweeps her things together and shoots to her feet. "Whatever. I don't need this."

"Wait," I say. "Are you sure?"

For a moment Chloe looks confused, like she's second-guessing herself. And that seems to make her even angrier. "Just leave it alone, Roxanne. Your infatuation with Kirsten is seriously weirding me out."

And with that, she stalks away.

Inez

Inez is driving down I-26 when the news report comes on:

> *More now on the law student found deceased near Bent Creek River Park early this morning. Police reports show that the suspected cause of death for twenty-four-year-old Evan Fowley was a self-inflicted gunshot wound. The young man had been reported missing almost two weeks ago. Friends and family were not available for comment. More as this story develops.*
>
> *You can expect fine weather this weekend as fall colors begin to show on the highest peaks and—*

Inez changes the station. She keeps her eyes on the road, dotted lines sweeping past. It's almost lunchtime and she's hungry. Maybe she'll swing by the Rusty Nail and get something to eat. Those okra fries were delicious.

She channel surfs until she finds a pop song and sings along at the top of her lungs.

Roxie

I think I need a flowchart.

Kirsten wasn't seeing Evan. Or at least it wasn't Evan that Chloe saw her with. He went missing before she died. But then he showed up at Kirsten's house the night of her murder. He was at the lake weekend. And now he's turned up dead, apparently a suicide. So it's possible he killed Kirsten and then himself, but why?

Well before I get to Uncle Lenny's car, Hank peels off and disappears. So much for cornering him about his trysts with Kirsten. Was Chloe right about seeing them together? *They looked intimate,* according to her. But the idea that they had something going on doesn't feel right. I know Hank, and I just can't see him risking his career to get busy with a teenager. At the very least he would know how to be more discreet. But that raises the question: If they *were* meeting, what were they talking about? What would Kirsten know that the FBI would be interested in? And does it have anything to do with her death?

"What's Hank doing here?" I ask.

"Just saying hello," my uncle says.

"Mm-hmm. You ready to go?"

He winces. "Yeah, about that. Vincent called in sick and I can't find anybody to cover for him in the kitchen. I'm going to have to fill in."

I look at my watch. "Okay, but that still gives us a couple of hours."

"Can we do it another day, Rox? Monday, maybe? I'm already so far behind. If I don't finish payroll today, people aren't going to get their checks on time. I was planning on doing it after we finished at Montgomery House tonight, but now I don't know when I'll be able to."

My heart sinks. "Really? I mean, yeah, of course, people have to get paid. Monday?" That's two whole days away.

"Thanks, sweetheart. I know you're anxious to get to the next clue."

"I'm not anxious," I snap. "It's important." I hear myself. "Sorry, I get it. Payroll's important, too."

"Monday. It will be slow. I'll get someone to hold down the fort for me. I'll make it a priority. I promise. Come on, I'll drop you off at home."

After we've pulled away, he asks, "So, uh, did you hear the news about Evan?"

"Yeah. Crazy."

He nods grimly. "The police will connect all the dots soon. My bet is that they'll determine it a murder-suicide. Just a matter of gathering the evidence." He peeks over at me.

"Yeah," I say. "Sure."

I want to believe him. But I can't make it all shake out into a neat story. There are too many blanks. I still don't understand *why* Evan would have killed Kirsten.

I refresh my phone a couple of times on the way home, but details of Evan's death remain scant. No mention of a connection to Kirsten. I find myself thinking again about Mitch Montgomery-Wiggins. Surely he's heard the news. What's going through his mind right now? Does he believe that his friend killed his sister and then himself? And does he know why?

"You know, I'm proud of you for participating in the protests."

I pull myself out of my thoughts. "Don't be too proud. I mostly did it because Nina threatened to tweeze my eyelashes out while I slept if I didn't."

"Ouch."

"She's serious about justice."

"You can't fool me. You're the same way. And you know, I'm always too proud of you."

"Actually, I had no idea exactly what we were protesting until I got there." I sneak a glance at him. When we'd found the words *Bird Martin* written in the dresser, he'd acted strange, like they meant something to him. "But I talked to Marcus's grandmother. She said this sort of thing's been happening in Asheville for a long time now."

"Same thing happened all over the country," Uncle Lenny says. "The city leveled whole neighborhoods back in the late sixties. Said they were too dangerous and unsanitary to exist. Like it hadn't been them who made it that way in the first place."

"How?"

"There were all sorts of laws meant to keep neighborhoods segregated. Once your neighborhoods are separated, it's easy to decide to spend city money in the white ones. The Black neighborhoods get neglected and end up 'blighted.'"

"Ms. Martin said her dad lost his business when they tore everything down, and he died from the shock of it. And her sister went missing. She was one of the organizers against urban renewal back then." I watch him from the corner of my eye.

"Really?" Uncle Lenny's tone is suddenly casual.

I want to say her name, *Birdie Martin*, and see how he reacts. I want to ask him why in the hell Great-Aunt Regina would have written her name in that dresser drawer. But we've just pulled into our driveway.

"Sorry to kick you out and run," Uncle Lenny says. "You'll be okay?"

"I'm fine," I reassure him. "See you later."

As I walk to the front door, I decide that if we're not going to Montgomery House, there are still other ways to be productive. I get out my phone and make a call.

Roxie

Walking to Kirsten's front door later that evening, I steel myself. Lots of deep breathing and powering the hell out of my posture. As I ring the bell, I'm feeling good, actually, about how well I'm handling being back here. I'm calm. Serene, even.

But then the door is opened by a naked dude.

"Hi," he says, looking me over while toweling his wet hair. Another towel is dangerously close to falling down and revealing all the good Lord gave him.

"Uh, hi," I say, feeling the blood I had deep-breathed into my system rush to my face. Why is an underwear model answering the Montgomery-Wigginses' front door? "Is Mitch here?"

"Yep," the guy says. He doesn't move. His eyes rove down my figure, a sly grin on his face. "Are you Sexy Cindy?"

"Nope. Roxanne." I'm having a hard time figuring out where to look. There are pecs everywhere.

"Roxanne. Now, *that's* a hot name. Do people call you Foxy Roxy?"

"Almost never."

Mitch comes up and nudges the guy out of the way. "Give it a rest, buddy. She's a friend of Kirsten's. Roxanne, hi. Sorry about him. Come in."

Mitch is shirtless, too, tan and muscled. Why is everyone half naked? I follow him inside under the gaze of his friend, who seems not at all chagrined.

"Thanks for agreeing to talk. If now's a bad time . . ." I start.

"No, it's fine." Mitch leads the way into the kitchen. "I was rude the other day at the funeral. I'm sorry. I'm happy to talk."

"I think you're allowed to be rude at times like that."

I come around the corner, and suddenly Kirsten is there on the floor, splayed out before me in a pool of blood. Her hair a corona, arms outstretched.

"Are you okay?"

I start, blink. The hardwood floor before me is spotless.

"Yeah, fine," I say, my heart thumping.

"This is Kevin, a friend from school. He's staying with me for moral support."

"Here for you, bro," Kevin says, punching Mitch's shoulder as he walks past. "I'll be in the hot tub." He grins over his shoulder. "Feel free to join, Foxy Roxy. The bubbles are therapeutic."

Mitch sits down heavily on a barstool at the kitchen island and looks through a wall of glass at Kevin, outside on the patio. "Sorry about him. He's an ass, doesn't know when to shut up. But my parents have checked into the Four Seasons, and I really didn't want to be alone in this house."

I resist looking again at the floor, rub my sweaty palms on my jeans. "Who's Cindy?"

His head jerks up. "What?"

"Kevin asked if I was Sexy Cindy."

"Oh. Just a friend. So what was it you wanted to talk about?"

"I wanted to ask you about Ev— Whoa."

I have made the mistake of looking outside, where the white beacon of Kevin's bare bum glows over the in-ground hot tub, hands on his hips.

"About Evan," I finish as Kevin hops in. That's one way to get a new image seared into your brain.

Mitch slumps. "Yeah. Poor bastard."

"He was here the night your sister was murdered."

Mitch looks down.

"That car I saw was his. You knew it. Why didn't you say so?"

"Roxanne, all I knew about you was that you were the person found standing over my sister's dead body. I didn't know who you were and what you were all about. Evan was my friend. I didn't want you pointing fingers at him if there was some explanation. So I didn't tell you. I told the cops."

"I guess that's fair."

"And to be frank, I still don't know what you're all about. I mean, Officer Lamb was asking a bunch of questions that made it seem like he suspects you. He said you and Kirsten had beef."

"He'd be a pretty bad cop if he wasn't at least a little suspicious of me," I admit. "And yes, Kirsten and I had history. It's no secret. But I swear I didn't have anything to do with her murder. I don't know how to prove it, though, other than by figuring out what actually happened." I pause, then ask tentatively, "Do you think Evan killed your sister?"

Mitch sighs. "You're sure it was him you saw driving away?"

"Yeah. I mean, I'm sure it was a gray Porsche, anyway. Just like the one Evan drove." I shake my head. "I can't believe there's no security footage to back me up."

He glances at me. "Pretty convenient, right?"

I can't tell if he's making a subtle accusation or not. Does he think I somehow hacked into their security system and erased incriminating footage? Made it all up about the Porsche?

"Did you ever find the girl Kirsten was looking for?" Mitch asks.

I shake my head. "I think I'm getting close, though." I look in the direction of Montgomery House. Tall oaks and maples stand guard against prying eyes. "Her name's Inez. She worked there, at my great-aunt's house."

"She did? Regina Montgomery's your great-aunt?"

"Yep. Small world, huh? Actually, I was wondering if that's how Kirsten knew Inez. Did Kirsten ever go over there?"

"Not that I know of. To be honest, your great-aunt wasn't exactly my family's favorite person."

"Because of the divorce and everything."

"My mom always thought that Montgomery House should have been ours." He looks around. "Like we live in the servants' quarters or something."

Mitch's brown eyes are warm, with long, thick lashes. At the funeral he was cold and angry, but tonight there's something softer about him. More vulnerable. Droplets of water from his hair slide down his neck. I realize I am making a conscious effort to ignore how attractive he is. If only he'd put a damn shirt on.

"So this girl, Inez," he says, "you haven't talked to her yet?"

"I'm having trouble tracking her down."

He nods thoughtfully. "Let me know when you do."

"Sure. I mean, I'll tell the cops, too. They'll want to talk to her. Listen, about Evan, a friend of Kirsten's said that she was acting sort of . . . funny over the summer."

"Funny?"

"Like maybe something had happened to her. I think it might have had something to do with Evan."

"Who said she was acting funny?" Mitch asks. "Chloe? What did she say?"

"Not Chloe. Kelly Graham. The other intern in your dad's office. She said Kirsten started acting withdrawn around the end of June."

"I didn't know they were friends."

"She said it was after a lake weekend thing?"

Something passes over Mitch's face. He looks out the window. He's quiet for a long time, then finally lets out a heavy sigh. "You know, my sister could be sort of a bitch."

I have to force myself not to react. "What do you mean?"

"The other day you asked if she and Evan were seeing each other."

I lean forward. "Yeah?"

"Well, I sort of . . . not *lied*, but didn't tell you everything."

I wait, nerves humming.

"This summer there was a company retreat up at a lake house my grandfather owns. That's where it happened."

Roxie

Mitch runs a hand through his wet hair. "I've been thinking about that night, actually. We were all partying and Evan sort of . . . came on to her. We'd been drinking and . . . She wasn't into him. She laughed at him. It might have . . . It pissed him off. He started using a lot more after that."

The Montgomery-Wiggins kitchen seems to close in around me. My pulse thumps.

"Evan wasn't the sort of guy who was used to rejection."

Finally. Motive. Evan gets his heart shit on by Kirsten. Maybe he comes here to try to talk to her again and it doesn't go how he wants it to. He kills her in a fit of rage. Then drives out to the river and kills himself.

Except . . . something doesn't fit.

"But Kelly told me *Kirsten* was upset that night."

Mitch looks up. "She did? She saw her?"

"Yeah, she saw her crying. Late Saturday night. Why would she be upset? If *she* rejected *Evan*?"

Mitch shakes his head slowly. "I—I don't know. Maybe it was something else." He stands up, pads on bare feet to the refrigerator. "Do you want something to drink?"

"No, thanks. Have you told the cops that Evan had a thing for her?"

"Yeah," Mitch says from behind the fridge door. "I told Officer Lamb." He reemerges with a beer.

"I know you don't want to think your friend did this," I say, "but Evan ticks all the boxes. Means, motive, opportunity. And then there's the fact that he killed himself. Guilt."

Mitch picks at his beer label. "It was the same gun," he says. "Officer Lamb told us. He killed Kirsten and used the same gun to shoot himself." Mitch looks tired. Exhausted. I know the feeling.

We shall be weary.

My eyes wander back to the floor. Tale as old as time. Pissed-off, rejected dude axes pretty girl who rejected him. Add the extra layer of Evan's substance abuse clouding his judgment. But even though it seems clear enough, questions nag at me. Not only why Kirsten was upset that night at the lake. What about Inez? What's her part in all this? Why did Kirsten want to find her?

Echoing my thoughts, Mitch says, "I know Evan killed her. But I can't stop thinking about this Inez person Kirsten wanted you to find. I just wish I knew why my sister was looking for her."

It's a relief to know I'm not the only one who still has a million questions. I hesitate, then say, "I think she had your sister's phone."

Mitch takes a swig of beer. "A hooker stole her phone?"

"Exotic dancer," I correct. "And I'm not sure how she got it. Kirsten didn't say. Did she ever mention anything about it to you?"

"Nope. Never mentioned losing a phone, never mentioned hanging out with hookers. Bit of a mystery, my sister."

His handsome face has gone dark. He stares out the window.

I slide off my stool. "I should get home." The empty spot on the floor where Kirsten died pulls my eyes back to it. "You know," I say, "I think about how if I'd gotten here just a few minutes earlier, she might not be dead."

"Maybe. But if you'd gotten here earlier, you might be dead, too."

I reach for my phone on the counter and he puts a hand on top of mine. I start to pull away reflexively, then hesitate. The warmth of his hand travels up my arm. His touch is actually not unpleasant. My skin tingles.

"You'll let me know if you talk to her?" he asks again. "The dancer? If she does have Kirsten's phone, I'd like to get it back."

He fixes me in place with those liquid brown eyes. I see a potent cocktail of emotions. Pain. Desperation. Something else I can't put my finger on. His hair is still slicked and wet. He's a privileged, pampered man-boy, it's undeniable, but I can't help feeling drawn to him. I can see his pulse beating at his throat. Humans are so damn fragile. I have a sudden crazy urge to reach out and touch his bare chest. I pull my hand out from under his before I do anything ridiculous and turn to go, hoping to hide the blush that's risen to my cheeks. "Yeah," I say. "I'll call you."

Roxie

I'm taking my bike out of the garage to go to school when a car pulls up.

"Well, well, if it isn't the Federal Bureau of Investigation," I say when Hank gets out. I yell back toward the house, "Uncle Lenny! Hide the drugs!"

"Good morning, Roxanne."

"Agent Hank. Wait. Are you special now?"

He takes off his sunglasses. "What makes you think I wasn't before?"

Uncle Lenny comes out onto the porch. "Morning, Hank. Coffee?"

"Thanks. Black."

"It was nice of you to join the protest march the other day," I tell Hank after Uncle Lenny has ducked back inside.

He grunts. "What can I say? I'm woke."

Giving him a once-over, from his sensible loafers to his dress shirt and neat side part, I say, "Of course you are, sweetie."

I decide to just come out and ask before Uncle Lenny reemerges. "Were you meeting with Kirsten Montgomery-Wiggins?"

He does well. He stays blank except for a quick twitch of his lips.

"Lenny didn't tell me," I assure him. "I found out on my own."

Hank walks around me to mount the porch stairs. "If I was, it isn't anything for you to worry about."

Uncle Lenny returns with coffee. "Is she harassing you, Agent Riley? I'm sorry, the young lady has a problem with authority."

I smile. I know he's just playing around, but something about the comment needles me. "What did she tell you?" I ask. "Was it something about her family? Her grandfather? Was she feeding you information?"

"Roxanne," Uncle Lenny says. "You know you can't ask questions like that."

"I can always ask. He just can't always answer." I look back and forth between my uncle and the FBI agent. "Are you two having a meeting right now? About Mr. Montgomery's stuff in Great-Aunt Regina's cellar? It's to do with some white-collar crime thing, right? You guys wouldn't be involved otherwise."

Uncle Lenny points the way out of our driveway. "School. Remember school? The teacher who called me Friday to talk about your homework situation seems to think you don't remember."

I swallow. Damn meddling nuns. "Fine," I say. I put on my helmet. "We're meeting at Montgomery House at four, right?"

My uncle winces. "About that . . . Are you sure we can't go tomorrow instead? I've got so much work to catch up on."

"Uncle Len, you promised," I say.

"I know, but I'm still so behind. I've got orders, inventory, catering requests . . ."

"We're so close!" I look back at Hank. "You have time for *him*, why not this?"

"That's different."

"How is it different? Oh wait, that's right, you can't tell me." I get on my bike and start down the drive. "You promised," I say again.

"Rox, come on, you know how hard it is for me to get away for long enough to do this stupid treasure hunt."

"Stupid," I say. "It's stupid. Right. Two million bucks is stupid."

He gives me a look. He doesn't care about the money and he knows I don't either. That's not what this is about. It's about finishing it.

"Whatever," I say. "I'm going to be late."

I pedal away, and when Uncle Lenny yells after me, "Bike safe!" I just go faster.

Inez

The text wakes her up. It's nearly ten in the morning, but she worked the graveyard shift cleaning at the university last night. She's only barely closed her eyes.

Unknown: You have to do something about it.
She knows.

Inez sighs. It isn't the first text she's gotten like this. Unknown is getting very paranoid. She rubs her eyes and then types.

Inez: Like what?
Unknown: Meet me. Usual spot. Half an hour.

He doesn't like leaving a trail. He likes talking in person. As she's watching, his texts disappear. He's very fastidious about erasing them. Maybe it's overkill, but then again, maybe you can never be too careful. And now really is the time to be careful.

She drags herself out of bed and begins pulling on her clothes.

Roxie

I'm tempted to ditch first period and hide out in the band room closet, but decide I don't need any more teachers calling Uncle Lenny about my dipping GPA. As soon as class is over, though, I make a beeline for it. I check my messages on the way. There's one from Uncle Lenny.

Len: I shifted some stuff around. I can meet you at Montgomery House. 4?

I know I should be grateful that he's making time, but for some reason the text just makes me mad again. I write OK and put my phone back on Do Not Disturb.

In the band room closet I pull out photocopies of parts I, II, and III of Great-Aunt Regina's "The Robber Bridegroom" and lay them out in order on the floor. It's been a few days and I want to reread them all together as a unit.

Part I

Around four heads the angels flew
Silent in their keeping
Vanity thy name is mine
And paint masked all the weeping

Come in, come in, they called to her
Their goblin fruits to offer
To the bold dark maid who dared to rave
"I am this mountain's daughter"

Man golden tongued and high red checked
Girl lovely as a posy
Petting her and fêting her
Until the dawn spread rosy

Drunk of wine and velvet nap
Lust seen for affection
"Oh maiden brave," crooned crooked knave,
"Yon meadow thine reflection"

Clue:

The room was deep, the air was still
The worms, they did their part
To scour and hide the red blood tide
A witness: the tell-tale heart

Part II

A gift to give, a gem to see
Of wonder beyond measure
Descend the stair with your night-black hair
To view a nobleman's treasure

A-spy mine eye could scarce believe
My love in hand with maiden

I crept to follow, stone heart's hollow
A nook to hide and wait in

Ringed her neck with stars made plain
'Twas a noose of cunning making
A net of dreams of finer things
A thirst beyond all slaking

Clue:

The knowing gaze in knowledge hung
Once charming, proud and foolish
In death my jest, most bitter rest
Games played rough and ghoulish

Part III

Thirteen times they knotted round
The load post, castle bearing
And struck with belt till boil and welt
Upon her breast 'twas flaring

My once true love gray noble man
Cast goat-slit eye upon I
Saw me not, or with her lot
My life worth cubic zirconia

Scores of years, a thousand tears
Since bones became my altar
Around her neck a gem, a wreck
That bold young mountain's daughter

Clue:

A kingdom ripped in half by fools
A corpse in need of hiding
A nest for the prize 'neath the blind owl's eyes
A Bird in Hope abiding

By the time I'm done reading, my chest is tight and those squirrels are running all up and down my bones. Something is definitely *not right*.

"Why the gory poetry?" I mutter to my dead great-aunt.

Read all together it's clearly a story. A girl is brought down into the dark and murdered. Hence *the red blood tide*. All I can see when I read this is Kirsten's lifeless form splayed out on the floor. I squeeze my eyes closed, trying to get rid of the image so I can think. Different murdered girl, Rox. A *maiden* with *night-black hair*. *Ringed her neck with stars made plain* seems like a reference to the diamonds. Okay, fine, but still, why make the poem all about the girl? Why complicate things with the "Robber Bridegroom" story? Why not just lead us to Bart the Hart and the vanity and all the other little hidey-holes?

Whenever I played the treasure hunt game with Mama, each phrase in the clue was important. They all meant something and they all made a whole. Is it the same with Great-Aunt Regina's poem? Is there something more that we're not seeing? Or was it different with Regina? Was she maybe just being fancifully creepy? Is there any way to know other than by reaching the end of the hunt?

A nest for the prize 'neath the blind owl's eyes. That's the key to the next hiding spot. That's what we need to focus on. But I've racked my brain and can't remember seeing any owls anywhere in the mansion, much less blind ones.

I close my eyes to try to visualize Montgomery House, but all that floats up into my mind is Kirsten's dead body again. I growl in frustration and blink the dingy closet back into focus. I dig my lighter out of my pocket and begin to pace the tight quarters.

Why haven't the police made a statement declaring Kirsten's death a murder-suicide? *Flick.* What's the holdup? Are they still gathering evidence? *Flick.*

I sweep the poetry up off the floor, stuff it in my backpack, and pull out my notebook instead. I decide to leave off from thinking about owls for a little while. Great-Aunt Regina's motives are going to be a mystery until we finish the treasure hunt. All we've got to go on is the poem. But Kirsten's murder is real. Flesh and blood, right here in front of me. I can figure it out. I just have to shake out all the pieces and put them in place.

It feels like the answer to who killed Kirsten is obvious: Evan. But every page of my notebook is full of my scribbled questions that don't seem to have anything to do with him.

Great-Aunt Regina's clue in K's pocket?

FBI?

Inez?

Phone?

There are still so many things I don't understand. Tangled ends that don't go anywhere. *It's not an Agatha Christie novel,* I remind myself. Is this just how it goes in real life? A murder is solved but a million questions remain? *Flick flick.* I stop on the page of notes from my conversation with Kelly Graham.

She seemed . . . lost.

The squirrels go quiet.

Lost. From the night of that lake weekend until she died, Kirsten was lost and looking. Hunting through old files. What was she searching for?

Kelly answers my call on the second ring with a clipped "Yes? Did you find her?"

"Uh, hi. This is Roxie Hunt. We spoke a few days ago?"

"Oh, Roxanne. Hi. Sorry, I didn't recognize the number. I thought you were a detective I've been talking to."

"Detective?"

Kelly pauses. "I probably shouldn't say anything."

I flop back on the couch. "Kelly, come on, I found the body. I'm in the middle of this whether I like it or not."

"You found the . . . You found him?"

"No, I found . . . Wait, which body are we talking about now?" I feel a headache coming on.

"Evan Fowley."

"You were talking to a detective about Evan?"

"Yeah," she says. "I think I know who killed him."

"Killed him? You don't think it was a suicide?"

"No. Evan wouldn't do that. He liked himself too much."

"I mean . . . I know it's hard to think about your friend hurting himself, but—"

"No, listen. There's this girl. I think she did it."

"What girl?"

"I don't know her name, but I can ID her. I've been on the phone with the cops, trying to explain to some guy named Sheep or something."

"They put Lamb in charge of Evan's murder, too? Is he the *only* detective they have? What'd he say?"

"The thing is, it's taking less to convince him than I would have thought. It makes me feel like they're not entirely convinced it's a suicide either."

Is that why the police have been so quiet?

"Evan and I used to go for drinks after work," Kelly continues, "and this girl was always there at the bar. Well, not always, but she came in a lot right before Evan went missing. We'd roll up, she'd waltz in a few minutes later. She once even asked me his name. Anyway, I didn't think much of it until, you know, he turned up dead, and now I can't get her out of my mind."

"Did she threaten him or something?"

"No, not that I know of. I'm not sure she ever even talked to him. It was just . . . the way she looked at him. It was creepy."

"But why would she want to hurt him?"

Kelly doesn't respond for a moment. Finally she says, "Evan wasn't a nice guy. He was a player. And that's putting it nicely. There were some rumors going around that he maybe played a little rougher than he should have. She could have been someone he used and forgot about."

"Kelly . . ." I rub a hand down my face. "What the hell? You were friends with this guy?"

"*Friends* is a strong word. Drinking buddies, more like. We ran in the same circles. I wouldn't say I even liked him that much. But I don't think his murderer should go free. If I know something, I should say something, right?"

"You gave a description to Officer Lamb?"

"I did one better. I sent him a picture. I found her in the background of some selfies we took."

An odd feeling creeps over me. "Can I see?" I ask.

"Sure. Hang on. I'll text it to you."

I open the file already knowing. Still my stomach does a little backflip. Because there she is. She's everywhere and nowhere. The missing girl Kirsten wanted me to find.

Inez.

Roxie

The rest of the school day is pretty much a write-off. I can't concentrate in any of my classes, and as soon as school lets out, I'm on my bike and on my way to Montgomery House. My thoughts are a scattered jumble. Is Kelly right? Did Inez kill Evan? Is that why Kirsten was looking for her? But that would mean it wasn't him who drove his Porsche to Kirsten's house and murdered her. And in that case, I have to go back to the same old question. Who killed Kirsten? Inez? But why? Did Kirsten know too much? One thing's for sure, I need to find Inez. I need to talk to her. I know a sensible person would leave it to the police, but we've been through this—I'm not sensible like that. Plus, if Inez gets arrested, I might never find out why Kirsten was looking for her.

Saint Magdalene's isn't too far from Montgomery House, just a short zigzag through a nice neighborhood. Maybe it's because the traffic here is thin, but I notice a black BMW taking the same turns behind me. After this happens a third time, I speed up and make a quick swing onto a leafy street. The BMW blows past. I come to a stop, let out a little sigh. I chuckle at myself. *No one's following you, Nancy Drew.*

But then the car comes back down the street and makes the turn, heading straight for me. Fast. I start pedaling the other direction.

When I started biking to school, Uncle Lenny, in a fit of parental paranoia, kitted my bike out with these goofball rear-view mirrors that stick up like bug eyes off my handlebars. They may not look cool, but they do come in handy today as I watch the car. I bike at a normal pace for a couple of blocks, and then quickly swerve in front of an oncoming car and dart down a side street. I hear a horn blare and wheels screech behind me.

When I glance back, the BMW is turning.

Is this for real? Is someone *actually* tailing me? My heart begins to race. I make another turn onto a narrow street that curves around a park. The Beemer turns, too, no longer bothering with stealth.

I hop the curb onto the sidewalk and pedal hard into the park, scaring up a flock of crows pecking at a dead squirrel. I glance over my shoulder to see the car slam on its brakes at the edge of the grass. I can't see who's driving. What is it with these people and their tinted windows? For a second I think the car's going to come after me, over the grass, but then it pulls away. I follow the sidewalk through a patch of trees, down a hill, and out of sight.

I'm almost there. I just have to make it through the park, and then it's only a couple more streets to the Montgomery House gates. I pedal like crazy.

I swerve to avoid a little old lady who shouts "Hooligan!" and waves her fist at me. ("Sorry!") I pass a playground where kids play and well-dressed mothers give me disapproving looks. ("I know! I'm supposed to walk! I'm being chased!") I pass a couple making out on a bench who pay no attention to me whatsoever.

I hurtle over the grass, nearing the edge of the park. I see a straight shot ahead of me, the empty street. I'm panting and my legs burn. I'm drenched in sweat. Almost there.

From the corner of my eye I see a dark streak roar up the street beside me.

It's too late to brake or swerve.

The last thing I see is the car barreling toward me and a familiar face behind the wheel.

And then I don't see anything at all.

Roxie

A kaleidoscope of colors quiver before my eyes. Red, yellow, blue, black. I blink, and tree branches emerge from the blur.

A woman's face swims into view. "Don't move! Oh God, are you okay?"

She's hovering over me, the sun behind her head in a halo. In her suit and diamonds she looks like an executive-class angel.

Mrs. Montgomery-Wiggins?

"I saw the whole thing! That car just came out of nowhere!" Kirsten's mother says. "Don't try to get up—I'll call an ambulance!"

I'm lying on my back in the grass by the road. I hear the murmurs of onlookers. Against her advice I turn my head and see my bike a few feet away. Its wheel is bent almost in half. There's no sign of the BMW.

"I think I'm okay," I say, and slowly roll to my side. The small crowd of people who've stopped to check on me begins to disperse. I try out my arms and legs one by one. I've managed to get some gnarly road rash on my shoulder, and my leg hurts, but nothing seems to be broken. I take my helmet off, touching the crack down the center of it. "Wowee."

"Are you sure?" Mrs. Montgomery-Wiggins asks. "Please, let me call your uncle, at least."

"No, really," I say, and put a hand out to stop her. "I just need a second to catch my breath."

The image of the BMW hurtling toward me comes back. And the driver. I saw them. I knew them. I know who tried to run me over. But the face is a complete blank now. I shut my eyes, trying to remember, but it's no use. Whatever knock cracked my helmet also erased their face.

"You saw the car?" I ask Mrs. Montgomery-Wiggins.

"Yes! It just took off!" She's horrified, flushed.

"Didn't happen to see the driver, did you? Or catch the plate number?"

She winces. "I didn't even think about it. I just saw you there and I . . ." Her eyes fill with tears.

It takes me a second, but then I realize. Oh God. She saw Kirsten lying here limp in the grass, not me.

"I'm so sorry, I should have—"

"It's okay," I assure her. "I'm okay." I feel my wounds pulse with the inanity of comforting her as I drip blood.

Her hands flutter around her purse, and she tugs out a packet of tissues. Her hands tremble. She's more shaken up than I am. She begins to dab ineffectively at my knee.

"Lucky you came by," I say.

"I live around the corner. I was out for a walk. Trying to clear my head."

I take the tissue gently. She's dabbing hard enough to bruise.

"That car was following me," I say.

Her eyes widen. "Following you? Are you sure? Why? Should we call the police?"

I find myself shaking my head automatically. “No, it’s okay. There’s not much they can do if I don’t have the plate number.”

“I’m sorry.”

“No, it’s not your fault; you didn’t hit me.” I push myself to my feet with Mrs. Montgomery-Wiggins’s help. I’m wobbly, but in one piece.

“Mitch said you came over last night,” she says abruptly.

I nod.

“You heard about Evan, I suppose.”

“Yes,” I say. “Do you think he . . .”

She wads a tissue in her manicured hand. “That bastard.”

We say nothing for a little while.

“You saw him there that night,” she says.

“I saw his car,” I correct. “Mitch thinks maybe Evan liked her? And when she turned him down, he . . .”

“He did?” Mrs. Montgomery-Wiggins says. “Mitch thinks that?”

I nod, not sure how much more to say. Kirsten’s mom looks ready to crumble into a thousand little pieces.

“Yes, I think he did like her,” she murmurs. “And he was an addict. Unstable.”

“I . . . I should probably get going,” I say. “My uncle’s expecting me.”

“He killed her. And then he couldn’t stand the guilt of it and he . . .”

“Mrs. Montgomery-Wiggins, can I call someone for you? Your husband? Mitch? I have to go, but I don’t think you should be by yourself right now.”

"No," she says, and she straightens herself like she's on a pull string. "I'm fine."

She reminds me of Kirsten in that moment. Offended at the mere insinuation of weakness.

"I'm going to call the police right now and ask them why it's taking them so long to name Evan as the murderer. He was there. You saw him." Mrs. Montgomery-Wiggins takes out her phone. "Are you sure you're okay?"

"I'm sure," I say. I walk to my bike and pick the poor thing up. I turn to say goodbye to Mrs. Montgomery-Wiggins, but she's already marching away, her phone to her ear.

The words of Dr. Adams come back to me. *Everyone processes grief in their own way.* It hadn't meant much to me when he said it, but now I think this is what he means. People get weird.

As I limp my bike down the sidewalk in the direction of Montgomery House, it occurs to me that Mitch said his mom was staying at a hotel. She must be back home now.

Who was driving that car? Who would be trying to hurt, maybe even kill me? Nina's words float through my mind: *The person who did that to Kirsten is still out there. What if they come after you?* Am I close to figuring out who killed her? It definitely doesn't seem like it.

It takes me a while to hobble to the gate, and by the time I get there, my ankle is swollen, and I'm feeling like I need to sit down and put my head between my knees. But I stash my bike behind a tree on the long drive and make sure none of my wounds are showing. I pop a couple of painkillers I keep in my bag for cramps and force myself to walk normally, even though it makes me wince. The last thing I want is to give Uncle Lenny an excuse to reschedule again. I'm not that broken.

A nest for the prize 'neath the blind owl's eyes.

I let myself into the mansion and find Uncle Lenny and Aunt Lori already there, talking to Ms. Claverhill in the sunroom.

"There you are!" Lori says.

"Sorry, I had to stay behind for a little while and catch up on notes with Sister Ursula." No one is going to question my putting in a bit more effort at school.

Uncle Lenny nods. "Good, Sister Rebecca called and said she wanted you to do a few afternoon sessions to catch up with her, too."

I swallow, my stomach sinking. "Great," I say.

"Right, well, let's get to it," Lori says. "I think we should go room by room, look for owls, nests." She marches off down the hall.

Uncle Lenny hangs back. "You okay? You look pale. Is that blood?"

I rub at a spot on my blouse. "Ketchup. I'm fine." I follow Lori.

It takes me a second to call up the poem in my mind. Maybe I hit my head harder than I thought. My helmet did crack almost in half.

A Bird in Hope abiding.

Doesn't sound very hopeful. What's hopeful about *a corpse in need of hiding*?

A kingdom ripped in half by fools. I think of bulldozers and Marcus's grandmother's neighborhood. *Focus, Roxie.*

I hear Mama's voice. *"And I will give thee the treasures of darkness, and hidden riches of secret places . . ."*

I find myself becoming more and more agitated as I watch Lori poke her head in one room, then another. I've been eager to get back to the hunt, but that was before someone maybe tried to kill me. Now that I'm here, my brain is foggy and I can't focus. The poem is so vague. I'm tired of puzzles and games. I hurt all over.

An hour later, we're standing in the salon, wilted and dusty. We haven't found anything even remotely owlish. I let myself sink into a spindly chair, and bite my lip to keep from sighing in relief. My ankle is throbbing. I close my eyes and let myself rest for a second.

"This house is too big," Lori whines. "It's a maze. We need to plan our search out. Do you have a floor plan, Ms. Claverhill? I don't want to miss anything."

"A maze," I murmur.

"That's what I said."

"There might be a floor plan in Mr. Montgomery's old study," Ms. Claverhill says.

Uncle Lenny perks up. "Let's go look."

A buzz runs through me. I open my eyes. "No."

A nest for the prize 'neath the blind owl's eyes.

"We don't need it," I say.

"Why not?" Lori demands. "A floor plan would be very helpful, Roxanne."

A Bird in Hope abiding.

I stand up. It hurts, but the adrenaline rush I'm getting helps. "Not where we're going," I say. "Follow me."

Roxie

A small part of me hopes I'm wrong, but the deeper we go into the hedge maze, the more convinced I am.

"Roxie, wait!" Lori says, teetering on her ridiculous wedge heels. "We've already looked in here! This is a waste of time!"

The boxwood hedge maze is just as baffling as before. It hasn't been kept up, and in some places it's almost impassable, while in others branches have died or shifted, leaving gaps. I thought I'd remember well enough how to get to the center, but within minutes I'm already turned around.

"Are you limping?" Uncle Lenny asks.

"Lori, come on!" I yell, and then take off again as soon as I see her come around the corner.

Finally, after what seems like a hundred dead ends and back tracks, I make it to the center, panting. I put my hands on my knees. My vision is spinning. My ankle feels like it's being stabbed with broken glass. The obelisk grave markers wait placidly in the knee-high grasses. They've got all the time in the world.

Uncle Lenny is next; then Lori emerges into the clearing cursing, her shoes in hand. Her makeup is sweating down her face. "We should have brought machetes," she complains.

A few seconds later, Ms. Claverhill strolls into the center. She doesn't even look out of breath. I have the sneaking suspicion she knows exactly how to make it to the gravestones. That she just gave us a good long head start and then walked directly to it. She glances at me like she knows I know. I swear a little smile passes over her normally impassive face.

I straighten up. "Gang's all here? Good. Look." I point at the closest obelisk. *"A nest for the prize 'neath the blind owl's eyes."*

Lori shades her eyes. "Are those . . . ?"

We all squint at the intricate carvings on the facades of the other monuments. "Crows, herons, doves, and *owls*," I say.

"Holy shit," Uncle Lenny says. "You're right."

"Language. Now, look at whose grave this is. The one with the owl on it."

We walk around to the other side.

Lori's eyes widen. "Hope Montgomery."

The original owner of the house, William Montgomery's mother. Kirsten's great-grandmother.

"A Bird in Hope abiding," Uncle Lenny says. His red face goes pale.

"Nothing's more abiding than death," I say.

"But . . . where's the clue? Is it inside the monument?" Lori asks.

Ms. Claverhill comes up behind us. From somewhere in the hedge she's pulled out a shovel. "Not in the *monument*."

"Hope isn't alone down there, is she?" I ask the housekeeper.

A corpse in need of hiding.

She thrusts the tool firmly into the dirt of the grave. "Who'll dig first?"

—

We dig. And we dig. And we dig.

I keep waiting for Uncle Lenny to protest. Grave desecration is a crime, after all. But he takes his turn with the shovel after me. I'm still aching, and the digging doesn't help, but I can't stop. This is it. I can feel it.

We chop through deep layers of sod, black topsoil, and finally red clay shot through with the fibrous roots of the hedges surrounding the graves. The earth is hard. It doesn't want to give up what's within it. For the better part of an hour, we work under the hot autumn sun. Everyone knows without speaking to be careful, stopping when we hit rocks or roots. Then, about two feet down, well before we should find Hope Montgomery's remains, I catch the shovel on something. At first I think it's part of a root, but then I pull away a ruined strip of what is undeniably cloth.

"Look," I say.

No one speaks as I get down on my knees, reaching into the hole to continue excavating with my hands.

"Here."

I look up to find Ms. Claverhill holding out a small spade.

I have to wonder how long she's been preparing for this day.

And if she knows what's waiting for us.

I take the tool and silently go back to work. Uncle Lenny reaches in beside me to help, and even Lori forgets about her manicure and begins to scratch away dirt. I pull at the fabric, and the loosened soil reluctantly releases its hold, inch by inch. The cloth is thick, brocade. I brush away dirt until I've revealed about a foot square. I can feel myself shaking. The fabric gives up and falls apart in my hands. Under, the material is different, better preserved. Something satiny that might have once been light blue, stained brown. I peel back layers, revealing a pale geometry of bones.

"Oh God," Lori moans.

I keep pushing back earth and rotten fabric, even after I find the skull. I can't stop unraveling this horrible prize. My vision starts to swim.

"Roxie," Uncle Lenny says, trying to pull me away. "We need to call the police."

I finally tip back onto my haunches, panting. I have dirt and I don't like to think what else all over me. I'm dripping with sweat, and blisters have burst on my palms. Stars fly past my eyes.

"Wait," I say. I reach back into the hole and hook my finger around something under the skull's jaw. I tug it loose from the dirt, revealing it link by link. It catches the light of the afternoon sun, the only thing hard and bright, unchanged by time.

A muddy string of diamonds.

It's at this point that I sit back in the grass and pass out.

Roxie

AGE ELEVEN

The FBI's plan had been simple. Roll up on the dumbass hillbillies, isolate Pastor. Without their leader the others would be headless chickens, running in circles. Nab them. Cart everyone off to jail. Charge them with domestic terrorism. The Feds would pat themselves on the back, go for some beers. Wrap up an eighteen-month-long investigation, and get the hell out of this "back of beyond."

Thing is, Pastor was a hillbilly, but he wasn't a dumbass. I tried to warn Uncle Lenny that they were never going to be able to just roll up on us. And he heard me, and passed the info along, but his boss was from someplace up north, and although I have no doubt he was smart, he just couldn't quite believe that anyone who talked like Pastor could have more than two brain cells to rub together. Why should he listen to Uncle Lenny, who'd been watching Pastor all this time, and me, who'd been living with him my whole life?

Maybe Uncle Lenny's boss finally heard him in that moment he was watching a bullet speed toward his eyeball. But by then it was obviously a little late.

It happened on a Sunday evening, a few months after I first met my uncle in the park. Summertime, wet and sticky heat, everything grown up and jungly. When I heard the shooting start, I knew what I was supposed to do. Pastor had trained us for this. If we ever got in trouble, his orders were to drop back into the woods, disappear into the thousands of acres of Forest Service wilderness that surrounded us. We had caches of supplies in caves and hollow logs. We could survive for months out there. That was plan A.

There was a plan B, but it wasn't ideal. If we got surrounded and couldn't make it out, we were all supposed to hole up in our family's trailer. The walls had been reinforced with three layers of particle board, behind which we would make our last stand. We would not be taken.

To be clear, plan B was martyrdom.

But there was a plan C that Pastor didn't know about. It was simple, too. When the shooting started, I would grab Mama and we would light out, down the mountain, through the woods. We'd run until we hit the road, where a big black car would be waiting to scoop us up. We'd be out of harm's way while they took down Pastor.

That was the plan, anyway.

When I think of Mama and that night, I think of Lot's wife, from the Bible. Her husband told her not to look back on her burning home as she fled. The moral of the story was definitely do what God and your husband tell you to do. But I'd always felt sorry for Lot's wife, because who can blame her for wanting one last glimpse? She was leaving her parents and her sisters and brothers behind to die. Maybe your home is wicked Sodom, but it's still your home.

Lot's wife turned to a pillar of salt.

Mama turned to a pile of ash.

It was supposed to be a surprise raid, but of course Pastor had deer cams set up around the property that alerted him to movement. He and Brother Roger and Brother Mark had plenty of time to snatch up their guns and get ready. When the SWAT team was within range, two of them got picked off immediately by Brother Roger, who'd been a sniper in the army in Iraq. The SWAT team outnumbered us, though, and pretty soon the compound was surrounded. The SWAT guys started throwing tear gas, and I figured it was a good time to let Mama in on the plan Uncle Lenny and I had cooked up.

"We gotta go now," I said. We were crouched behind the chicken coop. "Lenny said the SWAT guys'll let us pass right there." I pointed at the woods, just a few feet away.

My mama wasn't stupid. She wasn't in on the plan, but it took her about two seconds to catch on, and about two seconds to understand that it wasn't going to work. Pastor was just a few yards away, shouting orders through a gas mask in a haze of smoke, and when he saw us run, he'd come after us. He'd never let us go. Mama knew my odds were better if I was alone. Better if she looked back at her burning home. Better still if she ran toward it and got in Pastor's way.

"Go," she said, and pushed me so hard that I stumbled and fell down the bank, tumbling through poison ivy and briars until I hit a tree, the wind knocked out of me. By the time I got my breath and crawled back up, she was inside, holed up in the trailer with Pastor and Brother Mark and Brother Roger, Sister Kathleen and Kathleen's teenage son, Luke.

Plan B.

The explosives they'd been intending to blow the clinic up with were stashed in that metal trunk in the bedroom.

I don't know what Mama told Pastor to make him give up looking for me and go inside. Maybe nothing. The shooting was nonstop at that point, and probably Uncle Lenny's boss was already dead, so nobody was leaving that trailer unless it was in a body bag.

I knew what I was supposed to do. Stick to plan C: Lenny's and my plan. Turn my back and run. But I couldn't. I didn't care if God Almighty himself and all his angels were telling me I'd turn to a pillar of salt. My mama was in there, the only person in the world I gave a shit about. She had to come with me, or I wasn't going. I started running toward the trailer.

Sometimes your home is a burning hell. But it's still your home.

Nobody knows what set off the explosion. Uncle Lenny says it was the FBI shooting a gas tank attached to the trailer. That might be true. But in my darkest nightmares I see Pastor taking Mama's lighter from her, scratching the flame to life, illuminating his flock's terrified faces.

His light shines in the darkness and the darkness has not overcome it.

Whenever I remember that night, I don't see myself watching the flames from the outside. I see myself in there, among them. I see my father touch the flame gently to a trail of lighter fluid. I see the flame skip over the shag carpet and down the hall and into the room with that trunk. I see the flock bend their heads to pray.

But in reality all I saw was white-hot nothing. The trailer exploded and I was blasted backward into the air. I saw only the power and the glory, kingdom come, forever and ever, amen.

Roxie

I wake up in my own bed from a dream of riding in the car with Mama. A memory, actually. We weren't doing anything but singing along with the radio, but I felt warm and special. Music, other than the hymns we belted out on Sundays, was forbidden. Especially songs like the one we were singing, where the singer was asking his love to lay down beside him and pretend, *For the good times.* "Al Green," Mama had told me. "He was a pastor, too." I'd gawked. Him? The one singing about warm and tender bodies? She'd grinned. Later she would remind me not to say anything to my father, but at that moment she just sang, lost in the sweet sadness. She had a good voice, loud and rich, and it filled the car. Filled me.

"Roxie?"

I squeeze my eyes shut, trying to hold on to the butter-yellow afternoon, the sense of being perfectly loved and safe within the confines of that car.

But it's no use; the dream slips away. It leaves a hole in the middle of my chest a yard wide.

I feel my uncle beside me, but keep my eyes shut. "All she had to do was run," I say.

He puts a hand out to touch my arm, but pulls it back when I flinch.

I lick my dry lips. My throat feels sandpapery. "I get that Mama was trying to save me, but she could have tried. We could have made it. Why didn't she try?"

I open my eyes. Uncle Lenny is watching me.

I look back up at the ceiling. "When you and I made that plan together, I thought the hard part was going to be running. Like the physical running part. Running without getting shot or something. I thought that when it came time, she would know she had to go with me. That she would choose *trying*. I thought that she just needed a clear way out. Away from him. I thought that's what she wanted. That she hadn't taken us away before because . . . I don't know."

"Oh, Rox," my uncle says, "she loved you so much. More than this whole world, more than a thousand Pastors. She chose you."

"So why didn't she try to come with me?" I demand, banging my fist on the bed. I feel tears running down the side of my face, but I don't care anymore about trying to keep them in. "Why didn't she let me save her? We could have both made it!"

"Or you could have both died."

I don't speak. It's not like I haven't thought of that before. In the long days and weeks after the explosion, that was exactly what I wished would have happened. The only thing that kept me alive was my rage. At her, at Uncle Lenny, at myself. Rage that made me set fires and led to my social worker writing "conduct disorder" in big red letters on my file.

"I could have saved us," I repeat.

Uncle Lenny hangs his head. "It wasn't your job to save her. If it was anyone's, it was mine."

I know I should say something. I should tell him no, it wasn't his fault either. But I can't. I'm too tired. I'm too raw. And truthfully, some small, furious part of me still thinks he's right. He should have saved her. He should have tried harder. Tried sooner. Before things got so bad.

After the explosion Uncle Lenny tried to take custody of me immediately. But I told the social worker no, that I didn't want to have anything to do with that asshole. He'd promised us we'd be safe. We. Not just me.

"Do you remember what your therapist said?" Uncle Lenny asks. "That we can throw people a rope when they're drowning, but they have to grab it?"

"So it's Mama's fault," I say.

"No. Of course not." Lenny sighs. "I never should have let you do the treasure hunt with us. I should have expected something like this from Regina. It was all there in the poem. I'm so sorry."

"It was my choice."

We're quiet for a while. The Al Green song comes back to me. *For the good times* . . . "You know," I say, "sometimes that game was all we had that made sense. We'd think we were doing everything right, that we were following all Pastor's rules, and then whoosh, all the rules would change." I feel the old scars on my back and buttocks as if they're fresh. They pulse, hot against the mattress. Signs of my transgressions. Of my willfulness. Signs of Pastor helping me find my way back. A belt. Sometimes a switch cut off a tree. Sometimes I didn't even know what I was being punished for.

It's taken me a long time to come to terms with it: Maybe it wasn't for anything.

"We'd be lying there," I say, "all stunned and trying to figure out how to get up and keep going, and she'd whisper, 'I will give thee the treasures of darkness, and hidden riches of secret places.'" I swallow, remembering how those words would pick me up with their promise of sweet, logical conclusions. It sort of felt like by playing, we were resisting. Fighting back in some small way against him. The game was the one thing he wasn't a part of. The ceiling swims in my vision. "I wish you'd come and found us a whole lot sooner, Uncle Lenny."

He looks like I've punched him in the gut. "Me, too, Roxanne." He puts his hand out again to hold mine, and this time I let him. It's not easy, but I want to feel what he's trying to tell me, so I let him. "Me, too."

Roxie

For the second time in one week, a body I've found makes national news.

Outlets trip over themselves to win the headline war: "MURDERED, BURIED IN NOTHING BUT DIAMONDS!" and "MACABRE TREASURE HUNT OF DEATH!"

(Me: "The first isn't true and the second is simply bad writing. Redundant." Lori, dreaming of podcasts and Netflix series: "Who cares? Truth is in the eye of the beholder.")

The police had been quick to determine that, unsurprisingly, the skeleton we found did not belong to Hope Montgomery, the original owner of the grave. Hope's remains were still tucked neatly in her walnut coffin six feet below ground, three feet below Birdie Martin, according to the technicians who'd come out to scan and dig.

Uncle Lenny had taken me home after I fainted, while Aunt Lori and Ms. Claverhill called the police. After many hours at the station, explaining and re-explaining, the police had disinterred Birdie Martin's missing-person file from wherever missing-person files go to die and matched the blue dress to a description of what she'd last been seen wearing. They're running her DNA against her sister's, Marcus's grandmother, but no one seems to have any doubt about who was in the grave. The activist Bernadette Martin, missing for almost half a century, had been found.

Murdered.

Uncle Lenny hadn't wanted to tell me all the details, but I'd been adamant. The police are guessing strangulation, but it's hard to tell after so long. Her jaw and wrist were broken, her dress torn and bloodstained.

The police had also taken note of Great-Aunt Regina's poem that had led us to her, sending people out to photograph the stanzas we'd found along with the vanity, the portrait, and the deer head.

"When are they going to haul William Montgomery in for questioning?" Nina asks, perched on a stool at the Rusty Nail. "It's obvious he did it. *He's* the Robber Bridegroom."

News updates roll across the screen behind the bar. Our newfound fame has had the positive effect of filling the restaurant with customers who want to be regaled with our tale. Lori is happy to oblige. When Nina and I got here after school, we found her holding court at a table of wide-eyed college girls, ignoring the orders piling up behind her. "I could just feel her calling to me through the years, imploring me to find her. You know, I've always felt a spiritual connection to the dead . . ."

On television a woman with perfect cheekbones tells us, "*William Montgomery is not speaking with the press.*" The businessman's face flashes onto the screen. It's an older headshot; his hair isn't so gray and his eyes are sharper, less lined. It's hard not to see Kirsten in his features.

"He was initially investigated at the time of Ms. Martin's disappearance but never charged with any crime. His attorneys have issued this statement: 'Mr. Montgomery expresses his deepest sympathies to the family of the deceased and continues to strongly deny any involvement with her tragic demise nearly fifty years ago. Our client is complying fully with the police in their investigation, but at this time he is focused on supporting his family through their own tragedy.' Mr. Montgomery's teenage granddaughter was killed in a home invasion just last week. Her murder is still under investigation. More as this story develops."

"They'll bring him in," Uncle Lenny says once the news moves on. "But I doubt much will come of it. They haven't got anything solid on him except this poison-pen poem written by his angry ex-wife."

"And he's got that whole sympathy-vote thing going on because of Kirsten's murder," I add.

"But what about forensics?" Nina demands. "All that *CSI* stuff?"

"They're running the body through forensics, but after so long in the ground . . ." My uncle shakes his head. "Cases this old are hard to investigate, much less prosecute."

"But Birdie Martin was found *in his yard*," Nina says.

"Circumstantial," Uncle Lenny and I both respond at the same time.

Earlier I'd confronted him about Birdie Martin. "You recognized her name when we found it in the dresser, didn't you? Did you investigate her disappearance?"

Uncle Lenny had answered grudgingly, ready to cut the

conversation short if I showed signs of spiraling. "That was before my time," he'd said. "But yes, ten years ago we looked into it, in relation to other . . . matters. We weren't able to link her to him then. I'm not sure they'll be able to now."

"What matters?"

He wouldn't say. "It's an ongoing investigation, Rox."

"And what about Aunt Regina?" Lori asks now, sliding up to the bar. "Isn't she a suspect?"

"Sure," Uncle Lenny says. "But she's also dead. Makes her hard to investigate, much less charge."

"I don't think it was her," I say. "She was a crazy old lady, but I don't think she murdered Bernadette Martin. If she had, why make up the treasure hunt? Why try to blame it on her husband *now*? Why not just let the secret die with her?" I look at my uncle.

"Please don't ask me to explain the machinations that went on in my aunt's head," he says.

"And why leave the diamonds buried there?" Lori laments.

The diamonds had been taken from Birdie Martin's neck and confiscated as evidence. No one is ready to tell us when—or if—we might ever see the sparklies again. Apparently the necklace we'd always seen Great-Aunt Regina wear was a fake. Ms. Claverhill had presented it to the police.

"I mean, this whole time, millions of dollars in diamonds were right there in the garden," Lori moans. "And she knew it."

"This whole time, *Birdie Martin* was right there in the garden," I remind her. "And she knew it."

Lori waves me off.

"I just can't imagine how Ms. Martin is feeling right now," Nina says.

"She's feeling pretty mad."

The words are spoken by Marcus, who stands in the kitchen doorway, a to-go bag in his hand. "And she's gonna be even madder when she hears her dinner's going to be late because Grubhub's backed up."

"I'll take it," I say. I look at Uncle Lenny. "If you can spare me."

He stops polishing the bar top. "Maybe you should stay here. I'll send somebody else."

"I'm fine," I say. He's been treating me like a Fabergé egg for two days now. "Really."

"I can go with you," Nina says, with a covert glance at Marcus.

I tilt my head at her, telling my uncle, "Mental health patrol."

"Okay, but then straight home when you're done," he says.

"You sure?" Marcus asks us. "That would be great. I'm about to need to clone myself back there."

Under her breath Nina murmurs, "We should be so lucky."

—

When we pull up in front of Marcus's grandmother's, the sun has just begun to set. There are a bunch of kids out on the playground across from her house, and the light has a sort of magical feel to it; the dust and insects are golden and dreamy. My heart pangs when I see a little girl sitting on a bench, dressed all in pink, her Pomeranian settled into her lap. I smile and wave at her. She looks at me, confused, then behind her. She has no idea who I am, of course.

Seeing the little girl makes me think of Chloe, and with a start I remember something she said. She accused me of following her. It's a long shot, but I wonder if the same person who was following her was following (and hitting, let's not forget hitting) me in a black BMW.

As we walk up to Ms. Martin's front door, I send Chloe a quick text. Can we talk? About whoever is following you.

Nina rings the bell. It strikes me again what a nice neighborhood this is. Not rich, no perfect yards, nothing fancy about it, just a sense that people feel like they belong here. That's what they're fighting to keep. It's going to break hearts if those bulldozers come through here and cut it all up into postage-stamp lots full of cookie-cutter houses.

The curtains on the door's window twitch back and we're met with a suspicious glare.

"Hi, Ms. Martin," Nina calls. "It's Nina Sanchez and Roxie Hunt. We're friends of Marcus? We were here the other day? We have your dinner." She holds up the bag.

Recognition spreads over Ms. Martin's lined face and she rattles the locks open. "Thought you might have been one of those damn reporters that keep coming around," she says, ushering us past. "Come on in."

She leads us into a cozy living room, where nearly every inch of wall space is covered in family photographs. *Jeopardy!* is on mute on the TV. A box fan propped in an open window ruffles the air.

"Can I put it on a plate for you, Ms. Martin?" Nina asks.

"Thank you, honey." She takes my arm to settle herself back into her chair. "It wouldn't be so bad talking to them if they'd just listen to what I say. All they want to hear about is the sensational bits. Was she naked? Was she Montgomery's mistress?" She makes a shooing motion. "Trash."

"What have you been trying to tell them?"

Ms. Martin looks at the silent game show on TV. "You know, we tried so hard to get them to care when she went missing. Filed the missing-person reports, went to the police station nearly every day for a year to follow up. They said there wasn't anything they could do. No trace of her. Said she'd probably just taken off somewhere to start fresh." She harrumphs. "She'd never leave like that. I haven't let myself think about her disappearing in so long, but now it's all come back, like it happened last week."

I sit down on a squishy plaid sofa. "What *did* happen?" I ask.

Her eyes go soft, remembering. "The night our Birdie went missing, she had gone out with some friends. One friend of hers in particular had somehow gotten herself into a relationship with a man who was a friend of William Montgomery. They all went up to a party at his home. I told her it was a foolish thing to do."

"Why?"

"Why, because William Montgomery was the one who

wanted to tear this neighborhood down! He's the one she was always out protesting against."

I start. "He was the developer?"

"Honey, he still is."

"What? I thought it was Blue Ridge Developers."

"Montgomery's an investor," Nina says, coming in with the plate of food. "Through SouthEast Holdings. Seriously, Rox, it's in the literature I sent you."

Ms. Martin has one of those swivel trays you see in hospitals. I unfold it so Nina can place the food in front of her.

"So yeah, okay, good question," I say. "Why would she go to a party at his house?"

Ms. Martin shakes her head. She picks up a plastic pill organizer from the table next to her, lifts her reading glasses onto her nose to examine it. "I can't tell you it surprised me. She hated that man, but she was human. There was a part of her that craved those fine things. A part of her that knew it wasn't fair. Why shouldn't she have them, too? Maybe she thought she'd go up there and give him a piece of her mind. Or maybe she wanted to taste that life. Maybe both. Our Birdie was complicated like that." She shakes pills onto her napkin. "I told the police that's where she'd been heading that night and they should start looking there, but they wouldn't touch him."

"I thought they investigated him," I say.

"They're saying that now, but it's a fig leaf. Maybe they talked with him at some point. Never went anywhere." She lines the pills up carefully as she speaks.

"Let me get you some water," Nina says.

The words from Great-Aunt Regina's poem float back to me.

Come in, come in, they called to her
Their goblin fruits to offer
To the bold dark maid who dared to rave
"I am this mountain's daughter"

The woman in the poem sounds exactly like the Birdie Ms. Martin is describing. Is that how it happened? Birdie went to a party at Montgomery House. Had Great-Aunt Regina been there? Had she seen Birdie's murder and said nothing? Simply turned the woman's death into a stupid cryptic poem? A treasure hunt? I start to feel like something jagged is lodged in my sternum and force myself to take a couple of quiet, deep breaths.

"Do you think Mr. Montgomery killed your sister?" Nina asks softly as she sets a glass of water on the tray.

Ms. Martin looks disinterestedly at the food on her plate. She pushes a salt packet across the tray, lines it up neatly with its brethren. Lays her plastic cutlery in its proper places around her plate. Readjusts the pills—red, turquoise, and white—on the napkin. They look like precious stones.

Finally she says, "Birdie was a thorn in William Montgomery's side. He was used to getting what he wanted, and she made that difficult for him. And then here she comes knocking on his door, beautiful and loud. I heard about those parties. They were wild, everybody drunk and high and all sorts of things happening. It was Mr. Montgomery's own little kingdom. Nobody gonna tell him what he can and can't do. Kings do whatever they want in their kingdoms."

She nods once, decisively. "I don't think. I know. That man killed my sister."

Roxie

"Oh, thank you, thank you so much, Amber—*phew phew*—you are just a lifesaver! And I will definitely send you a picture of our little—*phew phew*—angel when she's here!" I throw in a couple more Lamaze breaths for good measure.

I finally manage to hang up, Amber still gushing her goodbyes.

"*Phew.* Gotcha."

I've found the key to Inez's whereabouts: babies.

Five minutes ago, "Maria," Inez's "sister," placed a desperate call trying to locate her, informing Quali-Clean's ever-vigilant receptionist that Inez isn't picking up her phone, and her sister has gone into labor! She needs to get to the hospital—*phew phew*—ASAP! Because Inez's sister's husband is busy being a hero in the Middle East and Inez is the only family she has in the world!

"Maria" found out that Inez is at Montgomery House today.

I convince Uncle Lenny to lend me the car, under the pretense of wanting to say a final goodbye to Great-Aunt Regina's housekeeper.

"I didn't realize you two were so chummy," he says.

"Closure, Uncle Lenny, it's all about closure." He still looks suspicious, but agrees and gets Marcus to pick him up on his way to the Nail.

"I can't believe your bike got stolen." He shakes his head. "One thing after another."

I still haven't told him about the hit-and-run. I figure it will only make him lock me up and throw away the key. It's bad enough that he's overprotective of my mental state right now. He doesn't need to know that someone tried to kill me, too.

I'd wanted to go to Montgomery House as soon as school let out, but had been cornered by Sister Beatrice, who insisted I stay late with her to catch up on my schoolwork. By the time I finally pull into the driveway, it's getting close to five and the light is fading. I hope I haven't missed Inez. Clouds have rolled in and the wind has picked up, sending leaves darting across the ground.

I check my phone on the way to the front door. Chloe didn't want to talk to me, but after a little back-and-forth she confirmed my suspicions:

Chloe H: Black BMW has been tailing me.
Got plate number. It's a rental.
Daddy trying to track down
who was driving.

I have to say, I'm impressed with Chloe's resourcefulness. Even if she does still rely heavily on Daddy. She says she'll let me know what they find out.

Ms. Claverhill looks surprised to see me at the door but lets me in with no questions. I look around immediately for Inez, but I don't see any sign of life other than the housekeeper.

"Tea? I've just made a fresh pot. It's in the library."

"Sure." I follow her. "Am I allowed to touch things now?"

Montgomery House has the look of a cat whose fur's been rubbed the wrong way: indignantly ruffled. The police have been through since the last time I was here, ostensibly looking for clues about Birdie's murder, but I have a feeling a lot of them just wanted to gawk at the mansion. I mean, like Uncle Lenny said, what evidence are they going to find now? They must have wanted to make it look like they tried, though, because furniture has been shifted, paintings hang askew. Drawers hang out of desks like tongues.

"Of course. The hunt is over. And goodness knows everyone else has." In the library, Ms. Claverhill leads me to the tea service. "Sugar?"

"Oh, I can do it."

She returns to reshelving books.

"Did they find anything?" I ask.

"They took a lot of things away."

"From the basement?"

She looks up, still inscrutable. "Yes."

"Anything that will help them solve Bernadette Martin's murder?"

"I hope so," she says.

I sip my tea and spin an enormous globe, letting my finger trail over the continents. "You said you've worked here for thirty-two years, right?"

"I've been the housekeeper for that long, yes."

"If anyone knows Montgomery House's secrets, it's you."

Ms. Claverhill adjusts a painting on the wall. "Bernadette Martin was before my time."

"Still."

"What brings you here, Roxanne? It's not the tea and cookies."

"Actually I'm looking for someone. There was a woman working here the first day we came. Inez? I was told she was back today. I need to talk to her."

Ms. Claverhill doesn't stop tidying, but her movements slow fractionally. "And what did you want to talk with her about?"

"Um, it's sort of complicated. You know the girl who was murdered next door a few days ago?"

So much death in such a small corner of the world.

Ms. Claverhill stops what she's doing and turns to face me. "Mr. Montgomery's granddaughter? Yes. It was horrible, what happened. Your uncle said you were the one to discover her."

"Yeah." For a moment it feels like a cold blanket has been dropped down on my shoulders. "Finding her was sort of random, actually."

"Random? How so?"

"Kirsten and I weren't friends. I only went over to her house that night because I was trying to help her find someone."

Ms. Claverhill's face stays blank. "Inez."

"Exactly," I say. "Is she here?"

"She is," the housekeeper says. "In fact, she's standing right behind you."

Roxie

I spin. For a second I just stare.

I'd only caught a glimpse of Inez the time I saw her before, and I wasn't paying much attention. I was too busy with the treasure hunt. But now I wonder how that was possible. She's gorgeous in an old-fashioned pinup star sort of way. Like a young Mamie Van Doren. Her figure strains to escape her maid's uniform, as if the whole getup is a joke, a bad Halloween costume.

"Hi," I say, finally finding my voice. "My name's Roxanne Hunt. I've been looking for you."

"Yeah, I know. Roxie, otherwise known as my sister 'Maria'? My supervisor was very confused when she called to congratulate me on becoming an aunt and I had no idea what she was talking about."

"I'll leave you two to talk," Ms. Claverhill says, and walks out of the room. I watch her go, more confused than ever. She doesn't seem surprised by any of this. Did she already know I've been looking for Inez? I pull out my phone and find the picture of Inez that Kirsten sent me the day she died. "Is this you?"

The color drains from Inez's face. "Where did you get that?"

"From a dead girl."

She looks up.

"Let me start at the beginning," I say.

I explain how Kirsten asked me to find her. How she gave me nothing to go on except a photo and the fact that Inez was a dancer. I explain about walking in on Kirsten's murder scene. I watch Inez carefully as I speak, but she doesn't give anything away, just winces when I describe finding Kirsten. I don't bring up Evan, and I don't tell her that the police might be investigating Inez for his murder as we speak, based on Kelly Graham's information.

"I don't understand," Inez says. "I never even met this girl. The first time I saw her was on the news when they were talking about her murder. Why was she looking for me?"

"She said you had her phone," I say. "But it seemed like it was more than that. I think she wanted to talk to you, too."

"Her phone? I don't know anything about a . . ." Her voice trails off. "Oh." She reaches into her pocket and pulls out a phone in a sparkly purple case. "This is hers? I found it," she tells me. Something dark passes over her face. "Under . . . unusual circumstances."

"Can I . . . ?"

She hands me the phone and I pry it out of the case. When I flip it over, I find initials engraved on the back.

KMW

Kirsten Montgomery-Wiggins.

For some reason those three letters hit me hard, each one a punch in the gut.

Treasures of darkness.

Blinking, I say to Inez, "I would love to hear more about those unusual circumstances, if you don't mind."

Inez

Inez had found the phone under the seat of her car three days after the lake house party. She was cleaning. She had already scoured the entire trailer in a frenzy of energy, scrubbing, vacuuming, ripping clothes from her closet and stuffing them into bags for Goodwill. The only thing she didn't touch was her mother's room. When she couldn't find anything else to clean in the trailer, she attacked her car.

She'd stood there in the gravel driveway staring at the phone. Where had it come from? It was new. Not a scratch on it. Clearly the fanciest model available.

KMW. Who or what the hell was KMW?

Had someone accidentally left it in her car? But no one ever rode in her janky car. So how had it gotten there?

And then a chill had gone through her. Had it happened that night? She'd found herself in the back seat the next morning, sticky and sore, a wad of cash stuffed into her bra. They must have carried her out there, and someone had dropped it.

Her fist had closed around the smooth metal, gripping it so hard she was surprised the phone didn't shatter. Her first instinct had been to hurl it against a tree. She'd cocked her arm back.

But then again, no.

Puck that. A phone like this was worth a lot of money. She'd lowered her arm. She could pawn it. Or better yet, she'd keep it. Her phone was a cracked-screen piece of shit, and she deserved something nice after what had happened. She'd go to the forums, ask if anyone knew how to wipe it. Someone would. Someone always knew a trick. They were a goddamned resourceful lot.

She put it in her pocket and went inside.

Roxie

"But you have no idea how it got there?"

Inez shakes her head. "I don't remember much from that night."

"Why not?"

"I remember a good-looking guy handing me a drink at the door. And that's about it." She looks at me like, *Do I really have to spell it out for you?*

"Oh."

"Yeah. Oh. My body told me the rest of the story in the morning."

I feel sick. "I'm sorry." The words sound pathetically inadequate.

She twitches a shrug. "It's not your fault."

I let her story layer over what I already know: Kirsten's dad's law firm sponsored a retreat at Kirsten's grandfather's lake house. The men hired a stripper, Inez. A guy gave her a drugged drink. She blacked out and someone assaulted her. Maybe several someones.

And then later Kirsten was seen stumbling around in the dark, crying. But why?

"Inez," I say. "Is it possible that what happened to you might have happened to someone else, too?"

"I have no idea."

"Do you remember seeing Kirsten there that night?" I find a picture from the news on my phone.

Inez takes it, frowns at the screen for a long time. "I don't know." Her eyes dart down to the side, avoiding mine.

She's lying. She knows her.

"Are you sure?" I ask.

"Like I said, I don't remember a whole lot," she says coolly. "She could have been there. SpongeBob SquarePants could have been there. I don't know."

I take my phone back just as a message pops up. It's from Kelly.

> They found out who she is. A prostitute. She had a big deposit in her bank account. $10K. Exact same amount taken from Evan's account. They're going to bring her in for questioning.

I glance up at Inez. She's gazing out the window into the darkening evening, toward the hedge maze. She has a strange expression on her face. Like she wants to fight something. Like she probably *could* murder somebody right now.

And if what she's telling me is true, then I don't necessarily blame her.

Did Evan assault her? And did she kill him for it?

But how is Kirsten involved? I just can't make it all shake into place.

"Can I see your phone one more time?" I ask. "Maybe there's something on it that would help."

"I had it wiped," Inez says. But she hands Kirsten's old phone over anyway. "I'll get my things and be back in a minute. I was about to leave for the day."

For a second I wonder if I should do something. I've got a murder suspect right here in front of me. But do what? Tackle her? Tie her up? She doesn't know that I know about Evan. The police will take her in soon enough. The thought makes me feel tired and helpless. I can see it all playing out. If she did kill Evan, people will be outraged and it'll be scandalous and sensational. "Promising Young Lawyer Killed by Conniving Prostitute." She'll go to jail, but other than Evan, the men who hurt her will never pay for what they did. Men like that don't, when it happens to a woman like Inez.

And surely this wasn't the first time those men hurt someone just because they could. Maybe it happened to Birdie Martin, too, before they killed her.

I find myself sort of hoping Inez did kill Evan. For her and for Birdie.

Frankly, it's a shame you can't kill a person twice.

Inez

When Inez leaves Roxanne, she thinks she's going to the staff room to get her jacket and her purse. Instead her feet take her out the back door and across the patio. She walks across the wet grass. The dew quickly soaks through her new shoes. Beside her, a forest separates Montgomery House and the Montgomery-Wiggins property. She can see the lights of the smaller house in the distance. Is Buddy still there? He has been sending more and more agitated texts. We need to talk! Where the fuck are you?

The entrance to the hedge maze looms up in front of her through the low evening fog. No one comes to lose themselves in the boxwoods anymore, and the branches have been left untended. They twist and stretch, looking for sun. Inside the maze the shadows are deeper.

She steps in and cold washes through her. The living walls seem to grow higher. She's never been afraid of the dark or the woods, but this is different. The maze is nothing like the woods. It feels wrong, like a pet gone feral. She closes her eyes, forces herself to breathe.

She needs to see Bernadette Martin's grave for herself. She needs to see where Birdie Martin lay for so long while the world spun around her. Inez wants to crumble bare earth in her fingers, feel its grit under her nails. She wants to mourn Birdie where no one ever mourned her in all those years.

Inez is aware that it's just a hole in the ground. She's aware that the body—what's left of it—has been taken away.

She's aware of the risk. There could be police officers staked out, waiting for someone. Or cameras.

But she can't keep herself away.

The hole in the ground at the center of the maze at the center of a riddle. It's a maw, open and howling. Furious.

Inez knows how it feels.

—

It had been pure chance that Inez saw the handsome boy from the lake house again. She hadn't gone looking for him. She'd been heading to work that day, early again and driving slowly, the long way through town to kill time, and he had walked out of an office building, right in front of her. She recognized him immediately. She almost ran her car into a telephone pole. He had been wearing a gray suit and a baby-blue tie. She pulled into the first parking spot she could find and got out, heart pounding. She followed him and a blond woman down the street to a brewery.

Inez sat at the bar with a good view and stared, dumbstruck. It didn't seem possible he even existed outside of her nightmares. It was like seeing Freddy Krueger walk out of the TV. There he was, hanging out. Laughing. Drinking a craft beer. He even looked straight at her once, eyes skating past like she didn't exist. He didn't even remember her enough to *see* her.

The mere fact of his existence was simply wrong.

The thought filled her, echoed into all her cells:

His existence was *wrong*.

She waited, sipping a club soda until her hands stopped trembling. When the guy's blond friend came up to order another round, Inez leaned toward her. "Can I pay for his?" She looked over at the boy, smiled conspiratorially. "He's so cute. He's not your boyfriend, is he?"

The girl laughed. "God, no. Be my guest."

"What's his name?"

"Evan," the girl said pleasantly. "He's a total douchebag. You could do better. My name's Kelly. Want to buy *me* a drink?"

Inez had pulled a ten from her wallet and put it on the bar top. She winked at Kelly. "Thanks for the tip. I'll let you decide." Then she'd slipped off the stool and left.

—

Once she had his name, it wasn't hard to figure out the rest. The office building where he worked was a law firm, and he was the only Evan there. The brewpub was his regular watering hole; it was close and he walked there almost every night after work. He was a heavy drinker, often shutting the place down after his friends had all gone home.

He consistently drunk-drove himself home in his Porsche, which was interesting, given that he always parked it in the far corner of the law office parking lot to keep it safe from other drivers.

She spent several nights watching him and decided the parking lot was her best bet. It was fairly well lit, which was a strike against it, but with some careful planning Inez could easily avoid being caught by the security cameras. On the plus side, by the time Evan was getting to his car, it was always after midnight, not a soul around. Also he tended to park close to the fence. On the other side of the fence was a wooded area that pitched steeply into the French Broad River.

Most importantly, he would be shit-faced.

The fence was a challenge. It completely surrounded the parking area and was topped with barbed wire, but after poking around on the forested side, she found a section covered in kudzu where cutting a hole in the chain-link a few days in advance wouldn't be noticed.

She set the date. A Wednesday.

She bought wire cutters, heavy rubber gloves, a tarp, wire, and a crowbar from Lowe's, paying in cash.

She kept waiting to get cold feet, but they never came.

On Monday night, two days before, she cut a hole in the fence, big enough for her to slide through. She closed it back up with a couple of twists of wire. She stashed her supplies under a thick mat of kudzu.

Then she went home to her empty trailer. And waited.

On Wednesday night, she killed Evan Fowley.

Roxie

Flesh can burn. People die. But nothing on the internet is ever truly lost.

I begin my usual routine of tricks with Kirsten's old phone. I start with the easy stuff. The trash folder, the hidden files. Then expand the search. Cloud backups. Shared drives.

Digital dumpster diving.

I've made good money off the fact that it's hard to lose all those ones and zeros. Never photograph yourself naked unless you're ready for Grandma, God, and everybody on the internet to see.

But sometimes it's not you who does the photographing. Maybe it's consensual. Maybe not. Maybe the victim didn't even know it had happened until she found herself online.

I've seen my fair share of photos and videos that I really wish I could unsee. But I'm looking at Kirsten's old phone. And I've never seen anything like this.

The video starts out shaky. It zooms, goes in and out of focus until it finally settles. A wood-paneled room. A group of men to one side. It looks like the video is being shot through a window. I recognize Mitch, Evan, Kirsten's dad and grandfather. They're all looking at something. The camera shifts and I can see what.

A naked woman lying facedown on a bed, unmoving.

I can hear Kirsten breathing. Her grandfather says something to Mitch and Evan. The other men laugh. Mr. Montgomery thumps his grandson on the back and leaves the room, ushering everyone but the two interns out.

Alone, the two young men stare at the woman.

At Inez.

"Don't," I hear Kirsten whisper. Her breath becomes shuddery gulps.

Evan moves toward the bed first. He stares down at Inez for a few moments and then leans over and slaps her naked buttock. Hard.

"Stop them," I whisper to a long-gone Kirsten. But it goes on.

I can only watch what comes next for a few seconds, and then I have to put the phone down. *Sweet holy Jesus.* The time stamp says the video goes on for fifteen more minutes.

I close my eyes, but afterimages still crowd my mind. I grind my knuckles into my eye sockets.

I don't remember much from that night.

I stand up, feeling a sudden sense of urgency.

My body told me the rest of the story in the morning.

I dash across the room, fling open the veranda door, and vomit onto the terrace.

Inez

Inez had been early to meet Buddy the night Kirsten Montgomery-Wiggins was murdered. She remembered checking her phone on the walk through the rain up to his house, thinking that being ten minutes early all the time really was a bad habit. It wasn't like she wanted to be here any longer than necessary.

Shouts came through the cracked-open front door. Why was the door open? A girl and a guy were arguing. It didn't sound like Buddy.

"You asshole," she'd heard the girl say. "You think you can do whatever you want. That you're so fucking special. You think no one can touch you."

Inez paused at the threshold, wondering if she should go back to the car. Wait a few minutes.

". . . I told you, I don't have it. It's gone."

"Bitch, you're lying. I know you're lying!"

That voice. The guy's. She knew it. It held Inez in place.

"Don't call her that."

"Fuck off, Mitch."

Inez heard the girl's tinkling laugh. "What are you . . . ? Are you even serious right now? Put that thing down before you hurt yourself, Evan. Put it—"

A shot cracked the atmosphere.

Inez's entire body seized up. A second that seemed to last a lifetime passed.

Then:

"I didn't mean— Did you see that? She fucking grabbed it!"

Wet coughing. A high keening. The noise finally broke Inez out of her paralysis and she ran inside, even though every fiber in her body was screaming, *No! Turn around, get in the car, drive away!*

She came to an abrupt halt in the kitchen doorway, because inside were several very strange things. Worlds colliding:

The first: a ghost named Evan Fowley holding a gun.

The second: a girl gasping like a fish on the ground, blood pumping from her sternum.

The third: Buddy kneeling over the girl, red flowing out through his fingers as he tried to stanch the wound. Saying, "No no, Kirsten. No no no."

Inez pulled out her phone to call 911, and the ghost pointed the gun at her. "Don't. Fucking. Do it."

He was watching her. Her ghost. The boy who'd ushered her into that lake house, all smiles and good breeding, and handed her a drink. The boy who'd hurt her.

The boy she'd thought she'd killed last Wednesday.

His bright eyes, swimming-pool blue, missed the moment when the girl on the floor behind him shuddered and stopped moving. Those pretty eyes missed seeing Buddy twitch once, then stand up. Those eyes were watching Inez, taunting her with their aliveness—*Remember me? Thought you killed me, bitch.*—and they didn't see Buddy pick a rolling pin up off the counter, one of those fancy marble ones. They did not see Buddy come up behind him and raise the rolling pin over his shoulder like a baseball bat.

They did not see the swing.

The first blow dropped the ghost to his knees.

Inez watched Buddy methodically set to work, his face placid, almost serene. Like he was playing a round of golf. She watched him smash Evan Fowley's head in, and then some. She watched the light go out of those lovely eyes. Forever this time.

When Buddy was finally done killing his friend, he looked up. "What are you doing here?" he panted. His face was speckled in red.

"You invited me," Inez said.

"No I didn't."

They looked down at Evan.

"You know him," Inez said.

Buddy didn't reply.

"I thought I killed him already," Inez murmured. She felt strangely disconnected from what was going on, like she was floating several feet above the floor. These people were not supposed to be in the same place at the same time.

But here they were. Clearly Buddy and Evan knew each other. Evan must have texted her, using Buddy's phone. Or he'd called "Cindy," anyway. The name she uses with clients. No telling what he wanted. To kill her, too? Wrap everything up in one fell swoop? Maybe. She'd made sure she was the last thing he saw before he died. Or when she thought he had died, anyway. Her head began to pound.

"He just came in here waving that gun . . ." The marble rolling pin dropped out of Buddy's grip. He put his shaking red hands to his forehead. "Fuck."

Inez looked from the dead girl to the dead boy. Her mind was disjointed pieces, thoughts banging around into each other. *Think, Inez, think.* "You know Evan," she repeated.

Buddy nodded miserably.

She swallowed down bile. "Were you there that night? At the lake house? With him? With all the rest of them?" She knew the answer as soon as she asked the question, shreds of memory coming back to her. "You were," she said softly, almost to herself. "I remember now. That's how they got my number. From you."

Buddy didn't say anything.

"Who is she?" Inez asked, looking at the girl on the floor.

"My sister." He put his head into his hands and began to cry. "Oh my god. Oh my fucking god. What am I going to do?"

Inez stood absolutely still for a full thirty seconds, staring at the mess.

Finally she said, "Mitch."

He sniffed. "What?"

"Shut up."

Mitch did.

She opened her purse and pulled out a pair of latex gloves. (She always kept a pair for when her more adventurous clients asked for special services.) "I'm going to help you," she said as she stretched her fingers into the gloves. "And then you're going to help me."

His eyes were glazed. He was slipping over some edge.

Inez clapped her gloved hands in front of his face. A puff of powder fell on a spot of blood on the tip of his nose and stuck there. "Pull yourself together, shithead. We're going to need garbage bags. Paper towels. Go get them."

Mitch watched her walk to the stove. "What are you going to do?"

"Me? Don't worry about me. I'm going to make us some tea."

Roxie

I don't find Inez in the staff room. Ms. Claverhill, who is in the cellar, tells me she hasn't seen her either and to check if her car is still parked around the side of the house.

On my way to look, I catch a flash of something out the window. I shade my eyes against the glass. It's Inez.

"Where are you going?" I ask her figure. She strides across the dark lawn and disappears into the hedge maze.

I roll the wheel on Mama's lighter under my thumb. The scrape of it drives away the video images at the edge of my mind.

I have to show Inez what I've found, even though just the thought of it makes me want to be sick again. It's dark now. The half-moon casts a weak blue light on the grounds. I zip up my hoodie, open the door, and set off after her.

Inez

It doesn't take Inez long to get to the center of the maze. She comes around a corner, and then suddenly there's the hole in the ground. Even expecting it, the sight makes her heart take off like a startled grouse.

The emptiness gapes at her feet, wider and shallower than she'd expected. The bottom is uneven, and in the moonlight the red clay is gray. A ribbon of police tape like a dead party streamer has fallen to the ground.

She realizes she's dropped into a crouch. Her legs have given out on her. Her pulse accelerates. Breath coming in gulps. Little white spots dancing across her vision.

How close had she come to being this girl? A mosaic of bones in a hole? But no, she never would have had it this good, would she? No pretty grave site for her. They wouldn't have gone to the trouble. They would have left her in a parking lot somewhere with enough drugs in her bloodstream to leave no doubt that she was just another OD'd prostitute. She would have become a name on a file in the Buncombe County Sheriff's Office basement. Open and shut. Because who would bother to question it? Who would have missed her?

Inez feels herself spinning, like the hole is sucking her in. She comes back to the same question as she has a thousand times in the weeks since it happened. Why? What did they gain by drugging her that night? What was the point of it? She can't come up with any sort of satisfying answer. She'd been paid well. Her body was theirs for the evening. You'd think they'd have wanted to get their money's worth, make her strip and gyrate around their log cabin mansion. You'd think they'd have wanted more than just a puck with a corpse.

Fuck. A fuck, Inez. Say it.

She clenches fists full of grass. Fuck them. Fuck all of them. Fuck Evan Fowley, especially, whose face is burned in her memory. She had savored every second of killing him.

Except she *hadn't* killed him. She'd tried and clearly failed. She'd thought she'd hit him over the head hard enough that night in the parking lot. He had bled so much, way more than she was expecting. She'd checked his pulse and not found one. She'd been shaking, her adrenaline rushing. She must have missed it. She'd dragged Evan down the bank and dumped him into the French Broad.

But something had gone wrong, because a few days later there he'd been in that kitchen, alive and standing over one more girl he'd hurt. Kirsten. And it was too much. Because the one thing Inez had promised him, whispering in his ear that night as she dragged him to the river, was that he would never hurt anybody ever again.

That was the real reason she'd helped Mitch get rid of Evan's body. Because in her heart she had already murdered him, even if it was Mitch who'd actually accomplished the deed. She did what needed to be done to get rid of the evidence (again) because she felt responsible. She *was* responsible. She *wanted* to be responsible. It took away some of the fury at not having actually been the one to do the deed herself.

They'd wrapped him in contractor trash bags and put Evan in the trunk of his own car. They had wiped up most of his blood and then dumped green tea all over the floor because its antioxidant properties confused luminol. (Thank you for the tip, XXX message boards.) She would later douse her clothes with tea because she wasn't about to dump any more perfectly good articles of clothing on Evan Fowley's behalf. Only one body would be found on the floor, in only one pool of blood and tea.

The money Mitch gave her was beside the point. She'd really only asked for it because she thought that was what he would expect of her, and she worried he would be suspicious otherwise of why she was so willing to help. He had paid without blinking. Good old Buddy. He never haggled.

Once Inez had explained what they had to do, they worked quickly and carefully, making it look like a single murder scene. Mitch's parents were out of town and wouldn't walk in on the two of them up to their elbows in blood and suds, but they would need to stage things properly, which meant they would need to make sure Evan's car was captured on video surveillance fleeing the scene (in good time). Mitch didn't think it would be hard to log in to the security account and delete any video footage that showed either Inez or himself. He knew his parents' passwords. He would leave a trail of bread crumbs from Kirsten to Evan. Then they would make Evan's death look like a suicide. With Evan's history of violence and substance abuse, it wouldn't be hard for Mitch to nudge friends and family into believing Evan had killed Kirsten and then himself.

It hadn't been an elaborate plan, but then again, the best plans weren't. Everything had been going along fine and dandy until Mitch nearly had a head-on collision with Roxanne Hunt as he drove Evan's car out of the gate.

Inez had already left the house in her car, missing Roxanne by seconds. Mitch had promptly called Inez and freaked out about it for thirty minutes while they drove out to a lonely farm road in Arden. As they stood in a patch of weeds and beer cans next to the French Broad, she'd tried to convince Mitch that Roxanne hadn't seen him through Evan's tinted windows. They were getting ready to stage Evan shooting himself in the head (the best way they could figure to hide the mess Mitch had made of his skull). All the while Mitch protested. "Fine for you to say; you weren't the one driving!" He had looked down at the body at their feet. "I think we should go back and find her. Do . . . something."

"What?" Inez had demanded. "Do *what*? Kill her, too? You're an idiot. Concentrate on Evan. Make it clear that he's the killer, and no one will bother to ask any hard questions."

She had surprised even herself at how authoritative she sounded, as if she knew the first thing about covering up a murder. (Though, to be fair, she did, a bit.)

Mitch had put the gun in Evan's mouth, wrapped his finger around the trigger, and pulled.

Then they dragged him down to the riverbank and heaved him in. Time in the water would make it even harder to figure out what exactly had killed Evan. That's what she told Mitch.

But it wasn't just the need to cover up his murder. Inez needed to put Evan in the water. To finish what she'd started.

Mitch followed her instructions. He needed direction. His kind always did.

He had still looked worried when she dropped him off at his dorm room. She reminded him to take a shower at the gym and burn his clothes (he could afford it).

When days passed without police knocking on their doors, Mitch had started to relax and concede that Roxanne must not have seen him. Luck seemed to be on their side. Mitch hadn't even needed to erase the security footage. There had been a glitch. Nothing had been recorded after six p.m. It seemed like they were going to get away with it.

But then Roxanne showed up at Mitch's house, asking questions.

"She's fishing," he'd insisted when they'd met up later. "She knows something! She's messing with my head!" He'd been practically levitating with anxiety. He'd asked Inez for a blow job. "Just to calm me down! Please!" To which she told him to go puck himself.

Now, sitting here in the dark by an empty grave, Inez wonders, why *had* Evan been there at the Montgomery-Wiggins house that night? Why had he shot Kirsten? All this time and she hadn't really thought to ask, not with covering up the shit show that had come after.

It didn't seem like Evan had really even meant to kill Mitch's sister. He wanted something from her. The conversation Inez had heard at the front door that night plays in her mind.

Kirsten had said, *I told you, I don't have it. It's gone.*

What was gone? What had Evan wanted?

She thinks about what Roxanne has just told her, that Kirsten was looking for her. Looking for the phone that had somehow ended up in Inez's car.

Inez sits blinking into the darkness, thinking and thinking.

She's getting to her feet when she feels it. Nothing distinct. But she knows what it is immediately. The air has shifted. The crickets have gone quiet. The hairs on the back of her neck stand up.

Someone is here with her.

Inez

There is a sudden blinding light.

"I saw you. I saw you talking to her. What did you tell her?"

Inez shields her eyes. "Mitch? Jesus, you nearly gave me a heart attack!"

"What did you tell her?" The light in Mitch's hand quivers.

She makes her voice tough. "Tell who?"

"Roxanne Hunt! Don't fuck around like you don't know!"

"Put the light down," Inez says. "I can't see a thing. What are you doing out here? Did you follow me?"

The picture he presents when he lowers the light isn't good. Bugged-out, red-rimmed eyes. Oily skin. Definitely on something. "Talk," he commands.

"What do you want me to say? She's that dead rich lady's niece. I was working. She was at the house. She wanted to talk to me. I didn't tell her anything. How did you even see us? Were you watching through the windows?"

Pucking creeper.

Mitch ignores the question. "Fuck. What did she ask you? Did she ask about Kirsten?"

His words are rushed, running into each other. He's coked

out. Inez keeps her voice calm. "She said your sister was looking for me." She pauses. "Did you know that?"

"Roxanne told me, too," he says cagily. "Did she say anything about . . . Did she see me that night driving Evan's car?"

"She didn't mention it."

A nightjar calls somewhere and Mitch swivels the flashlight toward it. The shadows of the obelisk headstones leap. "She fucking knows." He turns and paces, and Inez catches a glint at his waist. He has a gun tucked into his pants. *He's going to blow his balls off.*

Inez knows she should probably be more worried that he's high and has a gun, but now that she's gotten over her initial scare, she's pissed. She wants answers. "Roxanne said your sister was looking for me because I had her phone."

A long pause. "You have her phone?" Mitch asks.

"It somehow ended up in my car that night at the lake."

The flashlight twitches. "Yeah? So?"

She waits. He'll talk. He's jabbery as a jaybird when he's high.

Mitch rocks from foot to foot. "Where is it?"

"It was a nice phone," she says. "I kept it."

Silence. Agitation shivers through his body.

"Why was Evan there at your house that night?" Inez asks. "What did he want from your sister?"

Mitch doesn't answer.

"I heard him before he shot her," she goes on. "He asked her where *it* was." She moves slowly toward him, maneuvering herself into a better position. "What was he talking about?"

Mitch keeps the light trained on her. "I don't know."

"I think you do." She edges closer. "I think you both wanted that phone. You and Evan. Why?"

His eyes shift from her to a gap in the hedgerow. He sees what she's doing. Too late.

She bolts.

Roxie

I curse at the leafy dead end in front of me. I could have sworn I was going the right way this time.

Once inside, it takes about five seconds to get completely lost in the hedge maze again. I turn around in a circle, squint up at the sky. Maybe I should just yell for Inez. I open my mouth but stop when I hear muffled voices. I backtrack and try to make my way toward them. The moon comes out from behind a cloud, and suddenly I can see the wet grass in front of me, a clear track where someone has passed. I speed up, keeping quiet but heading toward the sounds of an argument. Crickets and nightjars cry around me.

"What was he talking about?"

I freeze. That's Inez. Who is she with? I don't hear the reply, and start to creep forward again.

". . . think you both wanted that phone. Why?"

I lean in but the voices stop.

And then I hear a thumping noise. My heart seizes.

It's the sound of someone running straight toward me.

I spin and take off in the opposite direction. I hear the person speed up. They'll be on top of me in seconds. At a fork I hesitate and then lunge to the left, praying I'm heading for the exit.

No dice.

At another dead end, I crash into the hedge, hoping to shove myself through, but the branches are old and tough. They grab me instead, holding me fast. Not bothering to be quiet now, I thrash, trying to get past them.

Hands grab my arms and I'm about to scream when Inez's voice in my ear says, "Shh! Come on."

She runs and I follow, stumbling. At the end of the passage she jerks to a stop. We listen. My heart is thumping too hard to hear anything, so I just let Inez grab my hand and drag me to the left, down another identical leafy passage.

"Cindy!"

The shout makes us freeze.

"I only want to talk to you!" The voice is muffled, maybe twenty feet away.

Is that Mitch? Why is he calling Inez Cindy?

Inez pulls me in the opposite direction of his voice, crouching low to avoid the branches that hang over our heads. They yank my hair. My heart feels like it's going to explode out of my chest.

I'm looking back over my shoulder when I put my foot down on a branch that snaps like a gun going off.

Dammit.

We freeze.

No sound except footsteps shuffling through the grass, coming in our direction. We take off, not bothering to be quiet now. I follow Inez at a run. I have no idea if we're heading in the right direction.

She lunges across an intersection, and I'm five feet behind when a flashlight beam suddenly hits me.

"Stop!"

I don't.

But in the second I take to squint back into the light, I lose Inez around the corner. I run and quickly hit a split in the path. Shit! Which way?

I dash to the right, pushing past branches, desperate for these damn bushes to finally end. My breath is ragged. The walls are closing in on me.

I hit another dead end.

"No."

I turn, press my back to the foliage, which pokes and pushes against me like clawed fingers. The light comes around the corner, catches me.

"You!"

I squint. All I can see is his hunched figure moving toward me. In one hand, Mitch has the light. In the other, something shiny. I renew my struggle with the thorns.

"Roxanne!" he yells.

Moonlight suddenly spills down on us and I can see everything. Mitch. The gun.

"I don't fucking believe this," Mitch shouts. "You're fucking *everywhere*. Were you listening to us? Did she bring you out here?"

"I— No!" I look around, desperate. Blind panic fills me. There's nowhere to go.

A few feet away, Mitch stops, raises the gun so I can see its tiny unwinking eye. "This has got to stop," he says. He sounds broken. In the moonlight I see tears streaking down his face. "I'm so tired."

I hold my hands up. "Please."

He cocks the hammer.

I close my eyes. And as I wait for the explosion to hit my face, in the infinity that is the fraction of a second I have to live, I hear a metallic *thwang!*

My eyes pop open in time to see Mitch flying sideways. He bounces off the hedge wall and lands on the ground in a dark lump.

I look up, astonished.

There stands Inez with a shovel.

She reaches down and yanks the gun out of Mitch's limp hand. Then nudges his face with her toe to make sure he's out cold.

"What a *fuck*ing asshole."

Roxie

On the front stairs of Montgomery House we watch the last of the police cars roll away down the drive, their blue lights gaudy and surreal through the trees.

"Well, *that* was interesting," Lori says.

"Quite," Ms. Claverhill agrees. "Shall we go in for a cup of tea?"

Uncle Lenny looks at his watch. "I think we should be getting home."

"I wouldn't mind a word before you go," Ms. Claverhill says.

We've had a lot of words with the police tonight and I'm exhausted, but something in the housekeeper's tone makes me pause. "We can take a minute, Uncle Lenny."

"Are you sure?" He scans me for the thousandth time to make sure I'm in one piece.

I study Ms. Claverhill's face. Not that she gives anything away. "It sounds important."

"It is," she says, and steps inside.

We follow her to the library. "I'll make that tea first," she says. "It's the way of my people in times of trouble."

"I think I'll take a whiskey, actually," Lori says after she's gone, helping herself to the wet bar in the corner. "It's the way of *my* people," she adds. Uncle Lenny holds up a finger for one as well.

I lower myself onto a very uncomfortable brocaded couch to wait. The chase reminded all my bike accident wounds that they exist. Inez sits on the edge of a chair, rubbing her palms on her knees.

Lori slugs her drink, refills it, and then, because she's Lori, takes the opportunity to poke around, pulling out dresser drawers, peeking into cupboards.

"Just try to relax for now," Uncle Lenny tells Inez. "The police will want to talk to you again soon, but they're busy with Mitch Montgomery-Wiggins for the moment."

She nods. The vengeful angel of the hedge maze has faded. An hour of explaining herself to Officer Lamb has clearly left her exhausted. "Do you think they believed me?" she asks.

Uncle Lenny is too honest to placate her. "It's their job to question everything," he says. "But listen, you saved my niece's life. I promise I'll do whatever I can to help you. I won't let them chew you up and spit you out."

I feel dangerously close to tears looking at my uncle Lenny. He was again the first person I called once I was convinced Mitch wasn't going to jump up and try to psycho-kill anybody else. In the movie of my life, I'd like to be my own savior, thanks. But in the reality of my life, I'll take Inez with a shovel. There are worse heroes.

As she had skillfully tied him up with gardening wire ("Just one of the many services I offer"), I told Uncle Lenny between shaky breaths to get back to Montgomery House pronto, and to bring the cavalry.

When they arrived with lights and sirens, I had a moment of panic. I knew it was irrational, but I found myself back at our burning compound, eleven years old with my whole world in flames. Uncle Lenny found me curled up in a chair in the staff room, heart racing. He'd coaxed me out, and together we'd gone to talk to the police.

It had taken a while to get the whole story out into the open. Inez had told the police her crazy tale of walking in on Kirsten's murder and (surprise!) Evan's murder. This led her to the tale of being assaulted by Evan and Mitch at the lake house. As proof, I showed Officer Lamb the video I'd discovered on Kirsten's phone.

Lamb wanted to take Inez in for more questioning, given that she was an accomplice to murder, but Uncle Lenny called Hank, who pulled some strings. He managed to convince Lamb to let her come into the station—with a lawyer—bright and early the next morning. She was a victim before she was an accomplice, after all, Uncle Lenny kept reminding the officer. Inez keeps sneaking looks at Uncle Lenny like she can't figure out why he's being so nice.

Ms. Claverhill brings in a tray of tea paraphernalia, which includes an honest-to-god knitted cozy.

"Tea," Inez says. "Good for everything."

Ms. Claverhill pours steaming cups, filling the room with a bittersweet aroma. "You're a very curious girl, Roxanne," she finally says once we've all been served.

I take a scalding sip. "Guilty."

The warmth travels down my throat and I feel a sort of unraveling inside. Maybe there *is* something to this whole tea thing.

"There's nothing wrong with curiosity, of course," she says.

"It kills cats, I hear."

A rare smile passes over the housekeeper's face. "You know, Kirsten Montgomery-Wiggins was curious, too."

I choke on my tea. Very unladylike.

Ms. Claverhill politely pretends not to notice. "She came here," she goes on. "Many times, starting back in July. To talk with your great-aunt."

I put my tea down with a shaking hand, join the others in staring at the housekeeper.

"Mrs. Montgomery refused to see her at first. Bad blood and all that. Granddaughter of the enemy. But Kirsten was quite persistent. She would walk from her house every day and knock on the door. Stand there rain or shine, waiting. Finally Mrs. Montgomery relented, or grew curious herself, perhaps, and after that they spent several afternoons together in this room, talking."

My voice is hoarse when I ask, "About what?"

Ms. Claverhill looks out the window, though all we can see are our wavy reflections. "About something that happened a long time ago. And something similar that happened very recently." She takes a deep breath. "Kirsten came here with questions. She knew what had happened to Inez and had suspicions that it wasn't the first time the men in her family had done something like that. Eventually they got to Bernadette Martin."

“But . . . but why come to Great-Aunt Regina instead of the police?” I ask.

“Kirsten didn’t have any proof. By then her phone and the video on it were gone. Before she came here, she confronted her brother, tried to get him to come forward. He told her to keep her mouth shut.”

“So Mitch knew she’d seen the assault on Inez?” Uncle Lenny asks.

“And also that she had taken a video,” Ms. Claverhill says.

“Why did she tell him?” I ask. “Did she really think he was going to rat out himself, his dad, his grandfather, his friend?”

Ms. Claverhill sighs. “She and her brother were close, Kirsten said. She thought she would be able to convince him. But instead he told Evan Fowley that she had proof of what they did.”

“And Evan killed her,” Inez says quietly.

Silence hangs heavy in the air.

Ms. Claverhill says, “When her brother refused to help, Kirsten decided to dig, to look for other victims. Other proof. That’s how she came upon Bernadette Martin. She found out that her grandfather had been briefly investigated for Ms. Martin’s disappearance. She discovered evidence that he had kept tabs on her, had paid people to watch and harass her because of the protests she mounted against his business interests.”

I remember the file in the basement of the law firm that Kelly Graham found Kirsten looking at. *M* for Martin?

“Kirsten came to Mrs. Montgomery to ask if William Montgomery was involved with Bernadette’s disappearance.

She hoped that between the two of them they could bring his offenses to light," Ms. Claverhill says.

"Hence the poem," I say.

"Regina could have just called me," Uncle Lenny growls. "Told me there was a body buried in the backyard. Instead of turning it into a game."

Ms. Claverhill looks down at her hands. "Yes. She could have. Kirsten was very disappointed, actually, that Mrs. Montgomery wouldn't talk to the police."

"I know the feeling," Uncle Lenny says.

That little pop of rage hits me again, and I glower up at the empty space on the wall where Great-Aunt Regina's portrait once hung. The woman lived in her own universe. One where it was perfectly logical to make entertainment from other people's suffering. A fucking poem. A treasure hunt. And the kicker? She didn't say a word until she was dead, because that way she wouldn't have to risk anything. Not her mansion, not her fortune, not her place in society.

"And I could have spoken up, too," Ms. Claverhill goes on.

The housekeeper's face comes back into focus.

"It's no excuse, of course, but I'm from a different time. Part of my training was in the sanctity of discretion. To work for a great family is a great honor, and part of that honor is keeping that family great in the eyes of the world. That was the way it worked. You accept it, or you don't last very long in this profession." She looks up, directly at me. "And I was very good at my job."

"You knew," I say.

Ms. Claverhill doesn't look away. "I didn't lie when I said that Bernadette Martin's death was before my time here as a housekeeper. But I didn't mention that before I was in charge of the house, I was a maid to Mrs. Montgomery. I was very young and very naive, impressed by these dazzling people and their endless wealth and power. Again, not that that's an excuse."

"What did you see?" I ask.

"Enough. I saw William Montgomery and his friends charm Bernadette Martin that night, ply her with drinks, put the necklace on her, tease her with it. I saw him take her down into the cellar. Mrs. Montgomery followed. She hid and saw Mr. Montgomery and his friends murder that poor woman." She stops, lost in cold, dark memory.

"I didn't see the murder," she goes on, "but I saw the aftermath. I knew. I washed dirt and blood out of her husband's tuxedo. I was told to keep my mouth shut or I'd be shipped back to the coal-mining hole in England I'd been plucked from." Her eyes grow distant. "They didn't even really worry about me that much, truth be told. A couple of threats and then it was like it never happened. Like Bernadette Martin wasn't worth worrying about. I could have revealed everything. Maybe they knew me better than I did myself. Maybe they knew my type. The well-trained loyal servant. Discreet."

After a moment of stunned silence, I ask, "Will you talk to the police now?"

She nods slowly. "Yes. I promised Mrs. Montgomery I would wait until Bernadette Martin's body was found. My last act of discretion."

Inez slowly shakes her head. "I don't understand, though . . . Why didn't Kirsten have proof? How did her phone end up in my car?"

Ms. Claverhill says, "Kirsten told Mrs. Montgomery that it was a mistake. She said she was in a state of shock after filming and slid the phone into your car through a cracked window. She knew the video needed to get to you, but she wasn't thinking straight. She said she realized it was the wrong thing to do the moment it was out of her hands, but then it was too late. She couldn't get it back out. She tried to wait for you, but then she saw her brother and some of the other men carrying you out toward your car. She got scared and ran. And then she didn't know how to find you later."

"The video wasn't backed up anywhere?" Lori asks.

"Apparently the only place she had it was on the phone," Ms. Claverhill says. "All she could recover was a still, an image of Inez's face."

"She should have just asked me to find the stupid video," I say. "It might have taken a little longer without her phone, but I'm sure I could have." My throat starts to tighten. "She might not be dead now."

"It's not your fault," Uncle Lenny says. "Even if she had told you about it, Evan still would have come for her that night."

Silence permeates the room.

Ms. Claverhill straightens her back and says, "No more secrets. Tomorrow I'll go to the police station. I'll tell them everything I know."

Inez watches her for a moment. Then she reaches over and takes her hand. "We'll go together."

Roxie

Regina Montgomery looks down on her realm, her décolletage milky pale, her diamonds (were they fake by the time the portrait was made?) forever twinkly.

A toilet flushes.

The sinks turn on and off, and smells better left undescribed float and mingle with air freshener.

I towel my hands, watching Great-Aunt Regina in the mirror. "I like her here," I say to Lori, who is touching up her lipstick.

"Hmm?" She turns to look at the Rusty Nail's bathroom wall. "Oh, her? Yeah. Me, too. Fitting."

"Regina. The porcelain queen."

We walk back out to the bar, where Uncle Lenny is doing his never-ending inventory. From her booth Nina surreptitiously watches Marcus and Inez share a plate of okra fries.

"Jealous?" I ask, nudging in beside her.

She sighs. "It's so hard to work up the proper fire. I like her too much."

Lori leans her hip into our table. "I hope it works out. Restaurant romances can be so sticky."

"You know we can hear you, right?" Marcus asks.

Lori and I wave while Nina ducks behind her chemistry

textbook. Inez pushes herself out of her chair and ties her apron on. "I need to clock in and start my side work anyway."

"Thank you," Uncle Lenny says, with a pointed look at his sister.

Lori doesn't notice. She's watching the television above the bar, where an endless parade of Montgomery-related news is dished out with barely concealed glee by local news reporters. Nothing like a spectacular fall from greatness to really get people's blood pumping.

The public corruption case the FBI is assembling is barely mentioned, the bribery of public officials and insider trading lost behind the much more thrilling scandal of "Secret Sex Rituals of the Super-Rich!" and "The Bloodbath of a Billionaire Bludgeoner!"

(Me: "Try saying that five times fast.")

On a happier note (also barely touched upon in the press), the plans to develop Marcus's grandmother's neighborhood have been put on hold while their primary source of funds—SouthEast Holdings, aka William Montgomery—is investigated. "On hold for now, anyway," Nina says. "Amazing how many racist millionaires there are in the woodwork, ready to step in." She's keeping tabs on the situation, and definitely not throwing out her placards yet.

"Speaking of cash," Nina says, "any word on when you'll get your diamonds?"

Lori slumps. "Probably never. Officer Lamb says they could be in evidence for years." She glances at a customer who is practically levitating, waving his arm, trying to get her attention. "I mean, who does that? Murders someone and then—whoopsie—forgets to take off the two million dollars' worth of diamonds you put on them?"

I marvel at my aunt. Lori's self-absorption in the face of overwhelming odds will never cease to fascinate me.

In another interesting turn of events, Lori has gotten chummy again with Carol Montgomery-Wiggins, who is apparently a bit of a pariah in the country club scene now that her father and son are both facing murder charges. It doesn't help that Mrs. Montgomery-Wiggins herself is also being charged as an accessory to murder. Lori has been letting Kirsten's mother cry on her shoulder.

It's from Lori we learned that Mrs. Montgomery-Wiggins knew from the get-go that Mitch had something to do with the murders. That, in fact, she saw him and Inez bringing a body out of the house on a security camera app on her phone and decided that no matter what the story actually was, the video evidence needed to be wiped, pronto. Which she did. All of this whispered in secret to Lori, who obviously told us at the first opportunity. "She's probably been covering up her father's and husband's misdeeds for years," Lori had gushed breathlessly.

I'd asked Lori to find out if it was Mrs. Montgomery-Wiggins who had almost run me over on my bike, but Lori had assured me, "No, not her! That was Mitch. She was just a passenger."

"I'm not sure that's better," I'd said.

"She tried to get Mitch to stop. When they hit you, she jumped out to make sure you were okay. Mitch took off."

"I'm sorry, why are you friends with this woman again?"

Lori had reached over and squeezed my hand. I had started to pull away, but she said, "You know I'm Team Roxie, kiddo. No matter who my friends are. Always have been, always will be."

Team Roxie needs all the support it can get. Inez is being charged as an accessory to Kirsten's murder, too, and will have to appear in court eventually. The prosecution will just have her testimony to go on as to the real events around Kirsten's murder, and it's not clear that the word of "a cheap hooker" (as she's been called by her detractors) will hold up against the testimony of bright young thing Mitch Montgomery.

(Inez: "I was hardly cheap.")

Mitch's story is that Evan killed Kirsten and Inez happened to walk in at that moment and take the opportunity to kill Evan, and that poor Mitch Montgomery was an innocent bystander who decided to help Inez cover up her murder out of the goodness of his heart. He had even made up some crazy story that Inez had in fact *attempted* to murder Evan a week before, and that Evan had risen from the dead, only to have her kill him again. I mean, seriously, Mitch? That's the story you want to go with? Far-fetched much?

Sometimes I almost feel a little sorry for the guy, because honestly, who can blame Mitch for murdering a piece of work like Evan Fowley? He did kill Mitch's sister, after all. But then I remember Mitch is a rapist and that he tried to run me over with a car, and my sympathy—*poof*—evaporates on the breeze.

My guess is that Mitch will get a nice short "bright young thing" sentence and that he'll be walking free in a few years.

If that's depressing, at least I can hold out hope that his grandfather will rot in jail. The murder charges against William Montgomery are by no means airtight, but Ms. Claverhill gave a long statement to the police that included leads on other women he victimized over the years. And Inez's testimony, along with the video evidence, doesn't help his image.

Uncle Lenny comes over to where Lori is lounging. "Don't forget that it's not clear the diamonds are ours to pine over," he says, and then he takes his sister by the shoulders and walks her to the table with the flailing man. "This woman would like to take your order, sir."

"What do you mean?" Nina asks, when Uncle Lenny comes back.

Uncle Lenny lowers his voice. "I could be convinced that the diamonds belonged to William Montgomery and that he gave them to Birdie Martin before she died. That means they belonged to her, and now, her heirs. Don't tell Lori that yet. I don't want her to crack me over the head with a frying pan."

I look around the restaurant, at the shiny countertops and warm murmur of customers. At Marcus eyeballing a row of tickets stuck in the kitchen window. He's got that look like an orchestra conductor in the moment before they stab the air with a baton, starting a storm of music. He'll spend the next few hours organizing and executing rapid-fire. It's sure to be another busy night. (Our fame has only grown since our last entanglement with the Montgomerys. I have been called Nancy Drew more than once.) Maybe Marcus will get the diamonds and buy into the restaurant. Or maybe he's got other dreams and plans. One thing's for sure: Birdie's family certainly deserves those diamonds more than any of the rest of us.

"I can count on you for the protest this weekend?" Nina asks me. She's zipping up her bag, getting ready to leave.

"Which one is it again?"

"Against corporatized mass incarceration."

"Oh yeah, I love that one. Sure. Lori?" I yell across the room. "You want to come protest this Saturday?"

Lori looks at me like I've invited her to an eyebrow-shaving party.

"Come on," I tell her. "It'll be fun. We'll fight the system. Your followers will love it." I sneak a glance at Nina to see if I've crossed a line.

"I need bodies," she says under her breath so Lori can't hear. "Any meat sack in a storm."

"I'll think about it," Lori says. But I can tell she's already pondering what filter would work best with a clenched-fist selfie.

Ding ding ding.

"Hey, hello? Anybody out there? I know y'all don't think I'm running these plates myself." Marcus bangs the bell again for emphasis, his serious face on. Two plates of burgers and fries steam in the window.

"God, he's sexy," Nina says, shaking her head. "I have to go."

"Coming," I yell, and hurry over. I grab a fry off the plate and pop it into my mouth.

He points salad tongs at me. "I saw that."

"Ow, hot." I let the fry fall out.

"Keep your paws off the food, Scooby-Doo."

Honestly, though. What would we do if we were rich? Sell out? Nah. This place is too much like home.

Inez

If hard-pressed, Inez would have to say that the best part of her new job at the Rusty Nail is the okra fries. God, they're good.

Obviously being around Marcus is nice, but they haven't really defined their relationship, and she doesn't want to put too much pressure on it. He's very serious at work anyway, no time for canoodling. That's fine with her. She's serious, too. And good at waiting tables. If sex work has taught her anything, it's good customer service, which really just boils down to keeping your cool when people are acting like unwashed assholes.

The other great thing about working at the Nail? Health insurance. A girl can get used to anything if you throw in okra fries and health insurance.

Because she works mostly evening shifts, she's looking into nursing classes at the local community college. It's not as good a program as the one she saw in Oregon, but it's a start. It's at least a lot cheaper, and that counts for something.

The ten thousand dollars she'd gotten from Mitch had been rudely wrenched back out of her bank account as soon as the police got involved. She wasn't surprised, seeing as it had actually come from Evan. Turned out Mitch had stolen Evan's wallet off his dead corpse and taken the funds out of his account to pay her with. He was apparently both an awful human being and super conniving. He had hedged his bets to be able to set her up for Evan's murder from the get-go. How's that for gratitude? She should have just turned around and walked out of the Montgomery-Wiggins house as soon as she was sure he'd bashed Evan's brains in, instead of giving him her time and cleaning expertise.

Cleaning is behind her. She'd quit Quali-Clean as soon as she'd been hired at the Nail, but hasn't made her mind up yet about whether she'll still see her private clients. Marcus, to his credit, has never asked her to give up sex work. Not that she would necessarily let that influence her. She hasn't taken any jobs since Mitch was taken into custody, but she wants to keep her options open.

There are so many options, really. She's beginning to realize that her limits are actually shockingly fragile. Working at the Rusty Nail is just the beginning. Maybe she'll become a nurse. Maybe she'll bring down a titan of industry (fingers crossed). That freedom is dazzling, terrifying, precious. She isn't ready to give it up.

Still, there's the practical give-and-take to consider. Another reason she hasn't gone back to sex work is that her lawyer made it clear that turning over a new leaf would do worlds for her case against said titan of industry, William Montgomery. And that asshole needs to pay.

Her attorney, Kelly Graham, is still in law school, but that doesn't mean she isn't a force of nature. And she has several seasoned lawyer-professors supervising her. It doesn't hurt, either, that she's helping Inez pro bono. The meetings they have with

Kelly's professors about the case are full of legal terminology she doesn't know, but Kelly always takes her out for drinks after, breaks it all down without making Inez feel stupid.

She's found herself liking Kelly, despite her initial reservations. The young lawyer seems to be working extra hard to make up for the fact that she once pointed the police in Inez's direction. She even told Inez, "I can't believe I thought you killed Evan. I mean, I would have understood if you had, but seriously, I'm so sorry."

Oh, the irony.

Roxie

"I got an A on my English assignment," I tell Uncle Lenny when I get to the Nail to start my shift. It's been a couple of weeks since the arrests, and things are starting to calm down a little. "The one Sister Deborah let me do to try to pull my grade back up."

"Oh, really?"

"Yeah, I had to write a poem in the style of another author. I decided to use Great-Aunt Regina's 'Robber Bridegroom' as my starting point. Not exactly what Sister Deborah had in mind, but she let it slide. Do you want to read it? I mean, you can do it later. I know it's go-time here and—"

"Give it," Uncle Lenny says. He stashes his clipboard under the counter.

I find my ears burning as I hand over the paper with the satisfyingly large *A* marked at the top. I have to admit, I never get tired of Uncle Lenny's excitement over my good grades. I loved Mama, but she was apathetic at best about my homeschooling. Pastor, ha. He was suspicious of anything that did not directly quote scripture.

"I'm going to start my prep," I say, because like hell I'm going to stand here biting my nails while he reads. "Oh, and I might need to leave a little early. I have a new job."

He jerks his head up.

"Nothing dangerous," I assure him. "In fact, I'm sure I can do ninety-nine percent of it online." I do not mention the fact that online means dark-web online and involves searching for photos of a schoolmate's boyfriend's penis. (Possibly many penises Photoshopped onto various farm animals? We'll see. Life is full of fun surprises.)

I leave Uncle Lenny at the bar and find a tray of silverware and a stack of freshly laundered napkins. I begin rolling them into neat little tubes. I enjoy a bit of zen before the shitstorm of taking orders, flinging food, soothing grumpy customers, slopping and dishing and frying and pirouetting through the restaurant balancing ten drinks on a slice of flimsy plastic, the elegant chaos that is creating a space people need. A place to find friends, lovers, family. Not to mention a damn tasty trout taco.

One fork, one knife. Pleat, roll, stack. Next.

I glance up at Uncle Lenny. His lips move as he reads.

Treasure Uncovered

By Roxanne Hunt

The worms had eaten everything
By the time we came around
A ring of thyme and goldenrod
Were her only crown

He put her there to hide her heart
Its beat too fierce and loud

His kingdom strong, his reign was long
Her silence was profound

The years go by but wicked folk
Evolve rather than perish
A stroke of pen and 'round again
Gone, home that was cherished

It's as simple as it's ever been
To beckon for fête and feast
Maidens bold, bought and sold
Playthings for the beast

They take and take and call for more
These men of wealth and ind'stry
They bite and tear, they're here and nowhere
Ravenous for all and sundry

But Bird today's a daughter found
Writ "warrior, sister, friend"
In cemetery, her bones we bury
Gone, but not the end

For wicked men in docks will stand
In court all orange-smothered
And on the street and in a tweet
A smidge of justice recovered

You singing Birds, you wives of Lot
granddaughters, Jezebels
Stories varied, the weight you've carried
Passed through one thousand hells

To you who stand against the tide
Women wrought of violence
To you who fight for what is right
I salute you who will not be silenced

When Uncle Lenny finishes reading, he comes over to the booth where I'm rolling silverware. He sits across from me and reaches out. His hand hovers, waiting. I nod. He puts his hand on mine. He can't really look at me, and he doesn't say anything, but he doesn't have to. We stay like that a few seconds, and then he lets go. He takes a stack of napkins and starts to roll.

Acknowledgments

It's been a minute since my last book came out, and in the time between then and as I'm writing this now, the world feels like it's been on fast forward. Upheavals, wars, resistance, pandemics, changing world orders, an acceleration toward collapsing ecosystems. Maybe it's always been like this, but it feels like we're really in a moment. It feels, actually, like the world is on fire. I'm not sure how I would have made it through these last years without my tethers, personal and professional—those people who keep me and all the other creatives out there from floating away.

I would be adrift without my agent, Faye Bender, who keeps things in perspective, who is always a sage voice, and who manages to balance practicality and optimism with marvelous grace. Stacey Barney: wise and funny, canny and courageous, the publishing industry is damn lucky to have your voice, and I am damn lucky to have you as my editor. To the incredible team at Nancy Paulsen and Penguin Random House that does all the heavy and unsung lifting behind the scenes to kick our books out of the nest (and make it look like flying), thank you for your magic.

I am eternally grateful to the Associates of the Boston Public Library, and to the anonymous donor who funds the Writer-in-Residence Program. Thank you for believing in *City of Saints & Thieves* ten years ago and setting me on this path. The program continues to be a beacon and an anchor for so many new voices, and has profoundly changed our lives. Thank you, thank you, thank you.

No matter how far from home I go, I am fantastically fortunate to have family and friends who make me homesick for their care and company. Thank you especially to those of you who really get the magic of books. To my parents, who always read me bedtime stories and actively discouraged coloring within the lines. To my best friend, Siara, for all those nights of reading Nancy Drew under the covers with a flashlight. To my kids, who are now desperate for "just one more chapter . . ." I also sorely miss my BSpec gang and dream of popping in on you at a MurderBooze weekend retreat.

Of course, I'd be lost without my partner and kids, who hold my hands in the high winds and remind me on the regular what's actually solid and important and immovable. You have my heart.